The emotional well-being of my readers is important to me. If you would like to see specific content warnings before you dive in, please visit www.jesseverlee.com/cw.

THE GENTLEMAN'S BOOK OF VICES

JESS EVERLEE

ISBN-13: 978-1-335-67998-7

The Gentleman's Book of Vices

Copyright © 2022 by Jess Everlee

For questions and comments about the quality of this book, please contact us at CustomerService@Harlequin.com.

Carina Press
22 Adelaide St. West, 41st Floor
Toronto, Ontario M5H 4E3, Canada
www.CarinaPress.com

Printed in U.S.A.

For Michael. Every depraved word. Forever.

THE GENTLEMAN'S BOOK OF VICES

Chapter One

Charlie

London's West End.
October 1883

The front parlor of The Curious Fox had gotten awfully crowded over the past hour. It was fortunate that Charlie Price's lungs were permanently coated with a slick of cigarette smoke and perfume already; the air around some of the tables was nearly as thick as the fog was outside. In here, however, the choking mist was tinted pink by the vibrant glass lampshades, while flashes of crystal glasses and well-dressed gentlemen drifted through it like drunken ghosts. Charlie thought the dreadful weather would have kept everyone home in their beds, but then again, their own beds did not allow for quite the same company as the beds that lay beyond the Fox's parlor.

Charlie had arrived early enough to claim his favorite of the alcoves across from the gleaming, dark wood bar. With the curtains drawn back, he watched the crowd comfortably from his flowery chaise, a glass of gin in one hand, the other settled disinterestedly around the shoulders of the newcomer who had somehow become the newest timid barnacle to attach itself to him.

The newcomer ran his inexperienced fingers lightly along

the checkered wool over Charlie's thigh. He kept glancing over, more nervous than lustful, and when Charlie finally glanced back, the chap looked downright terrified. Not just new to the Fox, then: he was likely new to the whole business of it. Charlie wanted to say something encouraging, but he'd forgotten the chap's name, and... Damn, he was not drunk enough for this, was he? Charlie took a pull of bitter gin, the rings on his fingers clinking against the crystal.

As he scanned the parlor—from the tinkling piano in the back, past the crowded bar, and over the tables of cards and conversation—he caught movement near the front entrance. More? Really? Were there even this many men in the whole of London who were trustworthy enough to gain access to a club like this?

Trying not to squirm under the tickling attentions of his companion, he watched the patron hand a dripping overcoat and umbrella to the doorman. Perhaps he could manage an upgrade, if the newly arrived patron was more interesting than this one.

However, while the visitor was dressed like a man and came so indecently unescorted into a gentlemen's club as if that were her birthright, he realized with a happy little rush that it was not a man at all.

It was Miss Jo.

Charlie sat up straight, his heart leaping to his throat as he watched his friend work her way through the smoke toward his corner. He hadn't even realized what a dull night it had been until she came along and saved it. He adored her always, but particularly tonight. Because tonight, she held a folded paper in her gloved hand.

Without a doubt, it was the one Charlie had been waiting for.

He glanced sideways at his awkward companion. In light of

Miss Jo's arrival, he was no longer even passingly interested in educating this chap in the finer points of pleasure. But there were other lessons Charlie could teach him.

For instance: men you picked up in places like this were terrible.

He pressed a hearty kiss to the side of the fellow's head and then disentangled himself, waving his newly freed hand. *Shoo, shoo.*

"Wh-what?" the chap stammered. "Did I do something wrong?"

Charlie's eyes hardly strayed from the clutched paper in Miss Jo's hand. He gestured to the bar, to the smoke, to the various other sofas and alcoves. "Go on, lad."

"Lad?" The fellow was at least ten years older than Charlie.

"I said what I said. Now go on, *lad.* I'm busy, but there's plenty of other nonsense to get up to, so go get up to it. Over there somewhere."

"But—"

"It's been a pleasure, my boy. Godspeed."

Poor man. Charlie felt bad for him, slinking off to sit alone at the bar. He was a handsome thing, but he had that sadness about him that was as depressing as it was hard to escape on a Friday night at the Fox. It was when all the tragic ones came in.

Charlie watched affectionately as Jo darted around a particularly raucous table of fellows and other fine folks who positively dripped silk skirts and strings of pearls. Noah Clarke—another of Charlie's friends—was among them, done up in extravagant drag. His character, the lovely Miss Penelope Primrose, spent her Friday evenings hustling admirers out of their money in nearly every card game imaginable.

When Miss Penelope spotted Jo, she gathered her in and pressed a powdered face to Jo's bosom. The two of them talked a bit, going on so long that Charlie nearly gave up and went to pry Jo away before she got sucked into whatever game was going on. But Jo finally kissed Penelope's gloved hand and continued along the path to Charlie's corner.

She sat heavily beside him and took his drink right from his hand.

"Get your own." Charlie tried to take it back, but she downed the rest of the gin and tonic in a single gulp. He was left with an empty glass. "Don't let Penelope drive you to drink, Jo. There's nothing she'd love more in this life than to know it was she who caused your downfall."

"It's you who's driving me, by making me come in here." She straightened her pin-striped lapels and smoothed her tie. "I don't have to come into this rouge-soaked hellhole. I do it for you."

Charlie put his head on her shoulder. "Lucky me, then."

"Who's that man you sent off?"

"Oh, I don't know."

"Poor chap," Jo said. "There was no need to banish him if you were having fun. I'm not going to be here very long. I only came to give you this." She brandished the paper between two kid-gloved fingers. Charlie reached out, but she tugged it back. "Ah, ah," she said. "I went to a lot of bother for this. A lot of snooping in places where snooping gets good little girls into barrels of trouble."

"Well, thank God you went instead of me," said Charlie. "Anyone looking at us knows which is the good little girl."

"I do hate you."

"I know. That's why I'm going to buy your drinks all night."

"All year."

He tried to snatch the paper again, but she switched hands with the deftness of a stage magician.

"Oh, come off it," he said.

"Six months." Her dark eyebrows danced up toward her bowler hat. She had the most devious eyes in England, set into a heart-shaped face with smirking lips. "Minimum."

"I have no money, Jo, and you drink like a man twice your size. What am I going to buy it with?"

"The money Daddy is going to slip you once your vows are final. That's why you're leaving us for a wife and twenty brats, ain't it? So you can afford to buy my drinks?"

"I'm not *leaving* exactly—"

"Six months."

"Three."

With a languid motion, Jo held the folded page over the candelabra on the table beside them. As the edges grew toasty and brown, Charlie's stomach knotted. They looked each other hard in the eye.

"If it was that hard to get it," Charlie said, "then there's no way you'll burn it."

"Don't try me, princess; I have no use for this thing."

The corner of the page caught, a thin line of fire dancing along the edge, adding a whiff of burning paper to the tobacco and incense already swirling in the air.

"Fine! Six months!" With a huff, Charlie snatched the page out of Jo's hand and blew out the flame.

Miss Jo wasted no time snapping her fingers at a young man who did not even work here, demanding a glass of top-shelf whiskey so commandingly that he nearly sprinted to the bar in terror. She kicked her shoes up over Charlie's lap and settled into the chaise. Though she complained about The Curious Fox—*so* much less *civilized* than the Sapphists' little place—she certainly knew how to get cozy here.

"Go on, then." She crossed her arms over the front of her three-piece. "Open it up. It's by far the best wedding present you're going to get, and if you wait too long, you'll have to share it with wifey. I have a feeling Alma won't be interested."

Charlie eyed the smoldering paper, suddenly nervous to see what was within. Why was he nervous? All he'd see was a name, perhaps an address or place of employment. The whole thing was a silly little fancy anyway, a last whim before all his scandalous souvenirs went into his safe deposit box until the end of time. If he was going to have to hide his most precious possessions from a wife, he at least wanted the satisfaction of knowing he'd squirreled away something special.

"Are you sure this is him?" He clutched the still-folded page to his chest. "He's well hidden, you know, and for good reason."

"If you don't open it, I'm going to set it on fire again, and you along with it."

Chastised at last, Charlie opened the paper and read, in Jo's scrawl of a hand, the address of a Fleet Street bookshop, and below it a name:

Miles Montague.

He allowed his lips to mouth the name. Miles. Miles Montague. A very normal-sounding name, yet somehow striking. "Better than his pen name," he said.

"How can you say that?" Jo laughed and took her drink from the onetime serving lad, who ran off before things could become more confusing. "*Reginald Cox* is a brilliant name. I'd take it myself, if he hadn't already claimed it."

Carefully, Charlie knocked the ash off the paper and into the cigar tray. He tucked the little treasure in his coat pocket. "How did you find him? Not to brag, but when it comes to uncovering the identities of notorious pornographers, you know I'm the leading expert."

"Yes, a rare and valuable skill you have there."

"I assumed you were kidding when you said you could find

him," he went on. "If I couldn't, I assumed no one could. What'd you do? Who'd you talk to?"

She sipped her drink luxuriously, staring at the gauzy ceiling as if unsure how much to divulge. The silence was cut through with the sounds of piano music, laughter, and something decidedly off-rhythm coming from one of the private rooms. "Well," she began slowly, "first, I drew a circle in chalk out in the chicken coop. I killed one of the birds—the worst of the birds, don't worry, real bitch—and with the blood and my pentagram—"

"I'm serious, Joey." Charlie nudged her with his elbow. "I'm really grateful, so I just—"

Jo took his hand and kissed the tops of his knuckles with her rough, unpainted lips. "If you're really grateful, Charlie, just let it go. I have a connection. It's that simple."

"Is it?" He raised an eyebrow.

She raised hers back. "That's exactly what I want to leave you wondering. I have an air of mystery to maintain. Don't take that from me, or I'll never do anything nice for you again."

"Alright, mate. I suppose I'll just continue to imagine you breaking into safes, sprinting away from pornographic printhouse goons, leaving maidens fainting in your wake."

"Thank you kindly."

They stayed a little longer, eyeing the crowd and gossiping. There was always gossip to be had at The Curious Fox, after all. Miss Penelope and her companions were constantly up to something amusing. Behind the bar, Warren Bakshi—the impossibly handsome barkeep—had memorized everyone's drink orders and flirted so mercilessly that his tips bordered on payment for immoral services. Meanwhile, the proprietor Mr. Forester set himself up with a ledger near the piano to oversee the renting of back rooms, a post he would keep until

Warren inevitably abandoned the bar to take up with his latest best customer. Forester was the best for gossip, since it was his job to know who was taking whom to do what, and the states of rooms when they were done.

"Warren's at it again." Jo pointed with her drink to where the barkeep was peeking over his own shoulder as he escorted a friend toward the back rooms. "And there's Mr. Forester, turning his back and pretending not to see. He's too nice."

"To Warren anyway. Anyone else tried to sneak into the back without paying, I'm pretty sure none of us would ever forget the sound of their screams."

"Too nice to you as well," Jo accused.

Charlie wished he could bury his burning face into the safety of yet another unpaid-for drink, but Jo had not ordered him one. "Let's, perhaps, choose a different subject."

"Alright. Who's that Warren is with, anyway?"

"That fellow?" Charlie watched the pair vanish through the door. "Oh, he's been here once or twice."

"Have you taken him for a test run?"

"You make it sound like I'm familiar with every last newcomer."

"You are, aren't you?" she asked.

"Well, *yes*," he admitted.

Jo looked a bit too judging. "I'm surprised they even come back after being subjected to you. You've been a right prick to them all, ever since—"

"*Anyway*. Warren's chap," Charlie interrupted. "He's alright, depending on what exactly you want him for."

He stared Jo down, daring her to turn the conversation back.

She shook her head, defeated. "Fine, I'll bite. What do you mean?"

"You'd never guess to look at him, but he's hung like a damned horse. Never seen anything like it."

"Isn't that good?" Jo asked.

"To a point. Warren seems to like him, though, bless his heart and his arse. He never does know when to quit."

Jo stood and stretched, then downed the rest of her drink. "Well, on that lovely note, I think that's it for me tonight. The Beast comes home from his latest expedition tomorrow, and I need to turn into a lady by morning."

She leaned down and kissed Charlie on the cheek. As she pulled back, he squeezed her hand. "Thanks again," he said. "You really are heaven-sent. Or hell-sent. Don't tell me which."

"Do you want me to come with you? When you go to meet Mr. Montague?"

Charlie thought about it. "No. All I want is for him to sign the book. I should go alone; I'd hate to scare him."

"Yet, I'd hate for anything to happen to you if he's scared anyway. Like you said, he's got good reason to be anonymous. He may not take kindly to being called on and identified."

"I'll be alright." He smiled to put her at ease. "You know me. No foolish chances. If I catch the barest whiff of danger, I'll make my escape, autograph be damned. I promise."

"It's a stupid thing to do, you know," she scolded. "It's just a signature, on a book you're planning to hide in a deposit box and never look at again."

Charlie sucked in a deep breath and swirled the boozy ice melt Jo had left at the bottom of his glass. "I'm sure I'll look at it again eventually."

"You know what I mean."

He wasn't enjoying this turn in the conversation. The line of her mouth had grown a bit serious. "You're not about to start *looking after me* again, are you?"

"Charlie—"

"Because I don't need it. The wedding is eight weeks out, and it's going to be lovely. So what if I have to tuck some of my more incriminating things away? All the better. It's the secrets that make it so delicious, isn't it?"

"Is it, though?" Jo asked.

"And I'm going to have a secret autograph from Reginald Cox. That should be more than enough to keep me from looking like that bloke over there." He gestured to where his rejected companion chatted morosely with Mr. Forester, who'd taken up Warren's spot behind the bar.

Jo smacked his arm. "It better be. If you get married and then start moping about like that, I'll break your damn jaw."

"That's very reassuring."

"And anyway, are you entirely sure Alma still wants to marry you? After all this time, you haven't managed to scare her off?"

"Quite the contrary." He sighed. "She's picked out her dress, and we're tasting cakes and wines for the wedding this week. All is going perfectly smoothly, and she's happy as can be."

"She must be mental."

"Don't insult Alma," he said seriously. "I'm the mental one."

Jo looked at him. She was doing it again. She was fretting about him. "Charlie... Look, I would just hate to see you—"

"Don't you have to go?"

"Charlie—"

"Please tell The Beast that I said hello, and reiterate my offer to have his babies if he grows tired of your refusal."

"Of course, I'll tell him word for word." She placed her bowler at an angle above the dark bun at the nape of her neck. "Good night, Charlie, you sodding idiot."

She mussed Penelope's hair on her way to the door, earning a most heartwarming scream and swat. But both were smiling as Penelope turned back to the card game and Jo retrieved her shape-obscuring coat from the rack and went out into the chilly night.

Miss Penelope turned her otherworldly stare on Charlie and beckoned him over. Charlie obliged, leaning in so that Penelope could stage-whisper in his ear, "Your girlfriend is a menace."

"Oh, Penny." Charlie cupped her face. Up close, he could see that she'd painted intricate butterfly wings around the corners of her catlike eyes. "You really mustn't talk about yourself that way."

The others at the table hooted happily, but then the lot of them were back to their cards, their cigars, their hennish chatter. They were every Englishman's very worst idea of mollies. Charlie loved them to hell and back.

"Sit down, *amore*." She patted her petticoat-padded lap. "You look a bit lost. Play with us."

"I'm fine. And I don't gamble anyway, which you well know."

She looked over her cards. "That's why I want to get you at the table. I'll have you cleaned out in ten minutes."

Instead, he went to the bar. If he was going to sacrifice his money to the ladies, he was going to decide what the losings were spent on.

"Charlie." Mr. Forester nodded a friendly greeting. He leaned his elbows on the bar, his closed ledger tucked safely beneath them. "Haven't managed to have a word with you all night. I've wanted to tell you, you look—" He laughed warmly. "Well, let's just say, I'm impressed. I can count on you to be on the cutting edge."

Charlie straightened a wrinkle in his indigo neckcloth. His trousers were checkered in a matching hue, and, really, it was a fine little getup. He was pleased to have it noticed. "Thanks, Mr. Forester. You're looking awfully fine yourself."

Forester looked amusingly doubtful. "You don't have to be nice, Charlie. It's been a very hectic night. I look something, I'm sure, but I don't think *fine* is the word you want."

"Oh, come off it."

"You been keeping busy?" Forester asked.

"Not as busy as Warren, but I've kept my hands occupied."

David Forester was a tall, lanky fellow with floppy hair the color of burned toffee and a close-trimmed beard. Though he couldn't have been any older than Charlie's thirty-three, he'd clearly seen a lot over his years at this place. He glanced down the bar at the sad fellow, then leaned in farther to whisper, "Are you looking for something in particular, Charlie? There's a few other new fellows tonight. If it's not working with that one, I could introduce you to Mr. Brady's friend. Sharp wit and money to burn. I think you might—"

Charlie held up a hand. "Much as I appreciate it, Miss Matchmaker, I'd most like to be introduced to another gin and tonic. And throw in a round for the girls while you're at it."

Forester gave Charlie a sideways sort of look, then glanced over at the card table. "You're feeling awfully generous tonight. I assume this is going on *the tab*?"

"Don't make it sound like that. There's money in my future, so a little more debt in my present isn't going to harm anything. You'll be paid in full in the blink of an eye."

The skeptical look remained unchanged. "If you say so, Charlie."

Charlie sat back on a stool as Forester busied himself with glasses, bottles, and what looked like quite a lot of extra ice in Charlie's drink. He felt eyes on him and peered around. The sad fellow was looking over from his own barstool, but quickly looked away when he was caught at it. Feeling sorry for him, Charlie went over and ran a hand from the fellow's feathery brown hair and down his shoulder. Bloodshot eyes turned back up to him.

"I apologize for my manners," Charlie said. "If you can forgive me, I'll pick back up where we left off."

The man really should have said no. Charlie did not deserve a second chance. But once Charlie had gotten his drink and started back to his nook, the man followed. They sat together. Charlie pulled him in close before he could change his mind, drew the curtain and finally got around to testing out the newcomer properly. Jo was right. He liked newcomers. They were too skittish to demand much of him, and since he never took up with any more than once, it was quite a sustainable arrangement and his friends did so love to hear his exaggerated retellings of the most interesting ones.

It would go on like this for the next few weeks, until he found himself with Alma waiting at home for him each night. He did not know what he'd do then. The future seemed alarmingly blank just now.

Well. Not the whole future. There was still a bright spot. As Jo's discovery crinkled in his pocket, he was glad to know he had one thing to look forward to.

Miles Montague. The name itself nearly made him shiver. Charlie could always rely on the white-hot imaginings of his favorite smut author to get himself going under nearly any circumstances. Though the newcomer's hands were stiff on Charlie's chest and his kisses were awkward, Charlie could find the pleasure in anyone.

Just so long as his mind remained a thousand miles deep in Montague's fictional filth.

Chapter Two

Miles

Smithy was silent for altogether too long. The stack of drivel Miles dared to call a manuscript—a manuscript he further dared to title *Ganymede's Feast*—sat on the desk between them, untouched.

With an air of gravity, Smithy folded his hands on the desk. His light hair was slicked so thoroughly that it shone even in the dim dregs of sunset that could filter through the October clouds and the inky mess of the print house windows.

"It's garbage, Reg," he said, using Miles's pen name.

Miles brought his index fingers to his lips, trying to keep the rest of himself impassive. "I see."

Smithy's face cracked into a grin and he held out his hand along with all three obnoxiously dazzling rings on it. "Which means it couldn't be more perfect."

Though he'd seen that coming—it was Smithy's favorite joke—Miles was still relieved as he took the smooth, glittering hand. "You're a monster, Smithy."

"Me?" Smithy laughed, picking up the first few pages of the handwritten manuscript. The labors of Miles's months fanned past. "The things you do to the boys in this book, Reg... There's a monster in the room, indeed, but it's not me."

Miles flushed upon commentary of his fourteenth pornographic novel no less than when Smithy had teased him about the first. "Oh, they all have a good time."

"And you mark my words, all the perverts of London will have one too, once they get their grimy hands on this. Best you've done since *Immorality Plays*. Better, even: jumps right into the action! It's the most self-indulgent mess I've ever laid eyes on, and I couldn't put it down. I may even be able to get a run on the Continent; you have the one lad rolling in French wine, after all. That's culturally relevant, that is."

"You know I have a terrible weakness for anything that comes out of Bourgogne."

"Well, buy yourself a good bottle, my lovely monster; you've sold another blasted pile of filth to me." Smithy opened his drawer and drew out an ostentatiously feathered fountain pen that Miles had bought him for Christmas last year. They both signed the barely binding contract and Smithy handed over the hefty stack of advance money. "I'll start getting it set as soon as possible."

Miles took the cash and tucked it securely in his inner pocket. He grabbed his bowler and overcoat from the rack, finding an ink smudge on the careworn wool from even this short time in the print house. "Take care, Smithy."

"Reg."

He turned back to see Smithy looking strangely earnest beneath his glistening hair. "You know I don't usually ask a lot of questions—"

"A fact I'm immensely grateful for," Miles grumbled as he pulled on his coat.

"Yes, but…" Smithy stroked the feather pen nervously. "Look, man. We've been working together for years. You're in and out of my office with ideas and pages and proofs. Don't get me wrong; your industrious nature keeps me and my lit-tle wifey here fed." He jerked his head to indicate the nearest of the scandalous photographs he had hung on his walls: a busty, dark-haired woman in nothing but knickers and corset. "Don't think I don't appreciate what you bring to the table. But it's all business with you."

"Yes, it is."

"Before you leave, can I simply ask, for once, how things are going?"

Miles paused with his hat halfway to his head as the perfectly normal question hit him like an outrageous absurdity. "How what's going?"

"Literally *anything* other than your work." Smithy smiled at Miles's awkwardness, yet there was a concerned edge to his boisterous voice. When Miles didn't respond, he twirled the feather pen slowly, prompting: "The shop, for instance. How's the shop?"

"The shop?" Miles settled his hat into its place at last. It was bad enough that Smithy even knew about the shop. Miles certainly wasn't going to hang around and *talk* about it. "The shop is still open."

"That bad, eh?"

Miles finished with his buttons and yanked his scarf tight. "It's none of your business."

Smithy tapped the nib of the pen on the manuscript's cover page a few times, staring at Miles and ignoring the blots of ink he left behind. "I do worry about you, Reg."

"You ought to stop that." Miles's voice came out as more of a growl than he typically used with Smithy, but this was getting to be too much. "You're my publisher, not my mother."

"How's your mother?"

"Dead. How's yours?"

"Come on, Reg. Let's get a drink. My treat. You look like hell, you know; you need to get out of that dusty old shop and have a little fun."

"I have plenty of fun."

"Yet you can't spare a bit for me, eh?" Smithy smacked the top of the manuscript with the back of his bejeweled hand. "Too busy kidnapping all the pretty lads of London and torturing them in your basement, are you?"

"Didn't I mention that *Ganymede's Feast* is practically an autobiography?"

Smithy finally dropped his head into a disappointed nod. He stashed the feather pen back in its drawer, closing it up with an air of finality.

"Good night, Reg," he said.

Miles pulled on his gloves. His fingers itched for the doorknob, but a twinge of guilt slowed his exit. "It's nothing personal, you know."

"I know, I know. Get out of here and enjoy that money. Blow it on whatever it is you blow it on—wine, women, men, whatever—and just know you have my full blessing and best wishes."

"Tell your wifey I said hello."

Smithy turned back to the brunette. "Reginald Cox says hello, dear."

The door to the printer's was heavy with the gale behind it as Miles pushed his way out onto the street. It was a particularly windy and miserable day, made all the worse by Smithy's horrible location on the horrible Holywell Street. Miles hated coming down here, to this dark, stinking, disheveled old nightmare of a place, but it was that or invite Smithy to his own. He certainly wasn't going to do that, so he skulked beneath the shadowy overhangs of the old buildings just as self-consciously as anyone else, his hat low and his coat pulled tight. The crumbling shop windows he passed were shaded or displayed cheap novels and almost-acceptable artwork. Most had a posture, picture, or turn of phrase that indicated secret stacks of inventory that might include some of Miles's own work. He enjoyed his work. He wished he could say the same for the places it brought him.

He clutched the cash tightly in the inner pocket as he picked his way around suspicious puddles and other men who were very happy not to meet his eye. It would serve him right to have it all nicked. He'd been lucky on that count so far—he'd yet to lose one of Smithy's payments to a thief—but how long could that last? As always, when he passed beneath the ugly crescent-moon sign that marked the narrow passageway back out to civilization, he held his breath. He had lost track of whether he did that for luck or for practical purposes.

The wind and fog were still making a fuss out in The Strand, but he'd made it off Holywell again, no worse for wear. With one hand, he clutched his hat against the air's assault, and with the other he clung to his chest. If he lost the money, he'd be in a real spot. Jokes of blowing his advance on fine wines were well and good (and often accurate), but not this time. Today, he had to go straight from the printer's to the bank. The money wouldn't stay there long—the storefront's rent was due in three days—but he was satisfied with the balance for the moment. It would see him through, thank God.

Or, rather, thank the devil. After all, it was more likely Lucifer's generous dictation that kept Morgan & Murray's open. The shop certainly didn't make enough money in its own right, not anymore. It was a shame. He could be living quite comfortably in proper rooms of his own, rather than in the drafty, musty apartment above his questionable inheritance.

Errand completed, he hunched against the wind again, finally arriving back at his dark, empty shop. He unlocked the door with rigidly chilled hands and stepped inside. As much as the shop's finances plagued him, it was comforting to trade the sharp, smoggy cold of the streets for the familiar smell of the bookshop. If he closed his eyes, he could almost pretend he was just a customer again. Or a lazy employee, sneaking words onto scrap paper when he should have been shelving. That had been easier to imagine back when the whiff of Ethan's herby aftershave still lingered. That was gone by now, though, so he could not kid himself out of reality for very long.

He flipped the Closed sign back to Open. There was only an hour until the official, posted closing time, but he needed any sale he could get. Neither the shop nor his writing quite covered his expenses, but so long as he kept up with both, he had a roof over his head, bread in his mouth, and the occasional vice properly indulged. So, while he was cold and tired and wanted nothing more than to give it up for the day and vanish upstairs, he got a fire going in the downstairs hearth and lit lamps against the darkness that was starting to seep through the windows along with the cold. Once the warmth and light were sufficient, he settled onto the stool behind the counter. The serial he'd started this morning was right where he'd left it, with Wilkie Collins's newest installment ready and waiting for him to put on his specs and dive back in. He could catch up on the shelving and the ledgers tomorrow morning. He'd turned in a manuscript today, damn it; he could afford to give himself a moment while he waited around for customers who likely wouldn't even come.

In fact… He checked the door. No one was coming in tonight; he was as sure of that as he was of anything. He rarely got anyone through the doors after dark as it was, and on a blustery, unpleasant evening like this one, any devoted reader would be hunkering down with an old favorite rather than mucking about with new purchases. With that in mind, why not indulge a bit? Another manuscript in, Smithy pleased as anything, and his bank account fuller than it had been in a year. Any normal man would celebrate such a success.

He made a quick trip up the creaky stairs to his flat. He lived a simple existence with very few extravagances, but he made two exceptions: novels and wine. His wine rack was as well stocked as his bookshelves, some of the inventory on each quite nice. He selected a sweet and celebratory burgundy, then brought it back down along with a glass.

Back behind the counter, he opened the bottle and poured a healthy portion. It was so lovely and rich that the delectable vapors crawled up his nose and seemed to spread to the rest of his head. The first sip was even better, delicious warmth that went right to the core of him.

There. A glass of wine, an empty bookshop, the long-awaited serial chapter, and the satisfaction that someone might pay him for his art. There was more to life, perhaps, but this was what Miles had, and it was something.

The wine was so delicious that before he knew it, he'd drained half the bottle and had moved on to the magazine's next story. His head felt pleasant now, and he was quite enjoying himself, so he poured a bit more.

No sooner had he righted the bottle, than the bell above the door chimed and a man stepped inside, clutching a ribbon-wrapped top hat tight to his head with one hand, clinging to a bag over his shoulder with the other.

"Good God!" the man exclaimed in a pleasant voice. "That wind's got me feeling like a paper doll. I'm shocked I didn't blow away." He looked up, revealing a smooth face set with a pair of intelligent brown eyes. A handsome devil, that one; it was probably the wine, but Miles caught himself looking the fellow up and down. He returned his gaze to the man's eyes. They seemed safer, at first, but the longer he looked, the more he doubted that. Good-looking, well-dressed men like this did not generally frequent Morgan & Murray's. What on earth was he doing here?

The stranger took in the sight of wine and magazine. His full mouth turned upward into a smile as bright and wicked as his eyes.

Miles felt heat rise to his face. He looked desperately at the clock. "Technically," he said, "we closed five minutes ago."

"Good." The man looked backward at the door, then nodded slowly. "Would you, ah, like to lock up behind me, then? I swear, I'll only be a minute."

Though his voice itself was lovely—a baritone rich and sweet as the wine, with a relaxed edge to an otherwise posh accent that pointed toward Manchester—something about the words raised Miles's hackles. "What can I help you find, sir? Something in particular?"

"Yes." He cleared his throat, suddenly looking uneasy. "I'm looking for a, uh, Mr. Miles Montague."

Miles froze. He tried to keep his voice casual. "Never heard of him. Do you know the title?"

"No, not… I'm not looking for a book. I already have the book, you see."

Miles stood. The stranger's sudden nerves, the way he kept looking at the door and running his fingers over the seams of his bag, stood out as suspicious. He wasn't a customer. He was something else.

He was trouble.

"If you aren't looking for a book," Miles said slowly, "then I suggest you leave. We're closed."

"It's you, isn't it?" the stranger blurted. "Mr. Montague, the proprietor of this shop?"

"Who's asking?"

The fellow approached the counter cautiously. "My name is…" He took a breath, looking at the door again. "Price. Charles Price. I suppose I should give you a fake, but that doesn't seem very sporting, does it? Given I know yours?"

No. Oh God. Oh *fuck.*

"What do you want, Mr. Price?" Miles stood with his hands flat on the counter. He was taller and broader than Price; he looked tougher with untamable hair and a voice he could make gravelly and straight out of the gutter if he wanted to. Maybe he could scare the fellow off.

Price did look intimidated, his face twisting with discomfort beneath the shadow of his fancy hat. But he stood his ground, reaching into his bag and tugging out a book. He revealed only the top half of it, just enough for Miles to see the title and author.

Immorality Plays. By Reginald Cox. Two moralists seclude themselves in a country house to pen a treatise against sin, only to find themselves compelled by dark forces to act out each crime they denounce. It was his best-read and most publicly scorned work. They said every copy should be rooted out and burned. Said that they should bring back hanging for sodomites and smut peddlers just for Cox alone. They said all that, and sales had boomed so spectacularly that Miles was still earning on the scandal.

And that was all well and good. That was the kind of thing to break out the good stuff over, in fact.

So long as no one knew that Reginald Cox was actually the unassuming bookshop owner, Miles Montague.

The very ground seemed to crumble under Miles's feet as he realized what this meant. He wished it would, actually, that the floor of the shop would open and swallow him whole. He could get it over with fast, that way. He wouldn't have to go like Ethan had, if only Satan would reach up and grab him now, thanking him for years of devoted service with a swift and painless end.

But Satan was not such a good friend. Miles was on his own. Unable to summon so much as a word, he stormed past Price to the door. He locked up and flipped the sign, then turned back to the demon who'd slipped in while he indulged in the few things he had to enjoy in this world.

"What do you want?" he growled, stepping in close. Price drew in a sharp, scared breath. Good. He should be scared. Blackmailers were murderers, as far as Miles was concerned, and should be treated as such. "Go on. 'Price,' you say your name is? Clever. Well, then, what's yours?"

"I, uh, I'm not sure what—"

"I won't play your head games, you know. I know how those end. So, tell me your price. If it's reasonable, I'll pay it. If not, well, I've got friends who will see to it I never have to."

Never was a strong word. Smithy had a few "friends" on retainer to step in on behalf of his authors, but they probably wouldn't take care of anyone permanently; just rough them up. But no need for Mr. Price to know that.

"I think you're misunderstanding me," Price stammered. "What...what exactly are you paying for?"

Miles narrowed his eyes. "Your silence?"

"Silence?" After a tense, confused beat, Price barked out a bit of nervous laughter. "You think I'm here to *blackmail* you?"

Miles hardly dared trust the amused openness on Price's pretty face. "What else? You barge in here with that book, saying you know my name, implying I should lock up behind you so no one comes in."

Price put a kid-gloved hand to his mouth, looking suddenly mortified. "My God, I'm so sorry. I've made awful fools of us."

"What's that mean?"

Now that the door was safely locked, Price took out the book and a fountain pen from his bag. "I'm not here to blackmail you, Mr. Montague." He hesitated, licking lips that were chapped from the wind. When he looked up, his face was strangely innocent. "I'm here because I want your autograph."

Chapter Three

Charlie

Charlie had never felt so foolish as he did standing there in a cramped, dark shop, holding out the dirty novel like some doting little schoolgirl while Montague stared as if Charlie were possessed.

"Autograph?" Montague's voice was low with a touch of gravel, quite pleasant on the ear and the perfect accompaniment to his broad shoulders, his black and silvered hair, and the decidedly cynical set of his dark eyebrows. He dressed like a writer and bookseller ought to—simple linens and tweeds, a pair of silver reading specs on his nose—but he did not otherwise look like Charlie had expected. A bit too big. A bit too rumpled. And far, far too intimidating for a man of letters. Charlie tried to imagine it, this rough-edged fellow sitting down to a candlelit desk, scribbling away and smirking to himself as he penned the phrases that drove Charlie into the folds of his own trousers.

"Y-yes." Heat rose to Charlie's face, a burning he couldn't quash. "I'm an enthusiast."

"An enthusiast. Of Reginald Cox. Interesting thing to prance into a bookshop and admit to a complete stranger."

His face burned brighter. "I, er, suppose it is, isn't it? Well, I guess that makes us even. I know something about you, perhaps, but now you know something about me. No need to fret about blackmail in that case."

Montague—Reginald Cox, and yet not Cox at all; a real man so close now that Charlie could smell the wine on his breath—didn't look convinced. He glared heartily above the rims of his specs. "You call that even? Being an *enthusiast* is not punishable by hard labor. Not punishable by anything, really, for a bloke whose coat buttons could pay my bloody rent." He lifted his glass toward Charlie's chest, nearly tapping the lip of it against an admittedly opulent disk of molded silver. "Someone might look sideways, but unless you're a complete fool, you'll get out of it. What you've accused me of, though, writing and selling it, could get me—" he gestured to his own simple, brown waistcoat "—in more trouble than I think you can imagine."

"I'm not accusing you! All I want is for you to sign the book. That's it."

"No one in their right mind wants Reginald Cox's bloody *autograph*. It's not *Dickens*; that's not how these things work." He crossed to the fire, then whipped back around. "Please take it and get out, Mr. Price. We're closed."

Charlie deflated at the look on Montague's face, something between panic and despair. There was nothing roguish about it, nothing reminiscent of the confident words he put on the page. With a nod of defeat, Charlie put the book in his bag and started for the door. He put his hand on the cold knob, but turned back. Montague watched him anxiously from his place by the fire.

"I'm sorry," Charlie said. "I didn't mean to alarm you. It's just that I *do* like your work. I like the work of a lot of fellows I really shouldn't like the work of, and when there's a signature on it, it reminds me that it was made by a real person.

I like that. Proof that I didn't make it all up in my own sick head. I've got Saul's, you know."

Montague's eyes widened. "*Jack Saul?*" he repeated. "You lying bugger, you do not."

Charlie beamed, glad to finally have someone who could appreciate the effort such a discovery required. "He keeps to himself, of course, but he's quite friendly in person. Got his scribble on the big one, and a few he's got under other names. And then I've got Dawes's."

Something near to a smile ghosted over Montague's lips. "Not as if that's difficult. Dawes might as well be a peacock."

Charlie laughed, remembering the night at the Fox when he'd gotten that signature. The poet Dawes hadn't cared who knew his identity at all, and wore purple and pearls with the best of them. "You're not wrong. But I've others. I have a very nice series of woodprints, for instance. They were supposed to be anonymous, but I found the chap, and the signature's hardly more than a line, but I've still got it." Charlie ran his fingers over the seam of his bag. "Yet, honestly, it's your work I come back to again and again. And *Immorality Plays* is my very favorite piece. My favorite piece and my favorite writer, yet I've never had any idea how to find him. I've asked all around my usual places; either no one knew or no one would tell me. Until now. I got excited. I apologize for storming over here and making you think you were in trouble. I swear on my life, Mr. Montague, I'll bring you no trouble. I'm just a collector, with a very small collection that no one even knows about except me and a couple close friends."

Montague stared. He had dark blue eyes and lovely long eyelashes, a surprisingly delicate attribute compared to the rest of him. He still seemed suspicious, but his countenance was softening. "How did you find me?"

"A friend did the investigation."

"What friend?"

"Um. To be honest, I don't know his real name."

Montague threw his shaggy head back and laughed, returning to the counter and picking up his drink. "To think," he said with a leisurely sip. "I was starting to believe you for a moment there. You don't know his name? Bollocks."

"I mean it. My friend is like you, I suppose. Can't afford to have too much information out there. Very cautious."

"And you're not?"

"I know how to protect myself. I'm cautious but see no need to be paranoid."

"So you admit to some kind of wrongdoing?" Montague snapped. "Something more damning than your little collection that you need to be cautious about? Sodomite, I expect? Most of my readers are."

Charlie had to laugh. "Of course not. I read your work for the satirical element and riveting plotlines only."

Montague didn't seem to find the joke amusing. He stepped in close, playing at intimidation again. He played it well, but Charlie prided himself on spotting red flags, and he saw, well, he definitely saw some, now that he was actually looking. This poor sod had circles under his eyes, wine on his breath, and a slump in shoulders that would otherwise have been beautiful. He looked on the edge of something bad even if he wasn't quite there yet. If one of his friends at the Fox had asked his opinion on whether to take Montague to a private room, what would Charlie have said? *Looks like rough trade, mate. Be careful.*

Charlie lived without fear only because he did not take any real risks. He knew the signs to look out for, always built himself escape routes, and never got close enough for anyone to wish him harm. But tonight, he hadn't looked. He'd provided no escape. He'd marched up unannounced to a writer whose books were filled with cruel sarcasm and violent sadomasochism. While that got Charlie's blood hot in a room by himself, he probably shouldn't have used such writings as if they were a glowing reference to the man's character.

Montague stared down at Charlie with the glass nearly at his lips. "Look, Price. I'll not be blackmailed."

"I'm not a blackmailer!"

"Maybe not, but I can't know that from your word alone, and I swear to God, I'll be hanged for murder before I let someone force the rope into my own hands." His voice rasped over those chilling words, raising the hairs on the back of Charlie's neck. "You could ruin me with this. If you're really in good faith, give me something that will ruin you in return." He paused for the rest of his drink, the scent of it swirling around them. "And then I won't ruin you. And you won't ruin me. I'll sign your bloody book, and you'll get out of my shop and never speak of this to anyone."

Mouth dry and heart fluttering, Charlie nodded. The man was clearly mad, but he also had a point. Charlie could only hope Montague was as earnest as himself, because he didn't think he was getting out of this without a secret divulged or a broken crown.

"Alright," he whispered. They were still uncomfortably close, closer than Charlie got to anyone he wasn't intending to get even closer to. "Call me Miss Molly if you like. It's the truth. Not particularly ashamed of it either, or I suppose I wouldn't have come here to have you sign the most buggery-filled book of the age, would I?"

The confession didn't relax Montague in the slightest. "So how do I prove it? Tell me the houses you go to. Your lover's name. Something as damning as whatever led you to me."

Charlie prickled. "I'm not dragging anyone else into this."

"Then it's useless. What am I supposed to do with what you've told me?"

"Tell everyone you know. It will get around and my reputation will be even worse than it already is. Reputation is everything for blokes with nice buttons." He tapped the silver and tried a smile, but Montague's grimness did not budge. "Look. My father is a big name in the Manchester branch of the Bank of England, and I'm about to be married. A scandal like that could really do me in." He reached into his pocket with shaking fingers and took out his card. "This is me. An identity for an identity. I think it's fair enough."

Montague glared at the card and didn't touch it. "Assuming this card is real, a poor reputation and a jail sentence are not the same. You can talk yourself out of the first much more easily, especially if you have money."

Charlie threw his hands in the air, laughing bitterly. "This is ridiculous. I don't know why you bother asking if nothing I tell you is damning enough. I suppose I shouldn't be surprised. You've a devilish mind after all; not impressed by run-of-the-mill sodomy and pornography. Takes boys chained to each other and ministers begging for flagellation to catch your attention, does it?"

"Mr. Price—"

"Oh, just stop it!" Charlie stepped in, pushed through fear into anger as he pointed his finger accusingly between Montague's suspicious eyes, a whisper away from the bridge of his specs. "You want me to name my friends and lovers to a snarling brute like you to prove my *trustworthiness*? Betray *them* so you can sleep sound, knowing I won't betray *you*? What sense does that make?"

Montague blinked wildly, taking the smallest of steps back. "I… I don't—"

"I don't wish you harm, Mr. Montague. Most people don't. Most people are too bloody wrapped up in their own business to care about yours."

They were truly toe-to-toe now. If he leaned in a bit, they'd be pressed up against each other. With Montague so startled by Charlie's pivot from politeness, he looked handsome again. These circumstances were a damned shame. Charlie, a hairsbreadth from his favorite filth artist, his lips parted in surprise, both their blood alight in their veins... There were much better ways this could have gone, weren't there?

Disappointing though it was, it gave him an idea.

If Montague wanted them even, well, then.

He'd make them even.

He reached out the remaining inch and grabbed the front of Montague's jacket. Before the fellow even thought to protest, Charlie dragged his head down and kissed him on the mouth, pushing his own cold lips into the warm taste of wine and a scratch of neglected stubble. With his other hand, he took the calling card and—before he could talk himself out of it—slipped it down the front of Montague's trousers.

He meant to stop short of anything too interesting, but around the edges of the card he couldn't avoid a searing brush of warmth beyond thin linen drawers. Muscles tensed up under his palm as Montague breathed in sharply, and there was a most enticing little twitch just beyond the tips of his fingers. He felt the vibration of Montague's hum of surprise, and a sudden grip on his upper arm. With their mouths still pressed together, Charlie nearly forgot what he was there for in the first place, was almost tempted to relax against this bookseller's broad chest.

After a few warm, terrifying, and confusing seconds, Montague let go and stumbled backward. He wiped his mouth, staring like he'd seen a ghost. "What are you doing?"

Charlie straightened his own lapels and cleared his throat. "Making myself into a criminal. If you'd like to cause trouble over this most offensive assault on your person, well, you have my card. You know where to find me."

They both looked down at the front of Montague's trousers. The front was noticeably more occupied than it had been, and certainly not from the addition of one little calling card. Charlie's face burned, but he tried to pretend he still had some dignity. He lifted his hat.

"Good evening, Mr. Montague."

He reached for the doorknob.

"Mr. Price."

Charlie turned. Montague's bluster had been replaced by bewilderment. "I... The book?"

"Forget it. I'll not ask anything more of you. In fact..." Charlie dug the book out of his bag and dropped it on the counter. "I've rather lost my appetite for it. As far as anyone's concerned, I've never even heard of Reginald Cox. Good evening."

He was reluctant as he walked past the confused writer, but he forced himself not to spare so much as a glance. He needed to escape this disaster, so he traded the warmth of the bookshop for the unpleasant slush of the streets.

The smell of paper clung to his coat and the taste of wine lingered on his lips the whole way home.

Chapter Four

Miles

Miles's lips tingled as he stared at the door. He brought his fingers to his mouth, as if he might find tangible proof that he'd not imagined the whole ordeal.

Nothing there, but he realized with a jolt that there was proof elsewhere. Though the curtains were shut, he still went behind the counter before slipping a hand down the front of his trousers. Price really had put a card in there, hardly an inch away from his traitorous prick, which was calming down more slowly than it had gotten going. Had it really been so long since his last fuck that he'd spring up at such an awkward and unwelcome fumble?

The card was a little crumpled now, but it looked as legitimate as anything. The same name Price had given was printed neatly on it, along with an address in Westminster. It *could* be fake, of course. While a sort of sinking feeling told him he'd made a mistake, he had no *real* way of knowing the truth without risking all to visit the address. And even then...

Oh, damn it all.

Guiltily, he picked up the volume that Price had left on the counter. It was from the first printing and was clearly well used. The cover was a bit battered, the pages very relaxed and comfortable in their binding. There were some odd glue spots on the edges, as if it had been most inexpertly repaired once or twice. As he flipped through, he found it preferred to fall open to particular pages, and that some of those pages were dog-eared.

Understanding swooped low in his stomach, catching the interest of his prick again.

This was not a blackmailer's book. That lovely man with his pretty eyes and soft mouth had read Miles's filthiest imaginings so many times that the binding itself knew where their tastes aligned. He really shouldn't have, but he could not help picturing it: the handsome Price in some aristocratic sitting room in his shirtsleeves, perhaps half-gone to a bottle of good claret. He'd be reading intently, the same passage two or three times, before furtively glancing at the door and...

Miles slammed the book shut and the image along with it. He had no business with that line of thinking after treating the man so poorly.

As he tidied up the front desk, he tried to talk himself out of his guilt. After all, with what he'd seen happen to Ethan, he had every right to be jumpy about blackmail. And Price—the spoiled prat—had clearly never given it a moment's thought in his life.

Yet, as Miles climbed the creaking and slightly crooked stair that led to his rooms, he couldn't stay righteous. He'd barreled well past the time of reasonable suspicion and embarrassed them both. Price was nothing more or less than a fan of his work, fan enough to risk his own exposure for a scribble on paper.

A fan and a bloody mad fool. He locked the door behind him and stood in the middle of his dark sitting room, lighting a candle that gave just enough glow to let him stare at the book and mull over the idiocy of such a gamble. He should have been thinking about whether an upstairs fire was worth the coal tonight, or what he was going to eat to soak up the wine in his stomach, but instead, he was fretting about how this preposterous stranger was going to get himself into real trouble if he did not learn to protect himself better.

That, however, was no concern of Miles's. So, Price liked his work, so what? Plenty of people did. Smarter people. People with sound, careful minds that had not been fluffed up by the sort of flashy, upstart wealth that made fools think they were invincible. *Manchester Branch of the Bank of England.* Well, bugger the Bank of England and all the pretty fops it fathered.

Candle in hand, he went into the single bedroom, floorboards squeaking under his agitated steps. He dropped the blasted book on his bureau and changed into his warmest flannel bedclothes with Ethan's old woolen dressing gown on top. The flat was cold and drafty, but at least it was sturdy enough to keep out the worst of the wind and all of the rain that started up shortly after he crawled under the blankets on his lonely double-wide.

He blew out the candle on his bedside and settled in for sleep, but the whistle of the wind and rolls of thunder kept him up. He could not seem to get comfortable; his fingers and toes were too cold, while his thoughts of Price had grown disconcertingly warm.

Giving up entirely, he relit the candle and ventured out of his nest to grab Price's copy of *Immorality Plays*. Just what passages had gotten to the fellow, anyway?

Gently, so as not to give an opinion, he allowed the book to open in his hands to whichever page it would. Which filthy episode was Price's poison? There was a folded corner when the magistrate buggered the priest with a shapely candlestick. The spine was weak near the end, during the part where the debased characters kidnapped a wayward flower-seller and committed rather unmentionable acts upon her in the basement. But the favorite part, the section of binding most abused with one of the corners having gone missing entirely, was much earlier in the story.

Take that, Smithy, he thought, his estimation of Price rising as he remembered old criticisms with a certain smugness. *Slow start indeed. My biggest fan likes the beginning, so put that in your pipe and stick it wherever you like.*

He was not in the habit of perusing his old work very often, but when he did, he always found his owns words to feel familiar and somehow marvelous:

> *"I'm glad we're of a mind, Reverend Collins," said the judge.*
>
> *The lights were low now, their few candles quickly becoming insufficient in the dissolution of the daylight. The lines of Reverend Collins's face came into sharp relief as he nodded his agreement.*
>
> *The strange light brought a waking dream upon Judge Humphry. Behind the tenderly aged face of the Reverend, he thought he could see something else. He saw the young man Collins had once been shine out as if behind a curtain of years.*
>
> *The Reverend, it seemed, had been a most dashing lad.*

Along came, then, the necessarily gratuitous description of the Reverend Collins as a nude young man—plump pectorals, tight backside, large and well-formed prick, etc.—seen through the lens of Judge Humphry's twilight vision. Miles hadn't left the vision in the domain of the eyes alone, though; he took it further, forcing Humphry (and thus the reader) to *feel* how wretched with temptation the beautiful body has always been. He'd forgotten just how cruel a hallucination he'd penned, both characters filled to bursting with painful, haunting lusts, forever on the edge of a damning crisis of pleasure, but never permitted to tumble over. He had concluded the furious passage without relief for character or reader, as Humphry awakens and realizes that Collins has seen him similarly. They swear on their lives to finish and protect their treatise against sin, that very writing being a metaphor for holding up and protecting one another from their own devilish natures.

Miles read the passage twice, to be sure he had not imagined it. Charles Price's favorite page was not among the scenes of most outrageous debauchery. It was Miles's own favorite part, the part that Smithy had tried to cut and Miles had insisted on keeping even if he had to cancel the entire publication over it. This first instant of sensual connection was necessary to the rest of the piece. *Immorality Plays* was both a darkly erotic escapade and a satisfying comeuppance for powerful hypocrites. Without that scene, though, it was a book about monsters. With it, it became the tale of two men who tried and failed to save one another from the darkness of life, until the only salvation for either was death.

He'd told Smithy as much, in an impassioned speech that sent the old bastard into rolling peals of laughter.

You're a glum chap, Reg, Smithy had said, wiping a tear of mirth from his cheek. *But have it, if you like. Just don't come crying to me when you don't earn anything. This is a risk, you know.*

He'd known. And he'd taken it. And both he and Smithy had been greatly rewarded, for it was indeed that raw, failed devotion that kept people coming back, even if they thought they came for the scandal. Anyone could write a scandal. Reginald Cox made his readers weep over it.

Had Price wept over it? It was hard to imagine such sentiment in a silly, smiling bloke like that. Yet, he'd dragged his pretty arse through the wind and cold, risking any number of frightful possibilities to secure the inscription of the sod who'd written the words. Whether or not he'd shed tears, he'd clearly felt *something*.

With a sleepy sigh, Miles left his bedroom and went to his writing desk. He dipped a pen, signed the title page, then tucked Price's calling card between the favorite pages.

He'd bring it by tomorrow.

Chapter Five

Charlie

It was an interesting time to be planning a wedding, wasn't it? October was shaping up most nastily. The winds had gotten so high that as Charlie waited for Alma and her mother to arrive, watching the street out his parlor window, he saw people hunched and dripping, their coats flapping about like wings. One lad's umbrella turned fully inside out and spun away from him, flipping right under the hooves of a startled carriage horse. It would be a unique wedding, that was certain. Memorable. Maybe, if November was cold enough, they could get icicles instead of flowers over the church steps. That would be pretty.

Overcome with a sudden restlessness, he scrambled to his feet. Once up, however, he could not think of anywhere to go but the brandy decanter. He poured a splash to keep himself company as he paced in front of the roaring fire for lack of anywhere else to go, waiting for the Merriweather women, who—he realized with an impatient jolt—weren't even late yet.

The ability to relax in this newly built town house was not coming easily to him. It would be better once Alma was here and they could fill the empty spaces with children, but he still had almost six weeks in it alone.

There was no reason to be so uneasy. Mum had furnished

the place beautifully. Pop had removed all stress of expense from his shoulders. But it was *dark*. That must be the problem. There was perfectly modern gaslight in almost every room. He'd lit every fireplace and wick and puddle of paraffin he could find in the place. And yet, it was still too gloomy on a day like today. His old bachelor rooms had let in more light than this, hadn't they? He had an uncanny sensation that the gloom itself was trying to invade his insides, tapping little nail-holes through his bones that would soon be filled with fog and ice water. He wanted to run right out into the rain. Go anywhere in the whole world where that feeling could not find him.

But he could not.

What he could do, though, was take a steadying sip of sweet liquor and focus on what was still warm and pleasant. He closed his eyes and inhaled the fascinating combination of sugary smells that had filled the place over the past few hours. Charlie had convinced Mum to sneak him the money to hire a baker and all his little minions, instructing them to put together a variety of cake samples for Alma to choose from for the reception. Now *that* was reason enough to wait around in this dim little parlor, wasn't it?

At one o'clock sharp, the bell rang. Charlie startled at the sound, nearly spilling his brandy. For months before his engagement, it seemed the only people who called on him were a rotation of increasingly infuriated debt collectors. It had left him a bit jumpy. He shot back the rest of his brandy, reminded himself that it was certainly only Alma and her mother, and made himself start for the front door.

Before he could get there, of course, the new butler swished past him to do the job.

How awkward. Charlie had not begun his life with any staff at all, and had never much liked how invasive it felt. His father's fortune had grown up right along with him. Given how much mischief he got up to as a boy, every pair of eyes hired on at home had felt like a shiny new shackle to deal with. He'd moved to London as soon as he finished school, into a boardinghouse and then a flat with no one looking over his shoulder other than his landlord's housekeeper.

Given how much mischief he got up to as a grown man, that's just how he liked it.

But that had not lasted. So, he did not answer his own door, peeking out from around the corner while the butler bowed the ladies inside and whisked them away to the drawing room.

Quincy the butler was far more Price Sr.'s man than he was Charlie's, and they both knew it. He raised a most judging eyebrow at Charlie as the party went past, then came back a moment later, utterly unamused.

"Your company has arrived, sir," he said dryly. "I'm sure this comes as quite a surprise. I do hope you're ready to receive them."

Charlie cheerfully clapped the man on the back. "Thanks, mate. I'll take it from here."

"I am sure you will, sir." Quincy bowed insincerely and vanished.

Charlie allowed himself one more splash of brandy, then went into the drawing room.

Alma and Mrs. Merriweather sat beside each other, chattering away as some other servant procured tea. As if anyone needed refreshment now. In addition to the cakes, the minions would be pouring some absurd number of wine samples from the crate the Merriweather family had delivered to Charlie's well-tended doorstep last week. The Merriweathers were horrified that Charlie had organized something so *outrageous* as a cake tasting, for so *frivolous* a reason as to *please their daughter and have a bit of fun*, but when they could not talk him out of the idea, they'd added the wine-pairing element so they could pretend there was some practical reason for it. A sommelier was also on his way, a gift from some obscure cousin or other, to help them make selections for the wedding that would impress all the right people.

"Charlie!" Alma burst up when she saw him come in, shining and squealing while her mother tried to shush her inappropriate response. Charlie's fiancée stopped just short of him, offering her hand.

He kissed it, looking her over appreciatively. It was true that Alma Merriweather was a bit skinny and unremarkable on the outside (a fact her horrid mother liked to point out whenever possible) but by this point in their engagement, he'd grown to see all her charming inner qualities reflected on her form. What were freckles but evidence of a love of sunshine? And an angular nose? Perfectly shaped to hide in whatever new and fashionable book she was bound to recommend to him next week. He wasn't marrying her for desire anyway, so he'd much prefer her warm, smiling face to some icy porcelain one.

"My sweet little dove," he said, lifting his hand so she'd twirl under his arm like they were in a ballroom. "You look stunning. That's not your wedding dress, is it? That would be terrible luck, but it's so lovely I wouldn't be surprised."

"Stop it!" Alma turned nearly as pink as her frilled frock. "Of course, it's not."

"I'm only teasing." He kissed her hand again. "Of course my little bride will be all in white. As for myself, though, I'm still deciding between the red and the violet for my suit."

Alma giggled guiltily at the horrified look on her mother's face. "Don't you dare! If I get to the church and see you standing by the vicar in your peacock-feathered hat or something, I'll never make it down the aisle for the laughing."

"Let's say I went through with it, though. Would you prefer the red or the violet?"

She gave it a moment of consideration. "The red. And fix your hair just this way. It's very dashing combed back like that."

"Thank you kindly. Now, enough of this; I think we're about to set your poor mother into a swoon." He felt a soft expression cross his face as she took his arm and led him back to the sitting area. "Are you ready for the cakes?"

"Of course! I cannot believe you've had them fix twelve, Charlie, and all of them different. It's absolutely marvel—"

Prudence Merriweather, dressed all in gray and black like every day was a bloody funeral, turned her sharp nose to Charlie. "It's decadent."

Alma's cheer faded, but Charlie did not let his waver.

"It is, a bit," he said. "But it's a wedding, you know? If ever there was a time for just a *touch* of decadence, it's now."

Mrs. Merriweather drew a tight breath. She was probably about to launch into one of her insufferable tirades that always left Alma very crestfallen.

Charlie wasn't having it. Not today. Fortunately, his future mother-in-law was easy to distract. Crassly refusing to wave down a servant, Charlie reached across the table to pick up the teapot and refill Alma's cup, spilling a few drops while he was at it. The extra lump of sugar he threw in horrified Mrs. Merriweather sufficiently to keep her quiet.

Alma smiled her thanks as she took the teacup from him, at least as grateful for the defense as for the tea. He tried not to pity her, tried not to think too much about *why* he ought to pity the poor girl he'd duped into this marriage. They would be alright, the two of them. After dealing with parents like the Merriweathers, Alma deserved a good life, some warmth, and a bit of fun. Charlie could not give her everything a wife might want, but he could at least give her those things. And she, in turn could give him...

One of those surges of panic hit his chest and he stood up all at once. It startled the women, so he cleared his throat and glanced at the clock. "Would you look at the time? I suppose I ought to tell the baker we're ready to get started."

Prudence Merriweather turned her disapproval to the grandfather clock. "The sommelier is late."

Charlie had forgotten all about that, and frankly preferred it that way. It was well past time to move forward with all this; another minute of stillness might just do him in. He waved a hand. "Forgive me, Mrs. Merriweather; while I appreciate your cousin's gift—"

"My husband's cousin."

"His...yes. That one. While I appreciate it, I do wonder if we strictly need someone to tell us what wines we like? Couldn't we just decide if we like them? I have a lot of experience, you know."

"With tasting wines?" said Mrs. Merriweather.

"With drinking," said Charlie.

Alma giggled. Mrs. Merriweather did not. Not at all.

"Taste is not subjective," she said seriously. "And mere *quantity* will not teach it. Have you ever tasted a poor pairing, Charles?"

"When you put it that way." Charlie suppressed the private laugh her words tried to shake out of him. "I suppose I have tasted a poor pairing or two in my day. And you're right. Dreadful. We can wait."

"Well, I for one think we should get started," Alma said. "I skipped lunch for just this occasion, and I'm certainly starting to feel it!"

"Alma." Mrs. Merriweather shot her own daughter with a glare that could shame a nun. "One cannot *get started* simply because—"

She faltered and turned to the doorway as the bell rang. Once Charlie got past his habitual shock, he had enough presence of mind to be relieved.

"Well," he said, as Quincy brushed past them to get the door. "That settles it at least. I suppose the old chap has arrived at last. I do hope he didn't encounter any trouble on the way."

Mrs. Merriweather sniffed. "I rather hope he did. Or else what is his excuse for being late?"

In came Quincy with a tall, broad fellow dripping along behind him. A man with long eyelashes and a scruffy face that was even more handsome in the light of day than it was in a dim, drafty bookshop. A man who crassly gripped an unwrapped bottle of wine in one hand and a bag in the other.

"A Mr. Montague," said Quincy by means of introduction.

Charlie stared at the man in the doorway. The man stared back at the populated room, his eyes very wide and lips parted in shock. He didn't seem to have expected Alma and Mrs. Merriweather.

And Charlie most certainly had not expected Miles Montague aka *Reginald Bloody Cox* to appear in his drawing room during his cake tasting. For a wild instant, he thought Montague might actually *be* the sommelier, in an insane twist of fate. He had a bottle of wine in hand, after all. But that wouldn't make sense, would it? Montague lived in a decrepit little bookshop, penning filth and getting drunk. There was no way Alma's uncle or cousin or whoever had hired this disheveled man to...well, to do *anything*.

"I apologize," Montague said in that same low, slightly rasped voice that Charlie had tried so hard to forget all night. "Perhaps I should come back later?"

Mrs. Merriweather stood, looking reproachful. "Come back later? When you're already late as it is?"

Montague looked sideways at Charlie, who was thinking

fast. He'd arrived with a bottle of damned wine. If he turned around now, without any proper introductions, it would lead to questions. Who's Montague? Why did he show up unannounced with a bottle of wine and a bag? And what's in that bag? Charlie thought he knew what was in that bag, and it was imperative that no one else find out, perhaps imperative that they not even wonder.

And so, though he knew he'd regret it, he bolted up and shook Montague's hand in a far more civilized greeting than the one they'd had the night before. His skin tingled at the memory of the only other place it had ever encountered on this man's body.

"Don't worry about it overmuch. Glad you're here in any case." Charlie widened his eyes, praying that Montague's paranoia would make him play along. He spoke slowly and deliberately. "My future mother-in-law doesn't trust me to select the wines for the wedding, and I can't say I blame her! A sommelier is just what the doctor ordered, I think, and you'll do nicely, late or not!"

He gritted his teeth behind his smile so hard he worried they'd crack as he willed Montague *to play along, play along, please dear God, play along.*

Montague held tight to his hand in an unnaturally long handshake while he absorbed the situation.

His eyes returned to Charlie's. "My pleasure," he said carefully. "And my sincerest apologies yet again. I found myself rather...tied up. Please accept, er, this, as recompense."

Charlie accepted the slightly dusty bottle of wine with a little rush of gratitude. The bottle was clearly an actual apology, though for last night's rudeness, rather than this made-up lateness. "How very thoughtful! Quincy, take this to the kitchen with the others. We'll give it a go along with the rest!"

Quincy took the bottle and immediately handed it off to

a minion who fled out of the room. Damn the man and his efficiency; Charlie had hoped to be rid of him. "Shall I take your coat, Mr. Montague?" the butler said. "And your bag, is that something—?"

"I've got it!" Charlie took the bag swiftly. He started helping peel the drenched coat and hat off him too, while the others watched his horrific decorum in a stunned silence. "Mr. Montague, please, make yourself comfortable. We'll all adjourn into the parlor momentarily."

He rushed back off to the foyer. As expected, Quincy followed at his heels until they were nearly at the door.

"Sir, if you'll allow me to—"

Charlie whipped around, drops of water flying off the bottom of the heavy overcoat. "If anyone else arrives at the door," he said seriously. "Do not let them in."

"But, sir—"

"If the person claims to be the sommelier, kindly give him a few pounds for his trouble, but tell him that we no longer require his services. In the meantime, please escort everyone into the formal parlor and begin the tasting. I'll be there shortly."

Quincy, for all his usual snark, nodded quickly and sincerely. "And Mr. Montague's things, sir?"

"Don't worry yourself about that, I'm already halfway to the coat closet."

"Sir."

Charlie swayed on the spot, every inch of him begging to bolt while he forced himself still. "What, Quincy?"

"It is my duty to protect your secrets, and I'm most glad to do so," he said. "But is this the sort of secret I'm going to regret protecting?"

Charlie ran a hand over his face and laughed nervously. "No, Quincy. It's simply in regard to *the collection*."

"Ahh," Quincy said with a disapproving sniff. Charlie had

been vague yet not altogether dishonest about the collection of books and artwork he kept in a locked cupboard in his library. He was hardly the first man to possess such things, and so long as the particulars remained obscured, he'd decided it was best to answer with something like honesty when Quincy had asked why Charlie possessed the only key. "One last hurrah before you clean up the house for your lady?"

"Indeed."

"You are quite the idiot, my good sir."

"Yes," Charlie admitted with relief. "Now go do what I've told you."

"In all haste."

Charlie hung up Montague's coat and hat, then dashed upstairs to the library to unlock the cupboard which held his collection. He'd had it all on display inside a dedicated wardrobe at his flat. The books had been lined neatly up on shelves; the wood carvings of a stunning pagan rite hung on the inside of the door beside the excellent nude sketches, and a rather gorgeous little sculpture sat beside equally pretty painted pottery, each suggesting the most illicit of lovemaking. A small showing, but his own showing nonetheless, and he liked to open the wardrobe, pull aside the obscuring curtain, and peruse his scandalous little treasures, feeling like he'd had one over on the world.

No longer. Since leaving the flat and coming to his comparatively enormous house, he'd had to pack it all in a trunk, lock the trunk, then the cupboard door to guard it. Two locks. Sometimes even that felt a bit too vulnerable.

He took the book from the bag in the shadows of the doorway, but could not simply tuck it away without examining it. He chanced a few steps into the sallow light sneaking through the window. It was indeed his copy of *Immorality Plays*. Belly on fire with nerves, he flipped to the title page. Sometime between the moment he'd pulled his hand out of Montague's trousers and right now, it had been signed by Reginald Cox in such an ugly swirl of handwriting that it was clearly one of the only signatures he'd ever given.

Charlie clutched it to his chest, a little overcome with something he did not want. He pushed the wave back before it could break right over his head, then locked the book up with the others.

Charlie met back up with everyone in the formal parlor, which was magnificently arranged. The baker had laid out a dozen different cake samples upon the various surfaces, each portioned into decadent-looking little cubes of confection and individually plated with tiny, gleaming forks. Beside each display were a few small glasses of red and white wines. Here and there between everything else were pots of coffee and baskets of biscuits to cleanse the palate, surrounded by hothouse flowers in vases, the petals strewn about on the tablecloths.

It had been a stressful morning, and there was more stress to come in this parlor filled with fiancées and in-laws and pornographers pretending to be sommeliers, but even in his heightened state, Charlie couldn't help but crack a smile at the simple elegance of a room filled with cakes.

Alma was in a state of bliss. She hardly bothered greeting him before getting back to her slow wandering around the room, leaning in to peer at and smell the various sweets with a joyful look on her face.

Mrs. Merriweather sat sipping her coffee, watching her daughter sharply as if unsure what trouble she might get up to. Bugger that old biddy in the worst way. Who could possibly look so glum in a place like this?

Even Montague—imposing, gruff Montague—had an eagerness about him as he looked around. It was a little awkward, and he was clearly fighting it, but it was charming nonetheless.

Charlie sidled over to the fellow and led him by the elbow a few steps away from the others. He gestured vaguely at the wines as an excuse before whispering though his smile, "Thank you."

Montague peered at him, downward a bit since he had a few inches of height on Charlie. He pointed at a cake, then muttered out of the corner of his mouth. "I'd say it wasn't a bother, but it does seem there's a bit of bother going on."

"All you need to do is eat some cake, drink some wine, and give us your opinions on them as if you know what you're talking about. Then you're on your way, I'm on mine, and we can forget all of this ever happened."

A look of skepticism told Charlie just how well Montague believed that.

Alma bustled up to the pair of them, her eyes shining about the cakes in a way they never quite did about Charlie. She clasped both her hands around one of his. "Oh, can we *please* get started? It's simply torture to look at them like this!"

Mrs. Merriweather was watching them from her spot near the baker with that look she always gave them, as if she were just waiting to catch her daughter at something she could criticize. Charlie was sorely tempted to give her something to look so grim about, but with Montague here, things were too volatile already. He settled on giving Alma that sort of *indulging* smile he'd been working on for the benefit of anyone who might question his husbandly affection: lips closed, head tilted, *ah my sweet angel, your needs are so simple, how could I ever reject them?*

"Of course, my dove." He squeezed her hand. "Let's get to it."

The assortment had an air of whimsical disorganization about it, as if each delight had popped into its place out of nowhere. However, the head baker clearly had an idea of how the tour should be conducted. He led them to the display nearest the entrance, and droned quite at length about a fluffy, creamy strawberry cake. It was indeed delicious but ultimately a lot simpler than the chap was making it out to be.

Alma was already eyeing the next cake over the sip of sweet white wine that was supposed to go with the strawberry. It was clear that she didn't give a whit about things like pairings. Charlie himself was more concerned with how drunk a particular alcohol could make him and could hardly tell the difference between the two that had been set out.

"Any thoughts from the lovely couple?" the baker asked. The assistant beside him had a pad and pen out, ready for their notes.

"The cake is divine!" Alma gushed, still eyeing the next, which had slivers of candied pineapple sticking out of the icing like little feathers.

"Splendid showing," Charlie agreed, lifting and draining the rest of his glass.

"Opinions on the wines?"

He faltered under the piercing gaze of Mrs. Merriweather. "I, ah, think I favor the second?"

Mrs. Merriweather turned her nose to Montague. Charlie followed suit. A few steps back, he was slowly sipping from one of the little glasses. He tasted another miniscule bite of cake, following it up with the other wine. Talk about splendid showings! Montague looked right official, smelling and lingering over each taste as if he could tell the difference.

"If you go with the strawberry," he said once he caught all the eyes on him. "I'd suggest the first wine. The second is delectable in its ice-cold state, but with weddings, we might find things are a little further from optimal temperature by the time they're consumed. The first is just a touch less astringent, and I think that would allow for more flexibility in serving."

Mrs. Merriweather's back went very straight as her feathers ruffled. "Are you suggesting our family cannot properly arrange the timing of our own wedding?"

Charlie clenched his teeth. Montague was not of means; in hindsight, this sort of thing seemed inevitable.

Montague's face dropped into a scowl for just a second, before he swept it away and gave a smile that did not remotely reach his eyes. He glanced knowingly at the serving staff and back again. "Mrs. Merriweather, I mean to suggest no such thing. My apologies, I assumed a large gathering to celebrate this lovely union."

"It *shall* be a large gathering!" said Mrs. Merriweather, a scandalized hand to her heart.

"Ah. Well, for my part, I've never been to a sizable gathering where nothing went slightly sideways. Have you? Sometimes a conversation goes on too long, someone is late through no fault of their own—"

"The groom has one too many at dinner," said Charlie helpfully.

This last one made Mrs. Merriweather's eyes go wide. She turned back to Montague for help.

"As I say," said Montague. "There's always a chance of something landing a half-hour long or short of the mark when human beings are involved. When I was hired to pick the best wines for your wedding, I meant to pick the best wines for your *wedding*, not your dinner table. There are different considerations. Don't you agree?"

Montague raised his eyebrows at Charlie. *How's that?*

Impressed, Charlie raised his empty thimble of a glass over Alma's head as Mrs. Merriweather's face relaxed.

"Alright," she said grudgingly. "I'm glad someone here is

able to take a practical view over the pleasure of the moment." Her nose turned back on her daughter and future son-in-law.

"Excellent!" Charlie said. "Did you get all that down?" he added to the note-taker. "Let's carry on, then. I'm eager for that frothy little pineapple trollop."

Alma laughed and led him over to the next cake. Mrs. Merriweather's scandalized look was quickly eased with more sweets and more wine, sticky-sweet reds this time. Charlie relished the cake—completely delicious, earning a squeal of delight from Alma—and he clinked his thimble against hers.

Though his thimble was with Alma, his eyes were on Montague, who was going through the same little song-and-dance of tasting slowly and thoughtfully, bit by bit. It was a striking sight. Even though Charlie knew it was an act, still he hung on it, wondering what was going on in Montague's mouth. Did he really experience more complex sensations than Charlie did? Where Charlie noticed only happy sweetness, was it possible that Montague tasted some dozen little nuances and partnerships?

A haunting recollection of the wine he'd had right off Montague's lips last night ghosted across his memory. What had Montague noticed on him? he wondered.

Charlie ought to have looked away. This whole act was having a near irresistible effect on him. But he stared until Montague caught him with nervous blue eyes.

"Well, my good man," Charlie said. "What do you think?"

Montague unconsciously licked a bit of icing off his bottom lip. Charlie had a giddy sort of feeling that he and Montague were partaking in a shared memory. Montague shook it off first, turning very deliberately away from Charlie to give his notes directly to the most unarousing person in the room: Mrs. Merriweather.

Unaware of the sudden tension, Mrs. Merriweather took

Montague's opinions with a solemn nod: *yes, indeed, pineapple sugars and acidity and lightness, serious business here.*

Charlie met Montague's eyes again over her steely-gray bun. They weren't exactly filled with sugar and lightness—he got the feeling Montague was incapable of such things—but there was something pleasant in them that hadn't been there the night before. Perhaps it was the sense of mutually assured destruction they now shared. Maybe it was just all the cake and wine. Either way, Charlie rather liked it; he especially liked how different it was from the frightening, gritty glare that the man was also capable of. It suggested complexity that Charlie himself probably lacked.

"On to the next one?" Montague suggested with a husky little smirk.

Charlie snapped out of his trance and put an automatic hand on Alma's back. "Yes. Yes, just..." He glanced at the note-taker. "Whatever the man said is fine with me. He knows his business."

As they went along, it became clearer that perhaps Montague actually did know this business. They sampled cake after cake, each with something lovely and delicious: peppermint icing, chocolate sponge, currant-specked cubes, or sugar-dusted violets. Along with them, wine after wine: sweet and dry, bubbling and still, red and white and yellow and pink. And Montague always had something to say about all of it. He had opinions about the pairings, questions for the baker, serving tips and bits of history about each and every splash of rotten grape juice that coated his tongue. Though the cups remained tiny, by the time they'd got through the last one, Alma was growing silly, Mrs. Merriweather had stopped sampling, and Charlie had completely lost track of the two women as he grew rather warm and hung on every word that came out of Miles Montague's brilliant mouth.

"I do hope you've all enjoyed yourselves," said the baker as the final crumbs were finished and the last of the notes were jotted down. "It has been a pleasure serving you."

Charlie dragged his eyes from Montague. "Thanks, old chap. I certainly can't complain."

The lot of them returned to the drawing room to discuss the selections and finalize them. Much to Charlie's dismay, Montague, after giving his final thoughts on the matter of cake, returned with an apology to the parlor to speak with the baker's minions, who were still cleaning up. Charlie tried to focus on the alarmingly in-depth conversation, but he could only care so much about the details. He kept glancing at the door, hoping it would open to reveal a slightly-too-bookish sommelier.

No. Not a sommelier. A writer. *Reginald Cox*. He could hardly contain the nervous giggle that built in his chest. Reginald Cox was going to pick the dessert course for his wedding. Jo wouldn't believe it. He couldn't wait to tell her; he'd have to get her to the Fox tonight or tomorrow.

"Something funny, Charles?" said Mrs. Merriweather, startling him out of his amusement.

"Not particularly," he said breezily, stretching a bit. "Just content."

"What did you think of the selections?"

"I'd eat any of them to excess any day. I'm inclined to take Mr. Montague's suggestions about what would be most palatable to the crowd." He glanced at Alma, an afterthought. "Or whatever Alma wants, of course, if there's disagreement between the two."

Alma giggled. Her face was pink, and her shoulders were a little liquefied. "If you'd been *listening*," she teased, "you'd have heard me say that I couldn't decide either! I want them all! Wee little samples all in a row, just like we had them."

It was a delightful idea, but Mrs. Merriweather put her foot down on account of some semblance of respectability. In the end, they went with two—the pineapple and the violets, along with Montague's preferred pairings.

"Where has that man got to?" Charlie mused as if he did not really care. "I'd like to thank him for his herculean efforts."

"Yes, the poor fellow!" cackled Alma in a little fit of laughter. "Working diligently at ardu…arduo…ar-ju-us tasks!"

"One too many thimbles, my little dove?"

"Oh no," she said. "At least three too many."

At last, the door to the drawing room swung open. Charlie's heart leaped to see Montague coming in behind one of the baker's fellows. The man placed a tray on the low table, which clinked with glasses, a brightly glinting decanter full of dark liquid, and the bottle Montague had come in with, now open.

"Before I take my leave," said Montague, "I wanted to present my gift to the happy couple."

Alma doubled over. "Oh, my goodness, I couldn't!" She wiped the mirth from her eyes. "Can't you see me? I'm already done in!"

Mrs. Merriweather looked reproachfully at her daughter. "Please forgive her, Mr. Montague. As much as we appreciate the kind gesture and your hard work today, I need to take Alma home now."

That little spark of pleasantness returned to Montague's eye. "Of course. It will be palatable for a few days after opening."

"Alma, dear," said Charlie. "You might find you want some come morning. Don't hesitate to join me for breakfast, if that's the case, and we'll take good care of your inevitable condition."

Mrs. Merriweather sniffed her disapproval of Charlie's humor, said a much friendlier farewell to Montague, and then ushered the loose-limbed Alma out the door.

Charlie smiled after them, relieved and satisfied. Alma had gotten the delightful afternoon he'd planned for her, with neither himself nor Montague coming out any worse for wear. Once the Merriweathers were gone, he dismissed the baking crew, thanking the head baker for his work and expressing his excitement for the upcoming event that he *just knew would be a hit, my good man, and the dessert course the very icing on top of it.*

That left Charlie and Montague alone in the drawing room. Bit warm after all that activity, wasn't it? Charlie tugged at his collar.

"Er, sit, Mr. Montague. If you'd like. You've been on your feet and, ah, working hard all afternoon."

Charlie laughed nervously and even Montague raised an eyebrow as he sat tentatively on the other side of the low table. He looked a bit large, his hands a little work-beaten, his clothing awfully rough-spun, compared to the delicate scrollwork and airy upholstery of the chair. How anyone had believed he was a sommelier was a true testament to his genius. He grew very quiet and the grimness returned to the edges of his being.

The silence was too much for Charlie. He couldn't bear it, just staring at Montague, at *Reginald Cox*, whose intimidating presence spread a few yards beyond his actual form.

"I am so sorry," Charlie said at last. "Thank you. For everything."

"You can't thank me for everything," Montague said, sort of a growl.

"Why's that?"

"You haven't even tried the blasted wine yet."

Chapter Six

Miles

Mr. Price's nervous smile faltered. He scooped up a glass, though much of the sturdy grace he'd put on for the women had been replaced with simple stiffness. He held the glass below his nose, not tasting it, just staring at Miles as though a bit worried it was poisoned.

"I realized when you left that it was *I* who owed *you* an apology." Miles suppressed a sigh that would make him sound as pathetic as he felt about the whole ordeal. "That's what the wine was meant for. I should have just signed your book."

"Oh, don't be ridiculous," Charlie said, feigning a casual air that didn't quite ring true. "I shouldn't have shown up like that. You were right to be suspicious; no sane person would just show up unannounced, waving that book about like a bloody lunatic."

Miles was more embarrassed than ever as Price waved his hand around in illustrative self-effacement, the firelight glittering manically off the amethyst on his pinkie. The fact that he'd mistaken such a pleasant chap for a villain suddenly seemed like a terrible indictment of his own temperament. Perhaps Smithy was right. Maybe he *did* need to get out of the dusty old shop now and then.

"Lunacy aside," Miles said, "once you clarified what you

were on about, it was obvious enough that you meant it. I shouldn't have put you into the, er, compromised situation you wound up in."

Price's face reddened spectacularly. He seemed to hide himself in the glass, which he pulled to the plump lips that had been so roughly pressed against Miles's not that long ago. He had an exceptionally good-looking mouth, Price did. The edge of the glass had an enviable position as he finally tasted the wine. His smooth, dark brows went up and he looked into the glass with something like alarm. "This is quite good, Mr. Montague."

Miles smiled before he could stop himself. "I'm a sommelier, ain't I?"

"Oh, God." Price gave a clear, easy sort of laugh, his face still charmingly flushed. "I cannot believe you went along with all that." He leaned his head back against the sofa. "Horrible. I simply panicked when you came in here. I don't know what's become of the real one."

"What do you mean?"

"Well, he was running late as it is. My dearest mother-in-law was getting very angry about that. And then you appear with wine in hand, looking like you're here to *woo* me. And that *bag*. I thought I knew what was in it, and I knew we could afford no questions about it. It was the best distraction I could think of. Perhaps it wasn't very good. But it's gone alright."

Miles helped himself to the extra glass, hoping a sip of the good wine would douse the little flicker of anxiety that lit his stomach. "So, the other likely came and went."

"No idea. If he did, Quincy sent him off with some money to keep him happy." Price glared out the window. "Hopefully, though, he had enough sense to stay home in bed on a day like today. I wouldn't blame him a bit."

The flicker turned into fear that all but tingled Miles's fingertips. "What if he comes back?"

With a flippant shrug, Price swirled his glass and stared up toward the ceiling. "Why would he do that? If he even arrived, he got paid extra to do nothing, and in the meantime, we won't spread the news of his lateness. Not to mention…" He rather suddenly slipped back into his handsome languidness, pointing straight at Miles's nose with a finger lifted from the glass. "You played the part so brilliantly that the worst that will happen is the old latecomer might end up with a few referrals he didn't deserve."

Miles examined Price until the fellow began to get uneasy again. But he couldn't help it. He was a little fascinated by the display of… What was it, exactly? When Miles thought of a bribe, he considered one thing and one thing only: what am I going to do when this bastard comes back for more? Price's little unravelling of all the ways in which everything was fine was an oddly *complicated* form of optimism. He didn't brush off the risk, but tidily assessed the mutuality of the transaction.

Price was clearly unnerved by the silence. He put his glass down and leaned his elbows on his knees, the whites of his eyes exceptionally white against the dark irises as he looked up at Miles with a nervous half smile on parted lips. God, those lips. He'd completely wasted his encounter with them last night. The things one could do with lips like that… His imagination wandered down some dodgy alleyways, finding ways he might write a fellow like Price into his next book…

"So," said Price, snapping Miles out of his professional musings. "Are you really a wine expert in addition to a literary genius? Or was it all fluff?" He cocked his head to the side, almost effeminate. "If it makes you feel any better, I can't think of any way divulging that bit of trivia would hurt you."

Miles stared at the label on the wine bottle, mostly so he

had something to look at besides Price's mouth, which had become unbearably distracting as it reddened with wine and went on with that constant stream of pleasant words. "I'm not an expert in wine any more than I'm an expert in writing. But I know a bit more than the basics, and I'm able to get by. I do think your wedding will be all the better for my advice, because, if you'll forgive me for saying it—"

"No forgiveness needed. Don't even say it. Because of my *nature*—" he waved his hand about a little, clearly referencing his admission last night "—I don't think that Alma and I will ever be united in true love. But we *are* united in an unabashed hedonism and lack of refinement. I think we will at least be able to have some good times together. That said, I appreciate that you were able to bring a bit of class to our menu. It will make all the parents happy. Alma and I are both disappointments, you see."

"I see," said Miles, though he wasn't convinced he did. "And this wedding?"

"Is supposed to appease the beasts that bore us."

Miles took that in, very aware of the anxiety that laced Price's airy words. "Getting married when you possess such a nature seems awfully risky. What if she comes to suspect?"

"She won't," Price mused. "For whatever reason, she's had trouble finding a husband willing to take her. I suspect it's her family—dreadful moralizers, the lot of them—but whatever the reason, I doubt she will ever go looking for things she doesn't really want to know. She wants a pretty home and some children to spoil, and to have dinner parties and the like. She's a good girl, with simple needs, and I do like her. I really couldn't ask for more."

Something odd crossed Price's face. He turned his gaze to the window, looking out of it a little desperately. As if through bars. As if he were caged. Miles spent a good deal of time imagining and writing about the twisted faces of trapped and bound men, so he recognized it when he saw it, even if it was more subtle in the bonds of real life.

"Well, then." Miles lifted his glass, hoping to cheer the fellow back up. "To your innocently hedonistic union. I wish you much cake and little trouble."

"Thank you, Mr. Montague." The pleasantness returned to Price's face as they clinked. He sipped slowly, as if considering something, then took a deep breath and said in a rush, "I know this is forward, but you can call me Charlie, if you'd like. Because of the books, I suppose, it feels like I've known you for a long time already."

The intimate notion managed to both warm and chill Miles at the same time. He bought himself a little time to think with a long drink of the wine.

"Alright," he said cautiously. "We've conspired now, after all, and could each ruin the other with a word. You can call me Miles."

"*Miles.*" The test of his name on those lips sent an involuntary shiver down Miles's spine. "Well, thank you again, for the book."

"What are you planning to do with it?"

Mr. Price—Charlie—rolled his eyes to the ceiling and then caught them on Miles's. "Read it yet again in secret and then put it in a safe deposit box with the rest of my nonsense before Alma moves in."

That same image that tormented him last night crossed Miles's mind, that of Charlie Price reading his work with a flushing face and a hand working at his buttons. It did not help that they seemed to each have leaned in farther and farther over the low table, such that they were much closer than they had been. Not close enough to feel each other's heat, but close enough to imagine it. Miles almost startled back with the realization.

He should have. Instead, he said, in a low, suggesting voice that hardly even sounded like his own, "Seems a shame your collection should be tucked away without anyone else seeing it."

"Y-yes." Charlie looked to the door nervously and then back at Miles. No longer trapped, he now looked like he was trying to puzzle out what he could get away with. "Would you...like to? See it? Before you go?"

He ought to say no to that. A look at Charlie's pornography collection? And that expression on Charlie's face as he took a slow sip of his wine... The surface invitation was risky enough, but he felt certain it did not end there.

Miles felt like one of his own characters, terribly tempted and about to make an awful mistake. Unlike his characters, though, he had volition. He could say no to this mad proposition. That's what he usually did, when such opportunities presented themselves. Too dangerous. He only accepted when his blood was so hot that it melted his reason.

It took just one more look at Charlie Price's suggestively smiling mouth to bring him to that point.

"Yes," Miles rasped. "Let's see it."

Chapter Seven

Charlie

Oh, Charlie was in a world of trouble now. Even Quincy knew it, damn the old bastard with that judging arched brow as the master of the house led the "sommelier"—wineglasses still clutched in both their hands like heathens—up the stairs to show the man the *library*.

"The library," echoed Quincy. "I'm certain he shall be impressed."

Impressed indeed. Charlie didn't exactly have a library. He had a small room with a couple of shelves and a handful of the proper books for a gentleman to have. Some histories, some war whatevers, the obvious great classics. Alma, a joyful reader herself, teased him mercilessly for it, and promised to fix the problem straightaway.

It was certainly not something you'd show off to anyone.

"I've got a history of the grape up there somewhere," Charlie said defensively as Miles followed him nervously up the stairs.

"Is he in the know?" muttered Miles when they'd arrived at the landing.

"Oh, he knows I've got some pervert's collection. Nothing a butler his age hasn't seen before, I'm sure. You'd be shocked how many gentlemen..." Charlie cleared his throat, peering back at Miles in the dark hallway. "Well. Perhaps you wouldn't be shocked."

Miles blinked. "What does he think we're up here to do, Charlie?"

"Giggle about titty pictures like teenage boys, I assume."

"Is that what teenage boys do?"

Charlie, warm from the wine and their proximity in this narrow hallway, elbowed the grim Miles Montague in the ribs. "You'd know more about that than I would, I expect."

He led Miles into the library and locked the door behind them. He lit a few lamps so he could close the curtains. When he turned around, Miles looked grumpy again, brow furrowed.

Charlie nearly snorted into his glass. "No need to look so cross."

"It's for the books," Miles said very seriously. "I ain't some chaser of young lads. It sells the books, you see, when some characters are innocent and others are corrupting. It's not meant to reflect real life, or even real desire. It's an idea, a notion, a—"

"I'm not accusing you of anything." He felt a surge of affection for the bewildered sod, and poked him playfully in the center of his chest. "I do understand the difference between pornography and reality, mate. If I didn't, do you really think I'd lock myself in a room with the fellow who wrote *Immorality Plays*?"

Miles batted Charlie's hand away quite unnecessarily, lingering a bit where their fingers touched. He put his glass down on the desk and crossed his arms tight. "Quite a library."

"Isn't it? It's got some, I don't know, *fifty books*. At least!"

Miles's face broke into a begrudging smile. Charlie wanted to touch him again, to poke or prod him, to find some excuse. He'd pounce immediately if he were certain he'd gotten his meaning across properly in the drawing room. Miles was still awfully standoffish, however, wandering around the room with his arms tight over his chest as he examined the sparse shelf of books, the dusty writing desk, the rarely used chairs. No one had bothered lighting the fire in here yet, so the air was chilly and a little damp.

"Where's your collection?" Miles said quietly.

"Hidden, obviously."

Miles turned back to Charlie, whose knees went a bit weak under that intense stare. "Shall we find it?"

Surely *that* was an invitation. But Miles's arms were still crossed, and he broke eye contact before doing anything to close that painful yard of distance between them. Charlie's whole body begged one of them to *do* something, but he couldn't, and Miles didn't. Why was this so difficult? In the club, he was practically a magnet; a look, a wink, a word, and he had whoever he wanted at whatever he wanted them for (sometimes for more than he wanted, if they were lonely). Though Miles was obviously interested—this had been his idea, after all—he was also completely unyielding. Charlie complained about the Fox's barnacles, but at least they were not boulders.

At a loss, he turned to the locked cupboard and dragged out the locked trunk. He knelt before it, and with fingers that would rather be running across Miles's broad shoulders, he opened it.

Miles's shadow fell over the trunk as he suddenly stepped in so close that Charlie could finally feel his heat and inhale the inky, woolen scent of him. His tweed trousers brushed against Charlie's silk sleeve, and the whisper of contact surged along all his nerves. Charlie swallowed hard, fumbling the lock. If he turned his head, he'd be on a level with where he'd left his calling card last night. He'd know instantly if Miles was as affected by the proximity as Charlie was quickly becoming. His breath caught at the very thought of what could happen if he just turned a little to the left...

But then as quickly as the shadow had come, it stooped as well. Miles knelt beside him, no less tempting shoulder to shoulder. Though his fingers still trembled, Charlie got the trunk open at last.

"It's not much," he stammered stupidly, feeling his face flush bright. "To even call it a collection is honestly a bit—"

"You weren't kidding." Miles reached right in with one of his rough hands and picked up Charlie's copy of *Sins of the Cities of the Plains*. He flipped open the cover and ran an impressed finger over the unintelligible signature scrawled on the title page. "You have Jack Saul's bloody autograph."

Charlie laughed, relieved of a bit of tension. "Yes, I do."

"They only printed about two hundred of these things, you know. And I doubt many of them are signed. This must be worth a damn fortune."

"Good, because that's what I paid to get a copy. And then I paid another to get the lead on Saul. As you can imagine, it was a bit of an undertaking. Managed in the end."

"*How?*"

"Oh, it's incredible what a few guineas and a sunny disposition will get you. I'd already proven myself down on Holywell; my friends at the shops knew I wouldn't bring harm to anyone."

Miles turned the book over, shaking his head in amazement as he traced a finger down the spine. "You go down there often? Holywell?"

"It's where one goes for these sorts of things, isn't it?" said Charlie.

Miles nodded, but did not say anything else about it. He started going through the rest of the trunk item by item. He was more interested in the books. The art pieces, he glanced at (sometimes with a knowing smirk), but he lingered over each bound volume, examining the cover with his gaze and the flat expanse of his hand before peering suspiciously at the signature on the cover page. With unbearable silence and slowness, he leafed through each book, stopping here and there. Charlie was fascinated. The slow, careful movements of Miles's hands; the gleam of his eyes moving back and forth behind his specs over the words; the way he licked his lips sometimes when he turned a page. It was all Charlie could do not to jump on him, crash him to the floor in a swift and impatient movement that would send books and specs flying.

When Miles got to *Immorality Plays*, he treated it no differently. He ran his hand over the cover, and by this point, Charlie shivered as if it had been run along the small of his own back. Of all the books, it was the most well loved, and opened without even the barest resistance. Miles stared at it a long time.

Charlie couldn't take the tension. He pressed his chest against Miles's shoulder under the very thin pretense of looking over it at the book. Each point of contact was scorching. He wanted to be consumed by it, but it was not so easy to curl up beside a boulder.

"This is the crown jewel," Charlie whispered, his mouth very close to Miles's ear. He felt Miles's breath catch as Charlie ran a light finger over the signature, taking care that his arm lined right up with Miles's, black silk nestled up against rough tweed. "The one and only autograph ever given out by Reginald Cox." He turned and brushed his lips against Miles's prickly jaw. "Thank you. For the book, of course, but also for coming here. For the wine. For playing along. For… I don't know, for just looking at these things before they go away." He rested his chin on Miles's shoulder. "I've no business caring so much about a pile of smut. But I can't help it; I do, very much. It's nice to show it to someone who might care a little as well."

Miles didn't answer. Silently, slowly, he started turning pages. He stopped where the book longed to fall open. "Do you read some bits more often than others?"

"Who doesn't? I assume the monster who wrote it fully intended for some bits to be read raw."

Those *hands*, God, Charlie swore his own skin was connected to the pages. His excitement swelled to an almost painful stiffness as Miles traced his fingers over the print of Charlie's favorite part of his favorite book.

"This one is an interesting choice to read over and over," Miles whispered into Charlie's hair. A little peck in return, on his temple. "What do you like about it?"

Charlie caught his breath enough to speak, though his voice came out very husky. "Fishing for compliments, Mr. Cox?"

Miles traced the words again, though this time, he trailed his finger over the back of Charlie's hand, swirling the skin and skittering over the lamp-lit gems on his fingers. "Maybe I am."

Something in his tone hit Charlie right in the chest. "You probably don't get many of those, do you?"

Miles swallowed, his throat moving against Charlie's cheek. "Most, ah, critical reception of my work has been accompanied by calls for my hanging," he said quietly. "People buy them, so I assume someone likes them, but no. When you write this sort of thing, the chance of a compliment is rather slim."

Charlie's heart was thundering so hard that Miles must have been able to feel it through both their jackets. He wasn't entirely sure they were still talking about the book.

"I imagine," said Charlie, "that it's particularly slim if you keep to yourself."

A sudden hand grabbed him under the chin and made him look into Miles's eyes. They were dark and gleaming in the low light. He was still tense, but his breath came heavy and his touch felt like fire.

"Yes," he whispered. "Particularly then."

Charlie couldn't stand it another second. He pressed a hungry kiss to Miles's mouth, and if that didn't get his meaning across, he didn't know what would.

"How's that for a compliment?" he said when they broke apart.

Miles stared at him wide-eyed, looking half-terrified. But the terror passed, and when it did, Miles Montague moved far more quickly than seemed possible for such a steady fellow. He put his hand firmly behind Charlie's head and kissed him back with breathtaking desperation.

It wasn't much like the humiliated little assault Charlie had subjected him to the evening before. Miles kissed like he opened those damn books, his hands wide over Charlie's back and neck, easing Charlie's mouth open with his tongue so slowly it almost hurt. And Charlie, like every last piece in his collection, yielded instantly.

Chapter Eight

Miles

The quick taste of Charlie Price from yesterday had been enough to keep Miles thinking about him the rest of the night. But this...full access to those plush lips, the twist of that witty tongue...

He couldn't remember the last time he'd been so overcome, and he didn't want to. Fortunately, he'd be amazed if he could remember his own name right now. Oh God, it had been *so* long, and Charlie... Charlie felt like pure heaven after so many months in an isolated hell. Charlie kissed wickedly, his body searing through the fine fabric of his clothes. His clothes, God, they were pretty, but not as pretty as Charlie himself. Miles hated them. He untucked the shirt impatiently and couldn't suppress a groan when his hands met the hot, bare skin of his lower back.

Charlie gasped and clung to him. Miles liked that, heart thundering as he wondered what other sorts of responses he could get out of this beautiful man. He scratched his nails over the spot, lightly, then harder until Charlie moaned softly against Miles's mouth. Even better. But not enough. He ran his hands desperately over every bit he could reach—sliding up his back, down his legs, cupping his face—but sitting like this, they could only get so close. He couldn't take it, needed more, and as he tried to get it, he wound up topping the poor fellow flat on the ground harder than he meant to.

"Sorry," Miles whispered, ragged.

Charlie's eyes were dark and starving; his lips were bright and more enticing than ever. He didn't answer. Just dragged Miles's head down and shoved his tongue back in his mouth.

They went on kissing like that, completely lost in each other until the need for air became too urgent to ignore. They broke apart, their mingled breath hot and labored. This would be a good time for Miles to regain his senses, but his body and emotions had left his mind out in the rain. He was so incredibly hard that even his buttons were in danger of giving up the fight; his reason didn't stand half a chance. Instead of doing something sensible, he worked frantically at the complicated knot around Charlie's neck, stealing quick pulses of pleasure against his leg.

Charlie seemed unaware that Miles had even passingly considered escape. With a rough movement, he helped Miles tear the tie off. Miles started on his collar stud, kissing his way down Charlie's warm neck.

"So," said Charlie on a low breath, tangling his fingers in Miles's hair. "I have to ask: which one am I? The innocent? Or the corruptor?" He arched into Miles's kisses as they reached his collarbone. "I'm...*mmm*... I'm afraid I've lost track." He slid his hand down Miles's chest, down his stomach, all the way down to where it was most needed. Miles grunted through his teeth, shocked in the best way possible as Charlie stroked him through his trousers. "*Oh*," said Charlie, his fingers wandering and his eyes going wide. "Oh God. I think you're the corruptor, love. There's nothing innocent about this thing."

Miles was surprised to find himself laughing at a moment like this, but he did. And he liked seeing the smile on Charlie's face along with his lust. It made him feel human again.

Connected. He was drunk on it as Charlie went on teasing him, closing his eyes and thrusting gently against his hand until the sweet sensation finally spurred him on. He grabbed both of Charlie's wrists and pinned them above his head. He moved full on top, settling his knees on either side of Charlie's hips and holding his wrists so tight he'd not get away without a good fight. He kissed that smirk and bit down until he got a delicious gasp.

Charlie's eyes closed and his hips bucked. "*Yes,*" he panted. "Yes, I'm definitely the innocent. Oh, poor me."

Miles dragged his lips and teeth along Charlie's neck until he found a sensitive spot that made him flinch beautifully. "Poor you."

It was overwhelming, too much and not nearly enough at the same time. They kissed and moved more and more desperately against each other in time with their tongues, building up into something truly delicious. It was well past time to start doing the thing properly, wasn't it? He reached between them to start on Charlie's straining buttons. God, he hoped he could last, considering—

Footsteps.

Footsteps in the hallway.

Hell came sharply back to Miles's mind, the terror, the death, and all the other reasons he could not do this. He darted up onto knees that were incriminatingly settled on either side of the man of the house. He wiped his mouth and looked down, horrified. The state of them was too obvious to hide, clothes disheveled, breathing labored, their bodies a beacon of evidence against them. And the *books.* The books and artwork strewn about everywhere, a lascivious mess spread too far to tidy in time.

"Shh," Charlie soothed. His eyes went sideways to the closed door, though the way he settled his hands on Miles's backside didn't express an awful lot of concern. The footsteps came and went, down the hall and back up it, and then vanished down the stairs.

After a moment of silence, Charlie gave Miles a solid squeeze. "They're after some linens. Not us."

But whatever had overtaken Miles was broken now. He disentangled himself from Charlie. His body was still glowing and reluctant to move, but Miles felt like he was floating a little ways above all that now. Unsure what else to do, he started piling the books back in the trunk.

"Thank you," he muttered. "For...showing me."

"Miles—"

"I should go."

Charlie sat upright just quick enough to grab the back of Miles's jacket as he stood. But Miles shook him off, deeply unsettled that he'd given in to something so dangerous.

Still on the floor, hair and clothes tousled, lips bright red and parted, Charlie Price looked the part of the real-life temptation that ruined the men in Miles's books. But he'd written those stories. He knew better. He knew how they ended.

"I need to go," Miles repeated. "Would you be so kind as to show me out, Mr. Price?"

Miles expected ice in return and was shocked when Charlie rolled his eyes and crossed the room to rather aggressively straighten Miles's jacket and push his unruly hair back into some semblance of respectability.

"You're being silly," he said.

"Silly?" Miles hissed. "If one of those servants came in—"

"They won't, because that's not what they've been asked to do. And all of them but Quincy are probably about to leave for the day anyway; they were here for the tasting." He peered suspiciously at the door. "That said, I take my dalliances out of the house, generally, so perhaps I didn't think this one through."

"Out of the house...where?"

An amused look crossed his face. "Likely not your kind of places, old boy."

Molly houses. Of course Charlie Price was out at molly houses. They probably loved him there, with his smart mouth and *obliging* nature. Miles could imagine it easily. Too easily, given he was trying to walk out of this house without an obvious erection.

"Damn you," he said. "Will you just show me out?"

Charlie went for the door, but rather than open it, he leaned against it with arms crossed. His tie and buttons were undone, his silk wrinkled, the perfect slick of his dark hair gone mad with a lock of it falling into his devilish eyes. He was too much. Far too much. Miles needed to get out before it was too late for both of them.

"Mr. Price—"

"Premature though it was, we agreed to Christian names, *Miles*."

"I'd like to go home."

"I'll let you go," said Charlie pleasantly, "*if* you promise I can visit your shop at closing later this week to pick up where we've left off."

Miles laughed nervously. "*Let* me go? What's the alternative?"

He wished he hadn't asked within half a second. Charlie's face darkened and he stepped in closer. "The alternative, *Mr. Cox*?" The look that crossed his face was wicked beyond all reason. "I've read all your books until the spines need regluing. By this point, I think I have *some* idea what to do with a beautiful man I've locked in my library against his will." He stepped right up until he could grab the front of Miles's shirt and drag him in for a sloppy, filthy kiss. "I'll stop by on Friday evening."

★ ★ ★

It was still wet and windy the whole way home, but Miles hardly cared. He was too deep in his head to notice much of anything, and his head was filled to bursting with Charlie, Charlie, Charlie. More than once, he found himself murmuring apologies to the people he'd bumped into on the street, but they were forgotten immediately. There was no room for them.

He arrived home before he knew it, and got the fire going nice and high without feeling himself do it. Once it got going, he stayed kneeling on the weathered old hearthrug, staring into the flames. His heart was racing. He felt like he'd hardly gotten out of there with his life. Now that he had, he wished he'd risked death to stay. It might have been worth it. What was here for him anyway? The longing he felt to return to this absurd, overdressed erotica collector was a sort of panic. He nearly put his coat on and went right back to Westminster, that's how mad he'd gone.

There was no way to manage that without looking like a lunatic, though, because the entire idea was lunacy. He couldn't go back. And it seemed very unlikely that Charlie would actually come here on Friday, either. Today had been a fluke, a bit of odd timing. Surely, Charlie Price had more interesting options for companionship, should he desire it. He'd gotten the autograph; now that that lust was slaked, he had no particular need for Miles until *Ganymede's Feast* came out. He would remember that by Friday. Or, more likely, he'd simply forget about his promise (threat?) altogether.

The thought that Charlie might not return made horrible, humiliating tears try to bloom behind his eyes. Christ. Miles needed to be more proactive about his erotic life, didn't he? His nervous attempts at celibacy never did end up working very long, and when he failed, he failed spectacularly. Like today. He'd nearly been caught humping a wealthy banker's son atop a pile of pornography. And if that weren't bad enough, he'd managed to acquire a nasty case of heartache on his way out the door. It was ridiculous. He knew better than this. He was thirty-five, for the love of God. Too old for this bollocks, by far.

He wiped his eyes and went to his cramped, chilly bedroom. He could not possibly be this heartbroken; he was probably just frustrated. Leaning against the door, he took out his handkerchief and released his prick, which rapidly hardened again at the merest suggestion of attention. He squeezed his eyes shut, gripped himself tight, and imagined he was sliding between Charlie Price's perfect lips until he came, shooting again and again into the handkerchief as an irrepressible groan escaped his throat.

He caught his breath and cleaned himself up. There. Everything was fine. He was fine. He changed into dry clothes with Ethan's dressing gown overtop so he didn't freeze. With a large mug of tea and his battered copy of *David Copperfield*, he settled in front of the fire. He sat in his usual chair, and tried very hard not to look at the other one, which was empty.

Chapter Nine

Charlie

The next two days were torture. Charlie went about his routine in a state of intense distraction and intermittent, inconvenient arousal. If his life were more interesting, like it had been only a few months ago, perhaps he could have gotten his mind on something else. As it was, he no longer even had to pick out his own clothes in the morning or brew his own tea. Once dressed and fed, he had a few hours at the bank where George Merriweather had gotten him a job doing accounting. He joined Alma's family for dinner, where they all talked animatedly about the wedding. All the while, the ghost of Miles's touch haunted his skin. At night, he read *Immorality Plays* again. Words that had mellowed over the years were freshly delicious, now that he could imagine Miles Montague penning them by candlelight.

By Tuesday, he was in such a state that he couldn't bear the thought of lying in his own bed, writhing into his own hand again. If he thought he could get away with it, he'd go to Morgan & Murray's early and unannounced, but he did not think that would be well received. Instead, he took a cab to a respectable pub, then walked the rest of the way to The Curious Fox.

It was not busy on a Tuesday, but Noah was there. His friendship with Mr. Forester was apparently long-standing, and so he could be found dallying about his old mate's place on almost any given evening. His Miss Penelope costume was tucked away in favor of a perfectly tailored velvet jacket and a silky red ascot. Penelope wouldn't return again until the weekend, but he'd still wrapped strands of pearls around his slim wrists and neck, his collar-length hair tucked behind his ears to reveal matching studs.

He was playing cards with three others, maybe hearts or, more likely, some vaguely adjacent game he'd invented that was too strange for anyone to understand. Many nights, Charlie had witnessed Noah flirtatiously bat his long lashes, claim his "wee little tweaks" would make the game *so* much more fun, and then, when he'd cleaned out entire tables of seasoned gamblers, he'd insist that it was not cheating if everyone agreed to the rules ahead of time.

It was a talent Charlie could really use right about now.

On a quiet night like tonight, everyone at the table literally knew Noah's games, and appeared to be holding their own for the moment, the lot of them talking and teasing each other as they placed bets and smoked cigars. When Charlie got closer, he found that the party included Noah's preferred partner in card-game crime, Miss Annabelle Archer. She, too, had toned down her weekend extravagance, in the modest sort of wool skirts, high-necked blouse, and simply pinned curls she preferred. Unlike Noah, Charlie had never known Annabelle to opt for trousers and her given name if it could be avoided.

Foolishly sitting between the pretty hustlers—and thus playing against them and doomed to lose—was Warren the barkeep across from the rather unexpected figure of Miss Jo.

Charlie perched on the edge of the round table. He peeked at Noah's cards.

"Eyes to yourself." Noah swatted Charlie in the chest, then turned beside him to Miss Jo. "Defend my honor, *amore*."

"Defend *you*? After that last hand? You're daft, ducky." Jo puffed her cigar and looked pointedly at Charlie. "What's he got? Mime it, or something."

"No, no." Charlie put his hands up. "I'm not getting involved in any bit of this."

"Traitor," Jo snapped, throwing her cards down and glaring as Noah smugly swept up the pot. "And here I thought I was your best mate."

"You are. But *his* best mate is Mr. Forester, who already has about a dozen reasons to kick me out." He tapped Noah on the shoulder, then pointed across to Annabelle. "And I don't see *her* best mate here tonight, but wherever he is, he's about twice as big as I am. I can't afford to be making enemies like that."

"Very clever of you, Charlie," said Annabelle, expertly shuffling the cards with a sly grin. "These days, Albert's less of a best mate and more of a husband. It's been making him feel very defensive."

Mr. Forester, who had been tending to the fire, suddenly turned toward the lot of them with his jaw practically on the floor. "More of a *husband*?" he said. "Since *when*?"

Annabelle shrugged with barely contained self-satisfaction, dealing the cards out mysteriously.

Forester pointed scoldingly with the poker from across the room. "I set the two of you up, so you can't go calling him husband until you've let me put a wedding on and consummated in the back. It's against club rules."

"Oh, it is not." She finished dealing and tipped back the rest of her cherry fizz. "You can't go making up rules on the fly, Forester."

"Right, only you and Noah get to do that, how could I forget?"

As the two of them bickered a little, Charlie met Noah's eye and chuckled. So far, the two of them had remained out of the reach of David Forester's meddling, though it was certainly not for lack of trying on the proprietor's part.

"Oh, leave her alone, Davy," Noah finally interrupted, not taking his eyes off his cards. "I need her to focus on the game for now. Jo's starting to cotton on to the rules, so things might get sticky soon."

"Shall I bring Jo another drink to tamp her wits down?" Forester offered. "Or a fresh one for Annie to build them up?"

"Oh, refills all around, I think," Jo said brightly. "And keep putting mine on Charlie's tab."

She finished off her glass pointedly at Charlie as the others cackled.

He cringed slightly at the damage she'd likely done to said tab, but seeing as it would all be settled soon enough, he liked the thought that his father was paying for all of Jo's debauchery. As Forester went behind the bar, she fixed Charlie with a mischievous sort of look.

"So tell me. Did you get your autograph yet?" she asked. "Or am I collecting on dreams you're too chicken to chase?"

"If I say no, will you hold off on running my tab into the clouds?"

"'Course not."

The lot of them finished another round, which Charlie thought was going to Warren, but, due to some inscrutable technicality, went to Annabelle instead.

"What?" said Warren. "But the ace should—"

"No, no, *amore*," Noah said, petting Warren's arm consolingly. "Remember? Aces are determined high or low for the round depending on their first appearance on the table."

Warren slapped a hand down on the coins and glared. "I want to switch partners. You and me, mate, what do you say?"

"I say I won't partner with someone who can't remember the rules of the game," Noah scolded. "Now give Annie her money. I won't have you cheating her, you know, it's not sporting."

As Warren released the coins and took the deck to deal, launching into an argument that inventing rules no one can remember *is* indeed cheating, Jo turned back to Charlie.

"So?" She popped her cigar in her mouth and spoke awkwardly around it. "Have you gotten the autograph?"

"I've gotten it," he said, mind sparking to life yet again with the sultry memories that had brought him here in the first place.

The assessment of their hands brought with it a moment of quiet, followed by the rearranging of cards and placing of bets. Charlie thought he was off the hook, until Jo managed to take the next trick to the sound of Noah's gasp and Warren's laughter. Then she went on with renewed swagger. "So, what's he like?"

"Who we talkin' about?" Warren nudged Charlie's leg, which was still propped on the table. Officially off-duty tonight, he had his sleeves down over his brown forearms and his collar buttoned properly—it was chilly, and he was after tricks rather than tips—but he could not seem to help but smolder and smirk. "Charlie, you ain't got a lover, have you?"

Charlie must have paused just long enough to cause suspicion, because Jo slammed her hand on the table hard enough to rattle the chips. "Charlie, you slattern, you've taken him to bed *already*?"

"Stop it," Charlie said. "No, I haven't. If I had, it wouldn't be your business anyway."

Everyone at the table laughed at the notion that anyone at the Fox might mind their own business. Annoyed, Charlie stole Warren's cigar and puffed on it.

"Give me that." Warren took it back. "Them's expensive."

"I know," said Charlie. "You're a bloody old man, Warren. That's the same kind my pop smokes."

Warren cocked a naughty brow. "You bet it is. Where you think I got 'em?" He waited for Charlie's groan and everyone else's chuckles to die down. "Now, come on, Charlie. Stop stalling."

From his other side, Noah ran a single finger down Charlie's arm. "Yes, Charlie. Tell us. Who is your mystery man?"

"He's my own business, is what he is."

Jo smiled out a stream of smoke. "I found Charlie his favorite author of sodomitical garbage so he could secure an autograph. Sounds like that meeting was more interesting than I thought it might be."

Another round of teasing commenced as Forester came around with the fresh drinks, pretending very unsuccessfully that he wasn't soaking up every drop of gossip like a sponge.

"It's an autograph," Charlie insisted. "Nothing more."

"What's he like?" Jo asked. "I wondered. What sort of man is he?"

"About...about what you might expect."

"Not sure what I'm meant to expect."

"I can't tell you much," Charlie said. "He likes his privacy. Jo knows his name and all that, but the rest of you lot don't, and I'm not keen to give any hints. He wouldn't appreciate it."

Jo rolled her eyes. "God, Charlie, there's plenty to say about a man that won't reveal who he is. I'm not asking where his birthmarks are, for goodness' sake."

"We only want the *important details*." Noah widened his mischievous eyes and put his own cigar to his mouth suggestively.

Everyone laughed, until Anabelle put her hands flat on the table, staring very seriously around at the others. "Careful, there, asking about the man's prick," she said. "Perhaps it's so uncommonly large as to be instantly recognizable."

"Couldn't be," said Warren. "Charlie's easily intimidated in that respect, you know."

They roared at that one, Anabelle barely saving her toppling glass before it spilled all over Jo's lap and Forester putting his head down on the bar to catch his breath.

Charlie stood, his face on fire. "You're all menaces. Each and every one."

"We just love you, Charlie," said Jo.

"That's your mistake."

"Come off it," she went on a bit more gently. "I'm curious. What's he like? I got you the name; I know I've gotten my repayment in the form of liquor, but I'd still like to feel connected to the end of the saga."

"Same," said Noah, who had had nothing to do with the name at all. "After how *hard* I've worked to secure the identity of this…*whomever it is*… I also deserve some information." He batted his lashes, unaltered by kohl tonight, but still long enough to get the job done.

Charlie thought about it. He really didn't want to give any information that could link anyone but Jo back to Miles. In fact, now knowing just how paranoid the fellow was, he hated the thought that even *she* knew who he was.

Where *had* she come by the true identity of Reginald Cox? It was a little troubling, now that he considered it. Charlie had been asking up and down Holywell Street for years, each time Cox put out another volume. His impeccably perverted reputation, an enthusiastic twinkle, and a heavy purse were usually enough to secure whatever book, art piece, or secret identity had captured his imagination. But those relationships had taken time to develop; these creators and shopkeepers were risking lengthy stints in jail for their work, and they gave nothing up easily. While Charlie had eventually coaxed out information about several very secretive artists, no one had ever been willing—or able—to tell him anything about Cox.

So how had Jo managed?

He adored Jo, but he'd meant it when he said he did not know her real name. He did not know if she was called Joanne or Josephine in her proper life, or if Jo was entirely fabricated from nothing. To say nothing of a surname. Their friendship was confined to a tiny corner of the world, and he suddenly felt that very sharply.

He'd just give them what they wanted, he supposed. "Like I said, he's very private. He assumed I was there to blackmail him."

He launched into a rather exaggerated tale of his attempt to even the playing field by putting his hand down the bookseller's trousers. Everyone was properly impressed and amused by the story, and Charlie leaned into his ability to entertain without giving away anything at all. Only Jo looked suspicious of his storytelling.

"So, did you get on with him, then?" she asked at the end. "Do you think you might see him again? Or bring him here?"

"I'd say we got on," said Charlie. "Though I certainly won't be bringing him here of all places. A *rouge-soaked hellhole* like this? He'd never forgive me."

After a final chuckle, the game of Noah's Hearts got started back up. He felt Jo's eyes on his back as he went to sit at the bar. She didn't say anything about it, but she'd clearly noticed that he answered only two of her three questions.

Chapter Ten

Miles

After a week of rain, wind, and—in some areas—flooding, Friday morning finally dawned dry. Cloudy. Cold. But blessedly dry. Fleet Street was swarming with coaches and pedestrians by late afternoon, as the whole of London took advantage of the novel ability to run errands without getting drenched. Miles had not been remotely ready for the influx of customers, and for the first time in a while, he felt he could have done with another employee to help.

The customers were varied and constant. A prim pair of governesses hunted for appropriate literature for their charges, unwisely assuming that his opinion on moralist allegories was worth something. A mother and daughter came in looking for fairy tales. A baker from across the street wandered around for a bit, then left him with a cloth-wrapped bun after buying an armful of mysteries. Things didn't slow down for a long time, and the minute they did, a gentleman in a dilapidated hat appeared to circle the place ten times at least, taking things slowly off the shelves and putting them back, before bringing two books on the most outlandish spiritualism to the counter for wrapping.

"Thank you," Miles muttered as he took payment. He handed over his change and the books wrapped in brown paper and twine. The man wandered out in the same distracted manner with his purchase tucked under his arm, the bell jingling overhead as he vanished outside.

When the door closed, the bell suddenly tumbled to the ground with a clang. Miles took it up in the pause that followed, unsurprised; the rickety shop had hardly seen this much action at once since he'd taken it over. He tried to right it, but something had rusted through. Ah well. He tucked it behind the counter for later and took the long-awaited pause to straighten up the shop and put any misplaced volumes in the back to be shelved whenever he found the time.

He ought to be more excited. He'd brought in a good sum so far, and it was still daytime with a lot of people strolling along to soak up the lack of rain like it was sunshine. This was the sort of day that could take the edge off the deficit the shop usually had at the end of the month; if the weather stayed like this for a few days, he might even profit a few pounds. Ethan would have been positively twirling with excitement, but Miles had always been better suited to the position of bookstore owner's lover. Owning one himself was much less amusing, and by the time the last customer was gone, Miles was just wondering if he had time to slip off to put some ointment on his hands, which were dry and paper-cut from the wrapping.

He was so tired that he did not even remember what day it was until the door opened again, and three boisterous lads with the air of students came into the shop laughing and chattering.

The sight of them—a bit pocked and not terribly well formed, having so little in common with imaginary "innocents" that it was laughable—reminded him of Charlie Price, who had threatened to come to the shop Friday after closing.

It was Friday today, wasn't it?

He recognized at once the source of the butterflies that had been in his stomach all day. He'd been a little agitated, a little nervous. He'd chalked it up to simple misanthropy, but no; he'd known in the back of his mind that today was the day.

And each hour that flew by in questions of this-or-that volume, this-or-that author, was another hour closer to finding out if Charlie was actually coming.

"Hey, old boy!"

The greeting popped him right out of his thoughts. One of the lads, one with fiery hair, was waving a hand in front of his eyes while the others laughed.

"Can I help you?" Miles said.

The lad looked annoyed with Miles's sharpness. However, at the urging of his friends, he shook it off and leaned over the counter conspiratorially. His face turned very, very red and he lowered his voice to a near whisper. "We're looking for things that might be, you know, *interesting*. Got anything like that in the back?"

Miles blinked rapidly at them as the two who hadn't spoken nearly choked themselves with suppressed laughter. He knew perfectly well what this was about. He decided to play stupid.

"Interesting?" he repeated carefully. "Indeed, I do. Come take a look at this."

He waved the boys along. They were still giggling. He went to the gap in the shelves where the eccentric had taken his volumes and removed a book on séances. He handed it to the red-haired boy, who flipped through it, disappointed. His friends looked ready to wet themselves with amusement.

"That's not exactly what I meant." He handed the book back and waggled his brows. "We're looking for something *really* interesting."

"I don't have anything really interesting in this shop."

"Come on!" The boy had reddened to an alarming degree. Embarrassment was clearly getting the better of him. While his friends were still entertained, he was getting angry. "You know what I'm talking about, man. I'm not a sodding child; you can show me the good stuff."

Nervous sweat sprang to Miles's palms and he couldn't keep his heart from thumping uncomfortably against his chest. He was no idiot—he really didn't keep anything illicit in this shop.

But he did have copies of his own work in the apartment upstairs.

He never liked to be asked about this kind of thing, but usually the asker didn't push it. Why were these boys pushing so hard? Had they heard something? If they'd heard something, it was no wonder they wanted to get their hands on it.

"Look, b—gentlemen," Miles corrected himself. "There's no good stuff. I don't know what you've heard—"

The friends finally collapsed into fits of laughter behind their increasingly enraged ringleader.

"Will you two shut up?" the boy spat out viciously. He rounded back on Miles, humiliation turning him near to purple and bringing him close enough that Miles felt a prickly ripple of fear wash over him. "Don't lie to me, you old sod! All bookshops got it. I know you've got it. So, quit holding out on me."

Miles put his hands out. "Please, let's—"

There was a creak of floorboards behind them all. Miles's head snapped up to see the lanky form of Smithy, his publisher, smirking beneath his thin mustache in the doorway.

"Leave the bloke alone, lads," he said. "You're barking up the wrong tree for sure."

The scene struck a chord of confused calm as Smithy sauntered over to the ruddy boy and slipped him a card.

"What's this?" the boy asked.

"Anything 'good' on this side of town isn't going to be nearly as good as what you'll get at the address on the card. Let the fellow know Paul Smithy sent you and you might get lucky." He turned back to Miles. "Now, Mr. Montague. I believe you have that book of psalms for my dear old mother held around here somewhere?"

The boys bolted, the door slamming shut as they went. Miles and Smithy watched them go through the window. When they were safely gone, Smithy pulled out a packet of cigarettes and a match. He leaned against the counter and put the cigarette between his lips.

"So, Reg—"

"Don't even think about lighting that thing. You'll make the books stink to high heaven."

Smithy rolled his eyes and put the stuff away. "Wouldn't want that. This is a *respectable* place after all."

"Yes." Miles sniffed. "It is. I'm allowed a respectable bit of something in life."

He glanced around suspiciously, eyes landing on the door to the stockroom and narrowing. "Do you really not have anything good in the back? Not a single postcard? Not even any of your own work?"

"Nothing at all, and particularly nothing of *Reginald Cox's.* As I've told you at least a hundred times, Miles Montague lives a law-abiding, God-fearing existence." Miles crossed his arms tight over his chest. "Which is why you really oughtn't be here at all. You know I need separation between my work for you and my work for…the shop. You ain't invited, and I'd appreciate if you'd clear off."

Smithy put a tortured hand to his heart. "You wound me, Reg."

"Stop calling me that in public."

"Public? There's no one here!"

"Someone could walk in at any time."

"You're more paranoid than I realized." He snatched Miles's serial off the counter and began flipping through aimlessly.

"They never do anything about you writer-types, you know. It's me they want, since without me you're just a pervert without a platform."

"It's only a matter of time before one of us writers is made an example of, and it ain't going to be me."

Smithy shrugged, unconcerned as ever. "Your loss. Maybe you'd actually make money off this shop if you read the market as voraciously as you read everything else. The good people of London want to feel like you've at least got a stash of low-level dirt in here somewhere, even if they never get up the guts to ask for it."

"Smithy," Miles interrupted sternly. "You can't be here. You know that. You've never overstepped like this before, so I take it there's some reason you can't wait until *Ganymede* goes to print to talk to me."

"I know, I know." Smithy drew a deep breath and returned the serial to its place. "I apologize for risking your very life to come in here in broad daylight or whatever it is you're fretting about. But I have a proposition for you. One that can't wait, and that involves me taking a good look around this place."

Miles glared, silent, until Smithy went on.

"This shop," he said, waving his hand around vaguely. "I looked into the ownership history. Not exactly a passion project of the respectable Miles Montague. Belonged to a friend of yours, didn't it? And you took it on when he passed?"

Miles had never discussed Ethan with Smithy. However, there was an unusual twinge of kindness behind Smithy's words that showed he'd put the pieces together and perhaps even cared about the sordid picture they revealed.

"What of it?" Miles said gruffly.

"And you've told me yourself you hardly make any money on it."

"Will you get on with it?"

"Have you considered selling it?"

An instant bubble of anger swelled within him. He blinked rapidly. It was amazing that his eyes did not whistle like a kettle with the release of literal steam.

"No," he said coldly.

"'No,' you've never considered it, or 'No,' you *would* never consider it and I'm a monster for the suggestion?"

"Get back to the print house, Smithy. This conversation is over."

"Hear me out: I've got a buyer. Friend of mine. I figured that if you wanted rid of the place, it could work out splendidly for everyone. He's willing to pay—"

"It's not for sale."

"You could continue to live upstairs, if you wanted. I'd personally make sure that—"

"Get out."

"Come now, Reg—Miles—you must at least listen to—"

"I do not have to listen. You shouldn't even be here. You aren't invited to this part of my life."

"He's passionate! He really wants to own a bookshop. Always has."

"Oh, and I don't?"

"Not as far as I'm aware, no. Look at it!" Smithy prodded a shelf of books on manners. "This isn't your shop. You didn't pick this inventory, and you haven't updated it since…" He checked the publication date and closed his eyes in disgust.

"Books don't spoil," said Miles.

"Books on manners do. That's why I don't bother with manners at all."

Miles took the book back in a fashion not consistent with anything in any manners book ever, nearly sending his publisher stumbling. "I care about bookselling."

"You care about books. They aren't the same, you know.

You'll make far more money selling the shop itself than you ever will trying to convince people to buy a bunch of trash you don't care about."

Miles grabbed Smithy by his bony shoulder and steered him forcefully toward the door. "I trade enough for your money, Smithy. I'm not trading Ethan's shop too."

Smithy turned to look at him, and Miles realized he'd said the name out loud.

"I'm sorry," said Smithy. Something about his naturally smirking face made it so he never seemed quite sincere, but he got very close to it this time. He took a folded piece of paper out of his pocket and slipped it between the pages of the etiquette book. "I don't mean to be insensitive to your situation. But I've known you long enough to know that this shop isn't your life. As your publisher, I know you're making enough on your work to live better than this; the shop is eating away at what you've built for yourself. It's going to eat your profits from *Ganymede's Feast*, too, and you know it."

Miles felt a flicker of uncertainty, but he squashed it down. "Get out, Smithy."

Smithy tipped his hat sadly. "I'll send word when the proofs are ready. I'll be sure not to waste my time providing any extra copies for your back stock."

Miles was still holding on to the book of manners. Once Smithy had gone, he took the paper out of it and hardly glanced at the informally written offer before he crumpled it up and threw it at the counter before turning back to shelve the bloody book.

Out of style, was it? He took a moment to flip through before he put it back in its place. He was so out of touch with what normal people of his station did that he wouldn't know the difference between a manners book published yesterday and one put out ten years ago. Still, he couldn't help but notice that the sketches did look dated. Perhaps he should look into acquiring something new… Dear God, the very thought of perusing a publisher's catalog for updated information on how to wear a necktie exhausted him instantly.

I can't choose only the books I want to read, Ethan had said once as he shelved some tripe about hunting. *And I certainly can't choose the books* you *want to read, my darling, or I'd have only hopeless snobs in the doors at all.*

Miles put the book back. Ethan would be horrified, though probably unsurprised, at how poorly Miles managed inventory. The shop was an endless source of guilt. He felt terrible for his incompetence, but when he considered ridding himself of the place, he felt even worse for his lack of loyalty. If only he could be certain Smithy's friend would tend it with the proper respect. There was no certainty when it came to people though; there was only trust, which was far too easily misplaced.

What a shame that the books didn't just update themselves. That would take care of something, at least. The thought put a smirk on his lips as he ran a finger down the spine he'd just replaced. A book of manners that kept up with the times…beloved by some status climber who began consulting it daily…and slowly, the advice would become more questionable, daring, and lewd, until the climber found himself seducing the aristocrat whom he'd been trying to impress in the first place…

Well, that was the next book, wasn't it? He flipped the sign to Closed—dusk was falling anyway—and went upstairs to make a note before he forgot the explosion of details that always seemed to flood his mind at the most inconvenient times. Perhaps this was the real reason for Smithy's interruption. Inspiration. Keep him moving, keep him writing.

Keep him making money he'd throw away in the end.

But he didn't worry about that. He had a roof over his head and a pen in his hand. The new idea flowed like sweet stream water, easy and sparkling. The details were delicious and hot to the touch, lascivious notions flashing through his mind and down to his pen. He'd hate it tomorrow, but tonight he let that wonderful feeling of discovery chase out all else.

Except for a small, nagging feeling that he'd forgotten something...

He paused in his scribbling, staring at the wall before him.

The bell. That's what it was. He'd forgotten the broken bell.

Oh, to hell with that. It was nothing to pause his pen over. He'd fix it in the morning.

Chapter Eleven

Charlie

Closed.

Charlie stared at the sign on Morgan & Murray's door and checked his watch. He *was* later than he'd promised, but Miles was certainly still in there. He peered through the window. Some of the lamps were lit. He tried the door.

It opened.

Guiltily, he closed it behind him.

"Miles?"

But the shop was empty. Empty with the Closed sign up, the lamps lit, and the door unlocked.

Should he leave? Investigate? The whole thing made him uneasy. He bolted the door. Last thing he needed was anyone else creeping around. As for himself, he tiptoed around the shop with careful steps, peering at the shelves of books, wincing when a floorboard creaked. He shouldn't be so nervous. He'd formally invited himself over, after all. He wasn't unexpected or unannounced, and the door had been left open. He did not linger too much on the suspicion that that had been an oversight.

He hadn't gotten a good look around on his previous visit, too focused on getting the autograph to make any unrelated observations. Charlie was not a frequenter of respectable bookshops, and it was interesting to have the chance to wander one so freely. It was small, but the shelves were up to the ceiling and stocked with dozens of subjects that had been handwritten onto little cards placed here and there. The single rug was worn, and things were a little dusty; yet beyond some surface neglect, there was a feeling that this was a well-loved place. It was...romantic. Charming. He liked it.

Yet, he'd not come here for books. He'd thought of little else but Miles for days, and to find him missing curdled his anticipation into something almost unbearable. He peeked behind the counter, realizing too late what an absurdly desperate action it was. Why would Miles be hiding behind the counter?

Still, he took a moment to glance around back there. His impatient gaze drifted over a wooden shopkeeper's stool, small piles of books and ledgers, a scatter of pens and ink bottles, and a few stacks of loose papers. Most of the pages were blank or marred with haphazard notes, but one angrily crumpled sheet caught his eye. Rubbish, probably. But... Charlie bit his lip. What if it was some page of Miles's writing that he'd destroyed in frustration? If it was, he should certainly not look at it. Miles was probably just in the washroom and would be back any second.

But the temptation was too much. He uncreased the balled-up paper and laid it flat on the wooden counter.

Not writing. Someone wanted to buy this shop, some Irish fellow who told Miles he could name his price for the place. Charlie wished he had something like a shop he could sell for a lump to buy himself out of his impending marriage. More than that, he wished he could have the luxury of crumpling such an attractive offer up and throwing it away. Charlie tried to put the thing back the way he'd found it.

He tapped his fingers on the counter. His guilt was climbing. He'd come in after closing, sneaked around, and now read a page of something that wasn't his business at all. Miles did not seem to be coming. Charlie ought to leave, but with his lips still burning from their last kiss he simply couldn't bear the thought. If he didn't see Miles tonight, he had a feeling he never would.

It was probably foolish, but he went up the staircase that he assumed led to Miles's flat.

The door at the top was cracked open. The gap was small, but through it, Charlie could see Miles sitting at a desk, mumbling to himself with his dark brows very furrowed. He had a pen in one hand, though he was not writing anything, just staring at a half-finished page. He scribbled a few words, crossed them out, then carried on with a little smile.

Charlie's heart grew so warm, he thought it might combust.

Miles—Reginald Cox—was *writing*.

The rest of it fell into place. The haphazard closing, the left-on lamps and unlocked door. He'd had an idea that couldn't wait. It was so deliciously writerly that Charlie could hardly stand it, so much better than the crumpled piece of thrown-out work he thought he'd found. It had been strange meeting the man who'd written his most beloved words. Miles Montague was big, gruff, and tinged with darkness, seeming like he might belong more readily on a farm or in a factory than sitting around penning filth.

But now that Charlie witnessed it, it all fit. The tension in those broad shoulders had melted. The words he so often left unspoken wandered quietly over his lips as he whispered to himself as he wrote. That was indeed where Miles belonged, and if it wasn't obvious before, it was only because he'd kept this part of himself hidden.

Miles paused and stretched, looking pleased. Charlie shrank back into the shadows briefly, then glanced again. With the shift in Miles's position, Charlie could see clearly that whatever wickedness he was working on, it was having its impact on the author. He watched as Reginald Cox gave his own cock a few seconds of attention though his trousers, sighed, then got back to work.

Charlie's breath was knocked out of him. Blood plummeted down from his head to his groin so fast he felt dizzy. By God, he could die a happy man if only he could bring himself off like this, watching Miles write himself into wantonness.

And, he realized, he might actually die if he did that. Because if Miles realized he was being watched, he'd probably kill Charlie, and Charlie would deserve it.

Two choices, then, he if wanted to live. Leave, or announce himself.

As he watched Miles continue writing with that cockstand, he realized there was only one choice. He'd die of fever if he had to spend another night thinking about this man without touching him again.

He knocked very gently.

The sound startled Miles out of his trance. He fumbled his pen and leaped to his feet, shoving his work into a drawer with a panicked slam.

Charlie pushed the door open. "It's just me."

Miles let out a huge breath. "Fuck, Price, you scared me half to death."

"Good to see you again too."

Miles softened a bit, crossing his arms awkwardly. "I'm sorry. I just didn't expect you to actually come. And then I got distracted by something. How'd you get in?"

"Flipping your sign doesn't lock the door or turn out the lights, mate."

Miles swore so spectacularly that Charlie couldn't help but laugh. "I drew the bolt behind me so no other shady characters could wander in."

"Yes, just the one, then. Thank you."

Charlie carefully stepped over the threshold into Miles's flat and closed the door behind him.

"Lock it," Miles ordered. Charlie stared at him, startled by the command. He liked the sound of it, though. He fumbled the bolt a bit as he did what he was told.

The flat was small and drafty, but well lived-in and homey nonetheless. No gaslight up here, but a fire hummed along happily in the hearth, and Miles had lit enough lamps and candles that Charlie could get a fairly good look around. A little kitchen area had a stocked wine rack, the bookshelves were stuffed to bursting near the single window, and art pieces and photographs were hung on the walls in nice wooden frames. The desk he'd seen through the door was clear of papers now, but cluttered with odds and ends, pens, and inks. It all smelled of beeswax and paper and the worn leather of Miles's desk chair.

A single door likely led to a bedroom. As he inhaled the scent of Miles's space, he wondered if he could make it that far.

"What were you working on?" he asked innocently, as if he had no idea at all. Miles didn't buy it, glaring over the rims of his glasses. "Yes, Miles, I know it's a book. But what book? Something new?"

"Must be, seeing as I've already written all the old ones."

"Fair enough." He took a few light steps over to the desk. He could tell by the amusement at the corner of Miles's mouth that he was not being successfully casual as he ran the tips of his fingers over the abandoned wooden workspace. But how could he be? To Miles, this was just a place to work, but as far as Charlie was concerned, this was a magical place where scandalous literary miracles occurred. "You did look busy with your work. I'm sorry to have interrupted."

"No, you're not."

"Perhaps not." He tentatively caressed the drawer pull. "Can I see it?"

Once again, Miles moved much more quickly than expected, coming up behind Charlie and taking his hand off the drawer. He turned Charlie so they were face-to-face, still clutching his wrist. "You can't be serious."

"Fine, you caught me. I'm not sorry *or* serious." Charlie let his hand slide through Miles's until their fingers were laced. "Just enamored. Nothing more or less than that."

"How long were you watching me?" Miles failed to sound accusatory, his tight grip on Charlie belying any actual suspicion.

Charlie leaned back a bit until he bumped the desk, a little space between them now, but the anchor of their laced fingers still held them together. "Long enough to get interested." He pretended to ignore how obvious his aching cock had become, but Miles did not. Those blue eyes raked over him. He did not seem scared in the least; a couple of locked doors and pulled drapes did wonders for the man's disposition.

Miles took a steadying breath. "How interested would you say you are?"

Charlie hopped up to sit on Miles's desk like an offering. "Extremely."

Miles crossed to him, putting his large hands on the tops of Charlie's thighs. The touch was utter bliss. He ran his hands up and down so slowly and softly that Charlie whimpered.

"I can't believe you actually came back," Miles whispered, so close to his ear that Charlie felt the words as much as heard them.

"It was torture even waiting this long." He tipped his head to the side to allow Miles to run scratchy little kisses under his ear. "I'm driven to distraction. I can't sleep. I fumble everything I touch. I tried rereading your books, but it only makes the situation worse."

"A bit pathetic," said Miles between kisses.

"Yes, it is," Charlie gasped. Between stroking hands and exploring lips, he was too overcome to be insulted. "Are you pathetic too?"

Miles looked into his eyes. After a moment of consideration, he put his specs on the desk and said, "Yes."

And that was that, now wasn't it?

Miles's mouth came down hard and greedy, so shockingly invasive and insistent that Charlie cried out in surprise. He did not melt into the kiss so much as scramble to catch up with it, opening his mouth wider and moving his tongue faster so he was not entirely devoured all at once.

Not for the first time, he felt a bit like he'd lost his mind, playing with unstable fire in the form of Miles Montague, but those flames were too hot to escape now. His hands were rough and seemed to be everywhere at once; pushing Charlie's coat off his shoulders, running through his hair, digging into his backside as he pulled Charlie off the desk and to his feet. Miles crushed their hips together so hard that Charlie nearly spent from the sudden force of it, clawing Miles's broad shoulders as he fought for something like sanity.

Miles's kisses were bruising. They'd been that way in the library, but the days apart had brought with them a new ferocity. He bit Charlie's bottom lip as he had before, but this time, he came down so hard that Charlie was finally overwhelmed by the pace, the intensity, and now the pain. He yelped and jumped back, feeling for blood.

That snapped Miles out of it. He took his hands off of Charlie entirely, holding them up. "I'm sorry."

Charlie laughed, glancing at his fingers. They were a bit shaky, but clean. "I'm alright."

Miles tried to catch his breath. He looked like the best sort of nightmare in the flickering firelight, disheveled and panting, with ink-stained fingers and a rigid cock. "I should have asked you."

"Asked what?"

"How you like it."

Charlie could feel the racing of his own heart through the throbbing in his bottom lip. "I liked whatever the devil that was just fine."

"Are you sure?"

"You surprised me, is all. I often wind up with the timid ones. I wasn't ready for...that."

A flicker of distress crossed over Miles's face. "Is that what you prefer?"

Charlie pulled Miles back to him by hooking his fingers into the waistband of his trousers. Coming back together after the seconds apart was so delicious that Charlie briefly forgot all words. He twined his arms around Miles's neck. "Don't worry about me, love. I've been around the block a few times, and I like it any which way. Right now, I want to know a little more about how *you* like it. It's intriguing, so far."

Miles didn't say anything for a moment, just placed a hand on the side of Charlie's face and pressed their foreheads together. It was sweet, but obviously a stand-in for whatever ideas were making him tremble and pant.

"Come on," Charlie said. "It can't possibly be any worse than what gets Reverend Collins fired up, now can it?" Charlie paused, thinking through the later chapters of *Immorality Plays*. "At least, I certainly hope not, or I'm in a lot of trouble."

Miles laughed. God, what a beautiful sound. He brought his head down to the bend in Charlie's neck again, putting a firm hand between his legs to cup his balls and then run straight up his cock. Charlie gasped and thrust his hips out, but the hand was gone already, scooping up one of his wrists and then the other, holding them behind his back.

"You'll tell me if you're not having a good time, won't you?" Miles growled.

"I promise."

With his spare hand and not a wasted second, Miles grabbed Charlie by the collar. He got the neckcloth off and had it deftly wrapped around Charlie's wrists faster than seemed possible. It wasn't tight or inescapable by any means—a good jostle would send it fluttering right to the ground—but somehow, that little bit of fabric made Charlie feel like the most deliciously vulnerable creature in existence. When Miles next touched him, it was to grab him by the hair—not a comfortable task, seeing as Charlie had it well styled—and push him down onto his knees.

Well, wasn't this a novel change from nervous newcomers?

From this unmatchable vantage point, Charlie watched Miles rub himself a few times through the gray wool of his trousers, then start on his lacings. He was tempted to shake off the suggestion of bonds around his wrists and speed Miles along, but before he could get up the nerve, Miles had freed himself. The tip of his swollen cock bobbed mere inches from Charlie's nose. It was just as it had seemed in the library: big and thick and just a tiny bit scary like the rest of the man. He was nervous he wouldn't be able to take enough of it, but every atom of him wanted desperately to try. He parted his lips and tried to lean in, but Miles's hand still gripped his hair and held him back, slowly stroking himself and denying Charlie so much as a taste.

"So, this is how you like it," Charlie panted. "I'm not sure why I was surprised."

Miles tipped his head back right to the edge of painful. Charlie looked up to find all fear and anger gone from the writer's face. There was nothing left but lust. "What did you just say to me?"

A delicious chill ran up Charlie's spine. "I said I shouldn't have been surprised that you like to go about it like a complete brute."

"Price," he said, pulling his hair just that much harder. "Charlie. There's better things to do with that pretty mouth of yours."

Still holding tight, Miles traced the taut head of his prick along the curves of Charlie's lips, then guided the first inches into his mouth with such an honest groan of pleasure that Charlie could have spent on the spot. But he pulled himself together and took as much as he could, which, based on the gasp he heard from above, was more than Miles had anticipated.

Keeping that barely tolerable grip on Charlie's hair, Miles set the pace himself as he slid in and out. Charlie had reign only over his lips and tongue, which he tried to put to the best use possible within his tightly controlled parameters. The arrangement was *very* inconsiderate, and Charlie loved everything about it.

As they went on like that, Miles's grunts and gasps turned to full-on moans of ecstasy. He sped up. "*Fuck*," he said. "Suck harder… *Yes*." At last, he went a bit slack, not holding Charlie back anymore but gently encouraging that faster rhythm with a hand on the back of his head. Charlie peeked upward to see the shaggy head thrown back toward the ceiling. "Like that, God yes, just like that…"

Charlie shook off the drooping tie at last and brought his freed hand around to make up for what he could not take in his mouth. Miles did not stop him, did not hold him back at all, giving silent permission for Charlie to finally give it his all. Miles's thighs started trembling and his fingers tightened in Charlie's hair. His cock swelled further, huge and rock hard, the tip of it getting wet and salty. He wouldn't last long.

Charlie let his hand take over for the finish while he grinned upward. "Guess I know what to do with it after all, don't—"

The wild look in Miles's eye told him what was about to happen a second before it did. He could have stopped it—it was not his usual habit—but instead he let Miles grab his head and push himself back in so deeply that Charlie's eyes watered and his throat protested. He could hardly breathe, but it was worth it as Miles let loose a low cry and shuddered with release that flooded Charlie's mouth. Well, *that* was awfully impolite. He should have been furious, but the brazen use of him was so overwhelmingly erotic that he took every last twitch of pleasure and drop of come with no complaint whatsoever.

After a moment of suspended time, Miles loosened his grip on Charlie and looked down as they separated. With his distraction gone, all Charlie could feel was the agonizing intensity of his own need. He was harder than he could possibly stand, and the front of his trousers was sticky all the way through. He stared up at Miles and fumbled at his own fly. If he could not release this throbbing pressure, he'd perish, he really would. This sort of desire was not survivable.

He'd hardly gotten the fly undone, when Miles pulled Charlie up by the front of his clothes so roughly that he thought he felt a button pop off of something. He thrust his tongue into Charlie's mouth for a bewildering second, then pushed him up against *Reginald Cox's actual, real-life writing desk* and dropped to his own knees. Charlie watched in wonder as Miles got his cock out and held it firmly a whisper from his parted lips. His breath alone might have tipped Charlie over the edge, but instead he started to lap teasingly at every inch until Charlie was shaking. With anyone else, he'd be selfishly chasing down his climax by now, but with Miles, he could barely even bring himself to slip his hands gently into all that wild hair. It did not seem to matter whether he was making Charlie gag on his big prick or was down on his knees himself. Obviously, he was not actually a kidnapper or torturer like his characters, but when it came down to it, the real-life Miles Montague was still absolutely in charge.

The realization brought a surge of pleasure so intense that Charlie gasped and tightened his fingers. "Fuck. Fuck, I'm going to spend."

Slow and unconcerned, Miles swirled his tongue to clean up the pre-come that Charlie was losing in critical volume. "Not if you keep pulling my hair like that, you're not."

"Oh, God." Coasting painfully on the very edge of bliss, he couldn't possibly argue. He took his hands off Miles's head like he'd been burned, clenching at the air and the lip of the desk instead as he started to really worry that Miles would just keep kissing and licking until Charlie died. "How about... how about now?"

"Say please."

Charlie's brain stuttered and gave up. He tried, but all that came out was an incoherent, pleading moan of desperation as his eyes squeezed shut and every muscle in his body tensed.

It must have been close enough. Finally, in an act of pure mercy, Miles took the entire length into his mouth in one movement. Seconds after Charlie felt that slippery warmth, he exploded, clasping a hand over his own mouth to catch the low, feral sounds that felt wrenched from the very center of his chest.

The absolute delight on Miles's face as he coaxed Charlie through the last shudders of his crisis was explanation enough for why he'd done the same to Charlie. Perhaps he was not rude. Perhaps he just could not imagine wanting anything else.

The moment faded into something dreamlike. Miles got

up shakily and pulled Charlie in close. He went to one of the lumpy armchairs by the gentle fire and sat Charlie down on his lap. The feeling of affection was surreal as tight arms wrapped around his waist and sleepy, scratchy little kisses tickled his neck.

Habit said to shake that sort of snuggly business off, so as not to send the wrong message. But he found that the message wasn't so terribly wrong when Miles was receiving it.

He stayed put.

Chapter Twelve

Miles

"Would you look at that," said Charlie, breaking a streak of silence as he examined the front of his shirt. "You did pop the button off."

Miles opened his eyes at last, mouth still pressed to the side of Charlie's neck. "You can't do it, can you?"

"What?"

"Let anyone sit quietly in your presence."

Charlie stiffened a bit. Miles realized how he might have sounded, and quickly kissed his cheek to show he'd meant no offense. Charlie relaxed against him again, but as the haze of consummation dissipated, Miles wasn't sure what he was supposed to do next. For the past five years, his encounters had either been meticulously planned and paid for, or so stupid and frantic that there was nothing to do but run when it was over. But he'd let Charlie into his own home. And so far, Charlie hadn't run. He hadn't asked for payment. He hadn't even simply done up his pants, wished him well, and left. Charlie's heart, it seemed, was not so dead as all that.

In fact, it was full of enough life to hop to his feet and say, "Perhaps a brew?"

Miles blinked. "What?"

"Cup of tea? I don't know."

"*Tea?*"

"Or wine." He wandered over to the rack near the kitchen. "Well stocked. No wonder you've learned a few things." He picked a bottle up and examined it like someone who had no idea what he was looking at. He put it on the table and glanced back at Miles. "Do you get quieter when you drink? Or do you talk more?"

"I.... What?"

"I'll just fix both."

Miles's jaw dropped as Charlie—in his flamboyant purple waistcoat, rumpled shirt, and stained trousers—put the kettle on the fire and started rummaging through his cupboards with a candle in hand.

"Stop it!" He got to his feet and slammed one of the cupboards shut.

"Stop what?"

"Digging through my things."

Charlie raised an amused eyebrow. "Is there really something in there you don't want me to see?"

Miles opened his mouth, but couldn't actually think of anything. They were cupboards, filled with the usual sorts of cupboard things. "It's the principle of it."

Before he'd even finished saying it, Charlie was laughing at him. "Go on, then." He stepped in and sweetly straightened Miles's collar. "Why don't you brew it if it will make you feel better?" He patted Miles's cheek. "Wouldn't want me to see the scandalous arrangement of your teacups, after all."

Miles grabbed his wrist mid-pat. He wanted to *want to* throw this bugger right out of his flat. But when he looked down, there was that smirking mouth, even more fascinating now that Miles knew what it was capable of. Not to mention the dark, clever eyes, full of good humor that Miles himself hadn't known in years.

"Watch it," was the harshest thing he could bring himself to say. And Charlie didn't seem to notice even that pathetic harshness, prancing on over to the table with a corkscrew in his hand that he'd apparently found within the few seconds of snooping.

Miles examined him with his arms crossed. "So, I take it you're making yourself at home, then?"

Charlie paused. He licked his lips as if thinking carefully, for once, about what he wanted to say. He seemed to come up short, scratching the back of his neck and grimacing. "This is very silly of me, isn't it? I should go." He put the corkscrew on the table and adjusted the wine bottle a bit, so the label was facing perfectly outward. "That's what you want?"

"No," Miles said instantly, startling even himself. He came over and took up Charlie's task, uncorking the bottle in a few smooth movements. "You, er, you're welcome to stay for a drink, if you'd like. The glasses…" He cleared his throat. "The glasses are in the second cupboard on the left, but leave the wine to get some air for a minute. I'm going to go downstairs to get the shop closed properly. Make yourself comfortable, I suppose."

What the devil was he doing? Miles cursed himself all the way down the stairs. This was madness, wasn't it? He'd lost his mind at last. Bad enough to have let things go this far already; letting Charlie stick around for wine and tea was so foolish he hardly recognized himself. He should cut it off now, before he got more attached. After all, he'd been in mad tears over this fop once already; what state would he find himself in if it turned out he actually liked the fellow?

But God, how could he make a man leave after that? Miles couldn't remember the last time he spent so hard. Charlie was temptation itself, and rather than quench the fire that had been lit during the wine tasting, this evening had left Miles burn-

ing even hotter. As he went about pulling drapes and snuff-
ing lamps, he was practically ready to go again just thinking
about it.

He stared guiltily at the abandoned counter. He ought to
count the drawer, especially after a busy day like today. The
task, though, sounded very dull compared to what was waiting for him upstairs. He'd count it in the morning; for now
he'd simply tuck it all in the safe.

As he started gathering up the notes and coins, he spotted
the paper Smithy had brought in, offering to buy the shop.
He glared at it, ready to throw it out properly, before realizing
that it was on the wrong side of the counter. For a moment,
he assumed he was confused, but thinking back… No, the
way he'd been facing wouldn't allow for it to land here. Once
he'd gotten the money locked up, he got the offer in hand. It
uncrumpled too easily, like someone had already been at it.

Back upstairs, he found Charlie sitting at his table with a
steaming cup of tea in his hands and a pot on the table before him.

"Been busy up here?" Miles growled.

Charlie poured some into the spare cup for Miles. "Idle
hands and all that."

"Yes." Miles threw the crumpled-up paper at his head. "Idle
hands might snoop."

Charlie guiltily caught the offer as it bounced off his forehead. "Sorry. How did you know?"

"It wasn't where I left it."

"Wasn't where you threw it, you mean?"

Miles shrugged. He picked up the teacup, but didn't sit
down. He took a silent sip. He knew Charlie wouldn't let it
stay quiet and awkward for very long.

Indeed, Charlie went on in a rush after only a few seconds.

"I'm sorry," he said, turning red in the face. "It's so silly, I hate to even say it. But I thought it might be a bit of writing you'd thrown out. The fanatic in me couldn't help myself."

That wasn't at all what Miles had been expecting. "You don't have to flatter me, Charlie."

"I mean it!" Charlie put his own cup down so hard it splashed out the side. "You saw my collection. Be angry that I'm a snoop, a spy, and a potential thief—if it had been writing, I'd have nicked it—but don't accuse me of flattering you."

At last, Miles let himself relax a little. He sat in the second chair. "I'm not selling the shop."

"Yes, I gathered as much." Charlie rolled the ball of paper back across the table to him.

Miles tapped the paper thoughtfully on the wood, then nudged it back to Charlie. "What did it say?"

"You didn't read it?"

"No."

Charlie laughed, threw it in the air, caught it. "Perhaps you wouldn't have been so hasty had you seen it. It says to name your price; the man is clearly quite motivated."

"Was there a name?" Miles caught the paper as Charlie threw it back and suspiciously opened it at last. It was creased beyond repair, so he flattened it out on the table. It was true: the handwritten letter said to name whatever price felt reasonable. He peered at the signature. "O'Donnell. I don't know him."

"Didn't he come in and give this to you?"

"No. He's some friend of my publisher, who stopped by with it an hour ago." He glanced at the clock. "More like three hours ago. Damn, is it really so late?"

Charlie peered over the rim of his teacup, his heated gaze settling upon the writing desk that he'd recently become quite intimate with. "You get awfully wrapped up in your work, don't you?"

"That's one way to put it," Miles muttered, half-tempted to see what other creative acts might suit such a surface.

"I'd love to hear about it. The writing, that is," Charlie clarified with a wink that let Miles know they were thinking along the same lines. "You looked so *enraptured*. Like you were in a different world. Now that I know how you go about, ah—" He broke off with a sort of happy self-consciousness.

"Like a complete brute, I know," said Miles.

"Indeed. Now I know about that, I'd like to know how you go about putting these stories together. Did you really just have an idea all at once and run up here to get started? The notion is so delectable, I hardly dare believe it."

Miles was shocked by the line of questioning. He didn't have the slightest idea how to talk about this, but Charlie looked so expectant and genuinely interested that he wished he had an answer dreamed up that would be as romantic as Charlie seemed to think it was.

"I, er, I suppose that's sort of what happened." He wanted to leave it at that, but then Charlie pointedly pushed the wine bottle across the table toward him, his expression very open as if to say *keep talking*. Miles snatched it by the neck and poured modestly into the goblets Charlie had laid out by the teapot, listening to the muddled-up words inside his mind and wondering if he'd forgotten how to have a conversation. He took a sip and tried his best. "The ideas sometimes just… come to me."

Charlie lifted his glass. "They *come* to you. Of course."

"Of course."

They clinked and sipped. Naturally, it was Charlie who went on, asking, "Why erotica?" He paused just long enough to accept Miles's need for more prompting. "Forgive me for saying so, but the stress of illegality seems to wear on you quite a bit."

Miles's first thought was that he didn't have the talent to write anything better, but that wasn't quite as true as it used to be, back when he was pestering all the publishers with winding imitations of Dickens. There had been reasons for his rejections back then, problems in craft he'd had more than enough time to fix in the course of five quiet years.

"I could write something else," he said carefully. "If I felt like it."

"But you don't?" prompted Charlie.

"No," he said. He wasn't sure how to expand on that, though, without killing that intrigued smile on Charlie's lips. There was no pleasant way to explain that his interest in writing palatably for the masses had died when his lover did.

It did not make for good conversation. Not at all.

"No," he repeated quietly. "I suppose I don't."

"Why's that, d'you think?"

"Isn't it obvious, Charlie?" He could not bring himself to ruin the moment, so instead he leaned in close, whispering, "My disposition is simply too depraved for anything better."

Charlie's eyes flicked down to his mouth. He licked his own lips. "That's not really an answer, but I want to kiss you so badly, that I think I'll let you get away with it this time."

With that, Charlie hooked a finger between Miles's waistcoat buttons and pulled him in for a very winey kiss. Miles's body couldn't help but go along with it, but his mind was racing. Why was Charlie even still here? Still spending his evening with a half-mad hermit like Miles when a man of his station and charm could be literally anywhere he wanted? He wasn't tipsy like they'd been in the library. He wasn't lost to delayed lust like he'd been earlier tonight. He was just here with Miles at the table over tea and wine, expressing curiosity about his artistic process and then kissing him slowly and decadently, like there was nothing in the world he'd rather be doing.

It gave Miles a strange feeling in the pit of his stomach. He wasn't sure what it was, at first. But as Charlie took a moment to look into his eyes and take an irreverent gulp of good wine, bringing such a spark of life into this quiet little flat, he figured it out.

He already did like this fellow. In fact, he enjoyed Charlie's company quite a lot. That would hurt terribly in time, but for now, the companionship was too lovely to resist.

"What?" said Charlie. "You're looking at me oddly."

Miles leaned back in his chair with his glass in one hand. "I want to know more about you," he said. "Tell me something about yourself."

"Well, that's not fair," Charlie said with a teasing lilt. "I was asking about your writing. Not only did you change the subject and distract me with various hedonistic pleasures, now you're going the turn the question round?"

"I don't discuss it very much these days," he managed, not quite keeping his eyes from darting to the always empty second armchair. "You'll get better answers from me if you ask again a few glasses from now."

"As I suspected," Charlie said.

"Something about yourself, then. While you wait for me."

Once again, that trapped look came over Charlie's face, quickly plastered over with a smile. "Well, you already know my most interesting secrets."

"Yes. It's all the other things I don't know."

"Where shall I begin?"

Miles rolled the balled-up offer around on the table a bit with his free hand. "Why are you marrying that silly girl? I want the honest answer: none of that tripe about having good times together. There must be something else going on."

Much to his surprise, Charlie looked at him sharply, lifting his finger off his glass to point at him. "Before we continue this, I want to make something very clear: don't insult Alma again, or I'll walk right out."

"I'm sorry," said Miles sincerely. "I didn't mean offense."

"I know you didn't, which is why I'm not walking out now."

"You really do care for her, then. It's not an act."

Charlie nodded into his glass. "We're in it together, she and I. Our parents are insistent on this union, and I'll be damned if I'm not as good to her as I can be. She deserves nothing less."

"But why are you going along with it? You seem like a confirmed bachelor if I ever met one, and I don't get the impression your family is under particular societal scrutiny. You're bankers, yes? Wealthy, maybe, but not nobility. You've made it this long without being bullied into a marriage. Why now?"

It may have been the longest Miles had ever seen Charlie pause.

Before he answered, he put on a show of self-deprecating amusement. "I may have gotten myself into a spot of...financial trouble over the past few years. I wasn't able to find a way out on my own."

"Considered selling your collection?" Miles suggested. "I'll take Saul off your hands, if you'd like."

Charlie looked a bit grim. "The situation is desperate enough that I did consider it. If I thought it would make more than a dent, I would. But as you pointed out, selling it is different. Of course, I've got safer nonsense to pawn." He wiggled his gem-covered fingers. "But you can't very well sell these things for what you bought them for, can you? It won't be enough, and I'll be dull in addition to indebted. I need my family's help."

"Can't they help you without making you marry?"

He swirled and smelled and tasted his wine very slowly to

buy himself more time. "This isn't...the first time this has happened. They're usually quite willing to help me—I'm Mum's
favorite, I think—but I am at the age where I'm no longer
cute enough to indulge. If I want help this time, I have to
take a respectable job and settle down like a 'proper, healthy
fellow' to prove I've changed my ways. For a while, I couldn't
find a job or a wife, and I swear my father might have let me
off the hook, but then the Merriweathers became involved.
They've provided both: a lady for me, and a position at Mr.
Merriweather's bank."

"*You* work at a bank? I assumed it was just your father." Miles
narrowed his eyes. He had quite the imagination, but it was
stretched by the thought of Charlie working at all, much less in
such a dull, stuffy environment. Charlie belonged in pubs and
parlors, his hands full of wine and his mouth full of...well...

"I'm talented at sums, believe it or not," Charlie said, in-
terrupting Miles's imaginings. "I'm no good with speculation
like my pop is, but I took quite well to accounting. It's easy,
and keeps me respectable enough to stop reflecting so poorly
on my parents and my brothers."

"You've brothers?"

"Two. Older than me. Proper, healthy fellows. I hate them.
They gave me a smattering of nieces and nephews, though,
so it's worth it, I suppose. Admittedly, spoiling the children
with presents has not helped my situation in the slightest."

Miles took all that in. "What kind of financial trouble are
we talking about, here?"

"A lady never tells her age, nor the size of her debts."

"Good thing you're a whore then, ain't it?"

Charlie threw the balled-up offer at his chest. "How dare you!"

"Are you going to tell me?"

Charlie slowly swirled his goblet, grimacing as he watched

the rich wine stick and slide down the sides of the glass. "Can we just say it's enough?"

"How on earth did you end up in such a situation?" The question made Charlie's shoulders slump, but Miles couldn't seem to help it. He was so intrigued by Charlie that he struggled to even give the poor bloke time to respond. "Are you a gambler?"

"I never gamble."

"Then what happened?"

"Is it really so hard to imagine? I moved to London as soon as I got out of school. They helped me for a bit, until it became obvious I'd come to nothing. When I refused to move back to Manchester to work for my father, they cut me off. I started helping a few mathematically challenged families and shops keep their accounts in order. Good work, fairly steady. Could have been a lovely situation. But then, well, I found these *gorgeous* rooms I couldn't afford, spending every other month traveling the Continent and every other day out with my friends. I was doing all these sums for others without caring that the work wasn't bringing in nearly enough to balance my own books. My mistake was nothing so glamorous as a poor bout of cards, I'm afraid." He threw back the rest of his glass, looking miserable. "Unless you mean the house of cards I built with my creditors."

Miles topped off Charlie's glass as he mulled that over. Apparently, he mulled too long.

"It's humiliating," Charlie said. "I can't believe I'm even telling you this. A genius like you. You must think I'm pathetic."

"Pathetic?" Miles laughed. He couldn't believe it. Run-of-the-mill debts? That was it? And all of it erased through marriage to a fine woman and a bit of work he enjoyed? "You aren't pathetic at all, Charlie. You're charmed, is what you are, if that's the worst of the troubles an obvious little Mary Ann like you has got up to in your life."

He'd meant it all in good humor, but a little bitterness crept in at the end. In general, Charlie did not make him think of Ethan; neither their forms nor their dispositions were terribly similar. Still, it was a bit difficult not to compare the outcomes of their lives.

Charlie pursed his lips, failing to look irritated. "I take it you've gotten up to some trouble, then?" He glanced at the desk. "Is that why... What I mean is, I can't help but notice that all your novels end in, well..."

"Death?"

"Yes, that. I'm reading along, you know, and one minute, I think I'm good and safe to have a wank, then next minute I'm weeping like a damned widow. It's confusing, really; I've not read anything else quite like it."

"That's partly a legal matter," said Miles, just to the side of the actual subject. "If the characters all get their comeuppance, then my publisher can argue that the books aren't corrupting, should he ever end up in court."

"Partly legal. Alright. But what's the other part? What's happened to make you come up with all that sordid stuff? You've hinted at it enough; if you didn't want to talk about it, I assume you wouldn't be so obvious. You've got my story, now—can I ask about yours?"

Had he been so obvious? Thinking back, he supposed so. He also supposed there was some part of him that wanted to confess it all to this strange apparition, this man who had stormed into his life full of compliments and curiosity. But when he considered putting the words out there—bald and plain, unembellished by artistic insinuations—he grew a bit clammy. He finished his glass off, hoping the wine might help him say it, to just admit out loud for once in his life that the man he'd adored died alone in jail, fevered and in pain, because someone decided that harmless desires should be punished just the same as monstrosities. That Miles had spent the intervening years with no tool to make sense of that love, that lust, and that tragic loss but his pen.

He wanted to say it, but the words would not move from his mind to his mouth. He feared there wasn't enough wine in the world to get him talking about this.

"No," he said quietly. "You can't ask that."

"Can I ask why you won't sell your shop?" Charlie asked, raising one of his dark brows in an unmistakable challenge.

Miles drummed his fingers on the table. His first impulse was to demand that Charlie take his good cheer and delectable mouth and get the hell out. But when he did not give in to that right away, the feeling softened. He didn't want Charlie to leave. He didn't want to sit here alone, thinking about him and Ethan and the shop. He did not want to go back to his desk, pull out the beginnings of his newest plotline, and start dreaming up the destruction it must ultimately end in.

He took up Charlie's hand and planted a sweet kiss on his knuckles. "Can we talk about something else?" he whispered. "I'll talk to you all night if you want. But it has to be about something else."

Charlie looked a little put out, but he squeezed Miles's hand all the same. "Good idea," he said, suddenly bracing. "Why should we become morbid when there's pleasures at hand? This, for instance." He picked up the wine and looked at the label on it again. "I'm still not entirely sure I understand what I'm supposed to be tasting aside from 'delicious.' There's more to it though, right? The sounds of it, or something?"

Miles knew Charlie was being stupid on purpose, but it softened his stress all the same. "Notes."

"Right. That." He ran a firm hand up Miles's leg and gave it a squeeze. "Why don't you tell me all about that?"

Chapter Thirteen

Charlie

In the weeks that followed, Charlie spent nearly every evening with Miles. He was given several proper tours of the dusty bookshop, with particular focus on the floor of the storage room, the underside of the counter, and—rather unexpectedly—the rolling ladder that led to the topmost shelves. In between learning new uses for things like book-binding tape, feather dusters, and rolled-up publisher's catalogues, Charlie and Miles drank beautiful wines with beautiful names, and talked. Just talked. When had Charlie ever *talked* to someone once he was through with them? Though they avoided a few unpleasant subjects, it hardly mattered; with a man as brilliant as Miles, there was an infinite number of things to discuss. Wine and books; food and France; spiritualism and philosophy. Once he got Miles going, the spells of surly silence were replaced by animatedly offered opinions and intriguing questions. Charlie knew a little something about everything, and Miles knew everything about some things, so the depth and breadth of their exchange hadn't reached its limits even after more nights together than Charlie had ever spent in the company of the same fellow.

Another Monday dawned as cold and miserable as the rest had this season, but Charlie found himself in good spirits anyway as he swapped out the weekend's lace and plush for his gray wool and starched banker's collar. Good boy that he was, he'd spent two Sundays in a row on his knees, and the promise of continued devotion this evening made a bit of sleet and a stack of ledgers insignificant detractors from his excitement.

The dining room was frightfully large and lonely by himself, so Charlie had started taking all home-cooked meals in front of the roaring parlor fire instead. This morning, he closed his eyes and was kept company by his vivid anticipation until he heard Quincy's footsteps in the doorway.

"Good morning, sir," the butler said as he put Charlie's tray on the little table beside his armchair.

Charlie accepted a cup of coffee. "Morning, Quincy. Big plans today?"

Rather unexpectedly, Quincy nodded. Charlie paused with the cup halfway to his lips as the butler procured the morning post.

"Send the notices on to my father," Charlie said quickly, joy chased out by dread at the sight of the stack. The bills and warnings and blatant threats had eased up since Pop had made arrangements, but occasionally one still slipped through. He hated to touch them, to even *look* at them, and so he kept hands and eyes both firmly on his coffee.

"No need for that," said Quincy. When Charlie still made no move for the post, he selected one piece of mail, a telegram, and placed it on top of Charlie's cup. "You can give it to him yourself tonight."

With a sinking feeling, Charlie grabbed the telegram.

Visiting London on business. Brief trip. Mother to come along to see the house. Arrangements made with Mr. Merriweather for Monday supper. Details handled via Mr. Quincy. We are much looking forward to the visit.

"Tonight?" Charlie exclaimed, taking in dates and travel details. "My parents are coming to London *tonight?*"

"I imagine they're on the Manchester Piccadilly as we speak."

He threw the telegram onto the table, barely managing to keep from pitching it right into the fire. "Why didn't you say anything before?"

Quincy peered grimly down at him. "It wasn't finalized until yesterday evening. Had you been home, I would have discussed it with you, but by the time you returned, you seemed awfully...*tired.*" He said *tired* as if he meant *drunk.* "I thought it best to let you get to bed. You don't need to do anything, after all. Your mother arranged extra staff to handle supper, so you just have to come home after work. Considering how difficult that is for you, however, I suppose you're right; I ought to have given you more warning. My apologies."

"Not at all, Mr. Quincy," said Charlie, his acceptance as empty as the apology. "What time is everyone set to arrive?"

"Your parents by teatime. The Merriweathers at seven."

Well, there went his night with Miles. "You could have mentioned it was being considered, at least."

"Your mother didn't want you to be disappointed if the plans fell through."

While that sounded like something Mum would say, Charlie didn't believe it. He had a feeling he was being checked up on, and all the better if he were caught unawares. He studied Quincy's surly face, wondering what sort of "details" had been passed back and forth between the butler and the Price gentleman he *actually* worked for.

"Well," he said as cheerfully as he could muster. "Not much I can do about it now."

"Is there any correspondence you need handled in light of the change of plans?" Quincy asked with an eyebrow up. "Anywhere your presence will be missed this evening?"

Though Charlie knew that a proper, healthy householder would come down hard on such a suggestive comment, the best he could manage was a self-deprecating grin.

"Who in their right mind would miss me?" he said lightly. "Don't trouble yourself with my correspondence."

After breakfast but before he left for the bank, Charlie locked himself in the library, putting his message to Miles as vaguely as possible on a little note addressed to Morgan & Murray's Bookshop. It felt like the composition took an age, but when he was done, his cold, tidy accountant's writing spelled out nothing more than, *Familial obligations have arisen unexpectedly. My deepest regrets for today and the next. I shall be in touch soon.—C*

Though it nearly killed him to do so, he left both their names off it entirely. After all, it wasn't as if Miles was inundated with callers. He'd know who it was from. Charlie folded the letter and got the stick of wax out of his drawer. He melted the end and sealed things up with a red splash and a press of his emblem.

Bollocks. He shouldn't have done that. The custom-designed initials and peacock feather was more unique than his own name. He quickly scraped the wax off and started over, using the wrong end to press a plain, unrecognizable square in the center of the red circle.

He stared at it, shocked at his own, unfamiliar behavior. When had he ever fretted so much about one little note?

The panic came back, a horrid hook behind his heart that was becoming as familiar as an old friend as the wedding drew nearer. All he could think to do to ease it was to pull the letter to his lips and kiss the still-warm wax.

Then he tucked it in his pocket to put in the post on his way to work.

It was alright.

It *was*.

In fact…*in fact* it was probably for the best. He chuckled at himself on his way out the door. How silly he was being. The letter was laughably beyond innocent, and this madness of missing Miles? If it was this strong now, why, the next time they saw each other, all this pent-up passion would make for a night they'd remember for the rest of their lives.

By the time he'd finished his day of ledgers and numbers and polite little conferences with polite little clients and clerks, he'd convinced himself fully of this truth, morphing the morning's dread and despair into a most delicious anticipation.

And that was good.

Because he got home to find that his parents had already arrived in London.

He'd hardly peeled the gloves off his half-frozen fingers to hand over to Quincy when his mother peeked her head into the foyer, her graying bun wispy and wilted from the day's travel and her dark eyes shining.

"There you are," she scolded as he shucked his slushy coat and then approached her with his arms out. She was very warm compared to him when they embraced, wearing a rumpled blue traveling dress and smelling strongly enough of soot and chocolate that Charlie had to assume she'd spent the past hour by the parlor fire, eating her favorite cherry cordials and rejecting offers to change before her son arrived. She squeezed him tight and kissed his cheek before leaning back to look at him. "You could have come home a bit early on our behalf, you know. I've missed you."

Charlie's eyes drifted to the doorway that led to the parlor and, likely, his father. "I would have, but that's, er, business. I suppose."

"Business, yes." Mum tried gallantly to keep a straight face.

"How strange to hear you say that, but you're right. Just imagine if mothers like me got their way and had all their boys at home all the time. Why, society itself would crumble!" She took his arm. "Come on, then. I'm sure your father will appreciate your prudent scheduling."

They went into the parlor to find Charlie's father, Mr. Basil Price, before the fire. He'd clearly been waiting, and sprang right up from his seat at the sight of them. He was of a height with Charlie, and they looked quite a bit alike aside from Pop's full, salt-and-pepper beard and narrower hazel eyes. Pop seemed a little weary, but happier than Charlie might have expected, striding over and stealing him away from Mum for a handshake, then a pat on the back, and then, as if he simply could not help himself, an embrace.

"Lovely to see you, my boy," he said. He looked around the parlor, a hand still on Charlie's shoulder. "Stunning in here, isn't it? My first time seeing it since you've gotten all the furniture in. It'll do, I say. It'll do you nicely."

"Well, it's Mum who ordered it all. I just sit back and…" Charlie could not bring himself to say *enjoy it*. "And I suppose that in the spring, when the sun gets through the windows, it will be a right paradise."

"Spring," said Mum with a dreamy sigh. He thought for a moment that she was as anxious for light as he was, but he noticed she was subtly counting on her fingers, pausing at nine, then backward rather scandalously to six. "I suppose by spring, all sorts of things could be livening the place up!"

Charlie's stomach flipped at her implication, and Pop's brow furrowed.

"By spring?" Pop said. "Maggie, your sums are off."

"Oh, bother *sums*." She sent a little wink Charlie's way. "They come when they come, don't they?"

Charlie's face burned so bright that he felt his chronically wind-whipped nose warming for the first time all day. "Mum, how many cherry cordials have you had since you got here?"

"Hush, now. I brought them for you." She chuckled and gave Charlie's hand a squeeze. "I suppose this is a fine time for me to take a little rest before supper, though. Why don't you go see if I've left any for you in the box?"

With that, she left. Charlie and his father stood quietly together until her footsteps had reached the upstairs landing.

"Pop," Charlie whispered, trying to keep his tone light. "She doesn't really think—? A nice girl like Alma. You know I'd never—"

Pop held up a very patient hand, as if he'd been dealing with this subject for days already. "I know, Charlie." He sighed with a slight air of something akin to disappointment. "Everyone knows that you would…never. Your mother is just excited to see you moving ahead with your life at last. Excited to the point of impatient, I'd say. Let's not judge her, eh? Not every mother her age would come halfway across the country for two brief days with her son."

He thought he caught an implication at the end there, that perhaps he ought to invite Mum to stay longer, to linger in London until the wedding while Pop returned to Manchester the day after tomorrow. But while Quincy could only ask so many questions of him, his mother would require much better excuses for the way Miles's presence in his life had taken his schedule from decadent to downright debauched.

So would his wife, actually, now that he considered it.

Oh *God*. He could not think about that, not with his father watching him with the sort of tired concern he always had for his mess of a youngest. Desperate for distraction, he took up the box of chocolates Mum had left on the table. He popped a cordial in his mouth, letting the sweetness soften his lips enough to speak.

"I have a question," he said after a moment. He couldn't stand still or look Pop in the eye, but he could play that off by busying himself at the teapot and making his voice sound normal. "You know *I've* no space to judge Mum's impatience. And you never would. We take her and adore her just as she is. But, Pop, has Mum met the Merriweathers yet?"

Pop snorted a little laugh and accepted a fresh glass of luke-warm tea from Charlie. "Briefly," he said. "We all met early in the engagement, but it was a rather hasty affair. And obviously, we've not had all six of us together before."

"Are you entirely certain, then," Charlie asked carefully, "that this evening is a good idea? We're quite different from them. There's unlikely to be as much, ah, *love* as there could be. Between the families. Are you certain we can't just…not?"

Charlie poured tea into Mum's empty cup and pulled it to his own lips so that he could pretend he was asking only the question he'd posed. Pop, in turn, cleared his throat and pre-tended that he had not heard the more dire question that sat beneath Charlie's innocent, deniable phrasing.

"Yes, Charlie," he said. "I am entirely certain that we *can't just not.*"

"But what if—?"

"Some things cannot be put off indefinitely. Life marches ever forward you know. And this *evening…*" He sipped his tea a little grimly. "I wish I did not have to put you through it, Charlie, I do. But it would be irresponsible to put it off a mo-ment longer than we already have. I'm sure it will be lovely in the end, anyway. Don't you agree?"

Charlie nodded, somehow disappointed even though he had not, for once, been expecting anything better.

The three Merriweathers arrived precisely on time as usual. There was something surreal about seeing Alma after the week he'd had. She was dressed in a mint green bustle with her hair piled carefully on top of her head, small and sweet and as different a creature from Miles Montague as any in creation, save for the blocky outline of a slim novel he could spy poking at the weave of her tapestry bag.

She smiled warmly at him, though, and he was glad to have her here as a friendly companion, for he could imagine no circumstance under which the Prices and the Merriweathers would enjoy one another's company.

Based on the way her smile turned to something like terror when she greeted Charlie's parents, it seemed that Alma was thinking along similar lines.

"L-lovely to meet you," she stammered. "I mean, lovely to see you again, Mr. and Mrs. P-Price."

Her eyes were painfully wide, an expression that was not softened by the way Mum was eyeing her waistline with a delusional little grin.

"Give Alma and me just a moment, would you?" Charlie said sweetly as Quincy started to lead the lot of them from the parlor to the dining room. He gave Alma that mushy sweetheart's look for all to take in. Mum smiled much too deviously at it; Mrs. Merriweather glared too suspiciously; their fathers both looked weary of the world and everything in it. But they allowed the couple to dawdle behind them in the parlor as they made clipped and tense conversation through the halls to start the soup course.

Standing alone before the fire, Alma turned wide, nervous eyes to Charlie.

"This is going to be a disaster," she hissed.

"Oh, darling, I'm sure—"

"Sure of what? That I'm right?" she said, crossing her arms over her stomach. "Come on, Charlie. You know as well as I do that there's no good that can come from this, considering the circumstances."

She seemed to be implying something, but Charlie wasn't sure what it was. Before he could ask, she started pacing in front of the fire with her fingers at her temples.

"Do you think I could get away with pretending to be sick?" she asked.

"Don't do that!" said Charlie quickly. The last thing they needed was to encourage Mum's impatience.

"Then what am I to do?" Alma said, voice shaky. "Just face them all and cover my ears when it goes bad halfway through?"

He'd never seen her so upset. Perhaps she thought his parents would be as cruel and critical as her own? Whatever the case, he was determined to make her feel better. He wandered over to the small table where Mum's cherry cordials had joined the brandy decanter. When he opened the box, he found there were still a few left. He held them out.

"What we shall do, my dove," he said, "is fortify ourselves."

Alma peered in the box like the chocolates had been plucked off the Tree of Knowledge. "It's a proper supper tonight, not a cake tasting. We shouldn't spoil our appetites."

"Oh, between the two of us, we've got enough appetite to get through the evening."

She looked curiously at him. He stood still and let her approach him. She plucked one out for herself and then waited for him to do the same. They ate them together, Alma smiling and putting a hand to her chest as the sugary liquid burst out.

"Charlie!" she giggled through a mouthful of chocolate. "You wicked thing, this has got liquor inside!"

"Just a wee bit," he said. Then he turned to the table and poured some brandy for each of them. "Which is why you really ought to wash it down with something stronger."

"I can't," she said, but she took the glass with her eyes sparking.

"Sure you can," he said. He lifted his glass so the amber liquid caught the firelight. "Now, do it all at once with me. It will burn, but the rush will be well worth it, especially once your parents see how excessively opulent a dinner my decadent mother has planned to appall them with."

She nervously brought the glass to her mouth and they both shot the brandy back in one go, same as he'd do with Jo or Noah or any friend at the club. It was conspiratorial and fun and absolutely everyone else in the house would despise them for it. The highlight of the evening, most likely.

Alma squeezed her eyes shut, covered her mouth, and squealed. Charlie laughed and encouraged her through the rough part until she removed her hand to reveal pink cheeks and a delighted smile.

"Would you look at that?" he said. "You didn't even retch."

"It was a near miss."

"You're a natural hedonist, my dove. Now. Are you feeling better prepared to face disaster?"

"Almost. Just one more thing."

"Oh? What—?"

He found out *what* pretty quickly, as she put a chilly hand behind his neck and kissed him right on the mouth, all sugar and brandy and that womanish softness that he'd stopped even pretending to seek out years ago.

She seemed to notice that Charlie had frozen and she pulled back with a bashful look. "I'm sorry," she whispered. "I'm so sorry, Charlie. Oh, that was so stupid of me. I just thought—"

"Not at all," said Charlie, his voice so awkwardly bright that he nearly cringed at the sound of it. "I—I mean to say, we're going to be married soon, aren't we? No sense, um, being shy."

Oh sweet hell, he'd really stepped in it this time. All that talk of hedonism and appetites. What did he expect? As his father had so helpfully pointed out, some things could not be put off forever. He was *marrying* her. Soon.

Less than a month, if he'd done the sums right.

Though his mouth had gone unpleasantly dry, still he forced himself to peek deviously over her shoulder as if they were the most devilish of conspirators, as if *this* were the sort of thing that could get him in all sorts of trouble, then pecked her bottom lip as briefly as possible. With any luck, she'd misread the bright burning of his face for passion.

He made himself smile. Soon, she did too, her embarrassment softening. They each had one more chocolate and another drop of brandy before they laced their fingers together and Charlie went to meet his family hand in hand with the sweet, fun-loving woman he would spend the rest of his life lying to.

Chapter Fourteen

Miles

Familial obligations have arisen unexpectedly. My deepest regrets for today and the next. I shall be in touch soon.—C

Considering the bright, swirling way that Charlie conducted himself, from his clothes to his laugh to the printing of his calling card, Miles was shocked to find such an unobtrusive little note included with his evening post.

He ought to have been grateful. After all, such simplicity allowed him to keep the letter in his pocket as he finished up with his last customers and got the shop shut down. Had it screamed *Charlie Price* within swirling foliage and purple-inked peacock feathers, foolishly including details of their regular meetings and signed with devotion, he'd not only have kept it out of his pocket, but would have burned it immediately.

And yet, once the door was locked and Charlie was not coming and it was just him and this note in the empty book-shop with its dying fire and ancient inventory, he wished it had been a bit less perfunctory. Just a little. Nothing mad, not a *love letter*. But would the tiniest of sentiments really have been so dangerous?

The realization that he'd had such a thought made him shudder. He thrust the note back into his pocket and went to bank the fire. He poked at the embers aggressively, wishing he could do the same to his brain. What the devil was he thinking? *Of course* setting a precedent for sentimental letters would be dangerous. Once the fireplace was settled, he stood up straight, wiped the ash from his hands, and stared around at the echoing shelves of books, knowing he'd be useless for the rest of the night. The shelving, the counting, the cleaning. It would have to wait until tomorrow. God, Ethan would hate that, just absolutely *hate it*, but as Ethan was not here and was never going to be, there was nothing for it.

He took up the last candle and used it to light his way up the staircase.

His flat, however, was even more unbearably empty than the shop, all dark and lonely and cold. He barely mustered up the energy to get a pan on the fire for a fry-up, the clop of carriages and patter of unceasing rain outside seeming to echo in an emptiness that should have been familiar, but took him quite by surprise tonight.

Miles was used to solitude like one gets used to darkness, the eyes adjusting, the shadows losing their mystery, until it felt quite comfortable. As the only child of a widow who passed on when he was barely twenty, it was a habit he learned early in life and had pulled back out in full force to see him through these past few years. However, one week of Charlie's blindingly brilliant light seemed to have reset his eyes. He suddenly felt lost and bored, the night stretching out endlessly ahead of him in a way it had not done for a very long time.

He cooked and ate his supper, then sat down at his desk, opening the drawer to fetch his new manuscript. Beneath it, he found the little shirt button of Charlie's that he'd lost on their first night together. Had it been fancy, he'd have given it back, but he saw no harm in holding on to this one. He rubbed it between his fingers for just a second before grabbing a stack of fresh paper and closing the drawer so he could get to work.

That was what he needed to do. He needed to work. Not the shopkeeping. Not *Ethan's* work. His own. This pressure in his chest would not find its release through any medium but ink on paper.

He read back over what he'd done already, his eyes blurring and mind wandering so much that it took twice as long as it should have. Once he got through it, he dipped his pen and tried to continue, but the words were clunky and laborious. His mind was still ringing with *My deepest regrets for tonight and the next,* and *familial obligations,* and *C,* just a single bloody *C* that was the poorest substitute for Charlie Price's company that he could imagine.

My regrets as well, he found himself scrawling out where he ought to have been putting a description of the status-climber's dressing routine. *I regret your absence most painfully, my darling, and shall be counting the hours until your return.*

He dipped his pen again, his hand racing as disappointment poured out of him:

When you do return, Charlie, my beautiful Charlie, I shall kiss you to the very edge of consciousness, press you up against the bookshelves and strip every scrap of status from your body. I'll run my hands and nails and teeth over your skin until you desire no obligation save for the ones I give you, when I spin you around and bend you over and drive such piercing memories into your flesh that you'll never do the same to your stupid little wife without thinking of me while you do it—

Oh God.
Oh, God, what am I doing?
What is this psychotic drivel?

I can't show this to him. I can't even use it in the novel; it's awful.
Well, maybe not all of it. I sort of like this line.

He drew a circle around the line about scraps of status, then held the page in front of his eyes and stared at what he'd done.

This was how it happened, wasn't it? The process by which real, living passion ended up smudging a bit of cheap paper on a pornographer's desk. When Ethan had been pronounced gone for good, there'd been nowhere else for that passion to go but the page. But he did not need to do that this time. Charlie wasn't gone. He had *obligations*. He'd *be in touch soon.*

This time, anyway.

It hit him that when Charlie's family expanded—first for his wife and then further from there—his obligations would too. Right now, the balance was perfectly tolerable; a few nights together, a few apart, a little unpredictability in the form of a broken plan or an unexpected chance at togetherness. But that wouldn't last past the wedding. Once he was married, there would be fewer nights with Charlie and more letters from *C*. The brightness of warm company would become blinding in-terruptions to his dark, quiet life, ruining the adjustment of his eyes until he found himself pouring his feelings for this fellow onto the page for lack of any other path to release.

He felt the chill of the night settle in for a shiver as he re-read his words. It was one thing to write like this about a man who was dead. But with Charlie alive and living in the same city, could Miles really trust himself to keep pages like this between himself and Smithy? Or might he someday be tempted to return one of *C*'s polite messages with a list of obscene promises signed off with love? He didn't want to do that today. But a month from now? Or, heaven forbid, a year from now?

The truth of the matter made him weary, but determined. They would enjoy this little affair while they could.

But once Charlie was married…

Miles took off his specs and rubbed his burning eyes. He ripped the page carefully in half once, twice, and then crumpled it up and threw it in the dwindling fire, where it brightened the flames briefly before leaving them just as dim as they'd been before.

Deciding it was one thing, but actually telling Charlie his conclusion about the ultimate fate of their acquaintance was another matter entirely.

Soon arrived sooner than he expected, late Wednesday afternoon when the shop was still open.

"I left hot on the heels of their carriage to the station," Charlie admitted, leaning over the counter in the empty shop. He looked up at Miles with a windswept, lovesick grin that should have been flattering, but instead reminded Miles of himself at twenty-seven, when he would visit this bookshop as an increasingly suspicious customer with one too many questions about literary criticism. "God, how I hated to put you off for them. If I'd had any other option, I'd have been here. I swear it."

Miles should have said something then. There were no customers. He could have done it. But instead, he listened to Charlie's outrageous report of how his hideous in-laws and his parents (who sounded suspiciously like the source of Charlie's determined cheerfulness) had spent the entire evening subtly insulting each other until it was a wonder the engagement had not been called off entirely.

"About that—" Miles said in response to this conclusion.

But the door opened just then, a creak and snap that startled them both, because Miles had forgotten to replace the bell. Miles greeted the customer while Charlie browsed the

adventure novels, selecting a few to bring home for his fiancée "while he was at it."

Charlie lingered in the shop until closing, at which point
he talked Miles into taking tea at a restaurant down the street,
and of course, Miles could not talk about these things in public. He planned to say it when they got back to the shop, but
then Charlie wanted to go upstairs and try a new wine. Half
a glass was excuse enough to start them kissing, and once that
got going, there just wasn't a good opportunity for that sort
of conversation.

It was still early in their acquaintance, and yet they'd de-
veloped habits already. Once they were spent, all bonds were
untied and everything was tidied up. Then Miles got the fire
going higher and sat in his usual chair while Charlie, instead
of taking the other obvious seat, put his warm underclothes
back on, wrapped himself in the heaviest quilt, and sat on a
pillow between Miles's feet with his head resting on one of
his legs. Eyes closed, he let Miles ruin whatever was left of his
careful hairstyle with caresses and petting while they soaked
in the warmth and comfort that seemed to permeate the sitting room.

Sometimes they talked. Sometimes not. Tonight, after a
comfortable spell of silence, Miles said, "Charlie?"

"Hmm?" He sounded half-asleep, so cozy and content that
Miles hated to kill it by carrying on.

But he did. "Do you have any other familial obligations
coming up?"

Another little sound came from Charlie's throat, this one
amused. "One."

"To your fiancée? Or your parents?"

"To my sisters."

"I thought you only had brothers."

Charlie looked up at him, his eyes like the richest chocolate. "I haven't visited my gentlemen's club in a while," he said. "I've had a little note from the proprietor, checking up on me. I'll need to stop in this weekend, or my friends are going to think I'm dead."

"Dead? Why would they think that?"

"Oh, they're worriers." The way he rolled his eyes made it seem like there was a story in that, but Charlie didn't seem inclined to share it. Instead, he said, "Do you want to come along?"

Miles was taken aback. Come along? To the molly bar in Soho that Charlie called a gentlemen's club? "No," he said immediately. "No. I'll take the excuse to get some writing done, I think."

Charlie clucked his tongue but didn't argue. "Fine. I suppose I am distracting, aren't I? You'll have to take your writing time when you can get it."

"Don't worry about it too much," said Miles, his voice very careful, even, measured. "Once you're married, I'll have time to make up for it."

All the amusement left Charlie's face for just a second before he slapped it back on. "Right," he said. "I suppose you'll have more time then. Though, I had thought that perhaps I could continue to provide distraction sometimes."

Miles licked his lips as his mouth went horribly dry. He could not believe he had a man this beautiful, this charming, this delightful, literally sitting at his feet and he was still going to say it.

"That's probably not a good idea," he muttered. "But I do hope you'll leave me with very little writing time in the interim."

Charlie kept the smile, but his eyes darted off somewhere. "Of course," he said, his voice sticking a bit. "I... That would..."

He cleared his throat without finishing the thought and turned back to face the fire. He was quiet for a moment, then:

"Miles?"

"Yes, love?"

"Can you..." He paused, like he was trying to keep his voice steady. "Can you tell me about your new book yet?"

With his chest so tight and a lump burning a hole in his throat, there wasn't much Charlie could ask for that Miles would deny right now.

"Sure," he said.

"What's it called?"

"Um. I'm calling it *The Book of Vices*, for now."

"Sounds delicious." He snuggled his head in more comfortably on Miles's thigh. "What's it about?"

"It's about...about a handsome clerk who's invited to dine with an aristocrat. He buys an etiquette book to make sure he doesn't embarrass himself, but the book is cursed. The advice is innocent enough to start with, but eventually it turns devilish."

Charlie laughed. "I love it," he said. "Tell me more. Tell me everything."

And so he did, detailing his work in progress to another person in a way he'd never dreamed possible. They talked and laughed at length about it while Miles went on raking his fingers through Charlie's hair, wondering how long the piney scent of his pomade would linger in his flat once he was gone.

Chapter Fifteen

Charlie

It had been a rough go, hearing Miles say that the wedding had to be the end of things, but as that night and the next several went on, Charlie started to suspect that Miles hadn't really meant it. How could he? Their time together remained so easy and precious, and the subject never came up again by the time the weekend rolled around. And if ever it did come up? Well, Charlie doubted that Miles's fears ran deeper than their happiness. He figured it would be simple enough to talk him out of it when the time came.

Optimism restored, he felt alright giving Miles a night to devote to his work while Charlie himself publicly asserted his continued place among the living.

He arrived at the club early enough to secure his favorite alcove. He had to admit, it was refreshing to return to his usual haunt after some time away. As things grew busier like they always did on a Saturday night, he watched Forester and Warren splash out liquor and sign people into the back so fast they appeared to have at least eight hands between the two of them. The usual crowd was all here, but others as well, both new fellows and rare but familiar faces. Everywhere was smoke and laughter, cards and kisses. Hands were filled with drinks while laps were filled with lovers. Jewels sparkled from necks and wrists, feathers and lace swirled about every table, and all the back rooms were so populated that Forester might run out of linens before everyone got their turn.

And yet, there was Charlie, lying back on his favorite chaise all alone, peeking out from behind the alcove's partially drawn curtain to smile at the festivities. The ice in his barely touched drink had melted, though he occasionally took a few puffs on a cigar he'd swiped from behind the counter when Warren wasn't looking.

He was warm and content, listening in on piano music and gossip. He tried to blow rings without really knowing how, sending smoke drifting up to a ceiling hung with gauzy purple folds.

At some point, the curtain drew back slightly as a lovely young chap peeked his head into Charlie's alcove. The fellow looked him over and licked his lips.

Charlie registered the look only enough to wave it off. "I'm not looking for company tonight, thank you."

The fellow seemed taken aback. "Then what are you doing here?"

"I'm relaxing."

At that moment, a heady shriek cut through the rest of the noises, likely from Miss Penelope's table. The stranger raised a brow. "Strange place for that."

"The Fox is a place for strange fellows, isn't it? Now go on, find your own strangeness somewhere else. I'm perfectly happy here on my own."

The man shrugged and took off, heading toward the shrieking. Charlie watched him go. Some familiar Easter-and-Christmas-type patrons seemed to have taken over Noah's usual table while he was getting into his drags. There was quite a to-do, and it didn't take long for the new chap to have two beautifully dressed heathens on his arms, complaining heartily about the situation. There. Let him get to know just how strange a place he'd walked into tonight.

Charlie grabbed the edge of the curtain and pulled it fully closed, not eager for another visitor to interrupt his peace. He took a small sip of watery gin and settled back in.

He was glad the man had gone, but he hadn't been quite truthful when he said he was happy here on his own. As one of his attempts at a ring wafted upward, he wondered whether Miles was awake at this hour. Was he still writing? *Could* he write, or was he, like Charlie, still floating along in a dream state, too inspired to even move?

Thoughts of what he'd like to do next time lit him up as he lay back in his cozy alcove. Threats of being tied, gagged, and made to watch while Miles wrote had been floated about recently, and had rather captured his imagination.

His favorite nook shared a wall with one of the private rooms, and while he was used to the whisper of muffled thumps and groans, with his mind swimming like this, tonight's lustful sounds were almost too much. The fingers not occupied by the cigar drifted lightly over buttons bulging with the beginnings of arousal. He'd gotten away with tossing strangers off in here without Forester making him take it to the back; perhaps he could get himself a bit of relief before anyone noticed. He gave his cock a more solid stroke through the fabric and his eyelids fluttered. It certainly wouldn't take very long...

With a dramatic whoosh, the curtain opened up entirely. Charlie nearly leaped out of his skin, pulling his wandering hand back like he'd touched a hot stove and drawing one knee up to hide his condition. He looked up guiltily to see that the entrance to the alcove was taken up by wide silk skirts and a smell of flowery perfume.

Noah—now Miss Penelope Primrose—had clearly noted his absence from the social sphere.

She was not pleased.

"What in *heaven's name* is going on in here?" She hit him on the side of the buttock with her fan so hard that he was startled upright. "Why are you back here by yourself with the curtains closed? Is there something wrong with that lovely man you sent away?"

Charlie looked through the crowd for the man. He hadn't thought much of it.

"I don't know," said Charlie honestly. "Does it matter?"

"He's here with Annabelle. She's rather irate that you've insulted her friend."

"Kindly tell Annabelle that I'm not her bloody rent boy, would you?"

Penelope hit him again, this time on the shoulder.

"*Ow!*"

"What's gotten into you? You disappear for an age, then when you finally come back, you lie around all night, useless as a lump. Forester thinks you're in here eating opium and has half a mind to tell you to go home. He says you're going to start bringing all the wrong sorts in." She took the cigar out of Charlie's hand, puffed it, and gave it back with a cough and a wince. "Good God, is that one of Warren's? Do you actually like those disgusting things?"

Charlie laughed. "Tastier than opium."

Penelope leaned in and took a good whiff of his hair. "I don't smell it on you either, and haven't ever known that to be your poison."

"That would have been well before your time, Penny."

She fluffed down on the chaise and linked their arms. While Miss Penelope rarely dropped her persona once she'd put it on, back here, just the two of them, she snuggled in comfortably against Charlie and let her voice relax into something a little closer to Noah.

"You do have the sort of delicious air of a lush about you, Charlie," she said with devious accusation. "I can easily see you lounging about in some den. I think Forester simply wishes to catch you in such a state, vulnerable for once. Who knows what we'd do to you, if we found you helplessly floating along?" She tickled the inside of his thigh, working upward until Charlie batted her off.

"No one will ever see me in that state," Charlie said. "Took a very bad turn in France, once. It rather put me off the stuff."

She swatted Charlie's chest. "Now, that's a story I'd like to hear."

"Not tonight." He took up her gloved hand and kissed it. It made him think instantly of when Miles had done the same thing to him, their first night in his flat. "Go beat those boys round the head until they give your table back, Penny, and have fun. It's a lovely night. Go enjoy it."

"Why don't you want to enjoy it?"

Charlie couldn't keep the smile off his face. "I am."

"You're lazing about back here, smoking Warren's disgusting excuse for a cigar, kicking out handsome new visitors. How on earth can you say you're enjoy—" She cut herself off with a huge gasp. She put one satiny hand on her enormous false bosom and clutched Charlie's forearm with the other so hard he worried about bruises. "*Charlie!*"

"What?"

Penelope grabbed him by the chin and turned his head so they were face-to-face. Hers was painted perfectly, a real work of art. In and out of paint, this face was comprised of perfect, smooth lines and elfin features. He worried, sometimes, that Penelope keeping her face so smooth and her brows so tidy might cause Noah trouble outside the safety of the Fox. Here and now, though, she really was a beauty, and he appreciated the dedication she had to herself.

Even if she was a meddling son of a bitch.

"Charlie," she hissed. "You have a lover."

He batted away her grip on him. "That's ridiculous."

"You're *smiling*!" There was no shaking her now; she had her claws in him somewhat literally. "You do! You bloody monster, I'm going to kill you! Who is it? Tell me everything. Is it that writer you assaulted? It *is* isn't it? Good God, I have to tell the others."

"Stop it!" Charlie hissed, but too late. Penelope was gone, floating across the club. She gleefully leaned so far over the bar that her heeled boots came up off the floor and crossed behind her in midair, flashing layers of petticoats. She flared the fan out as if she cared about hiding what she whispered to Forester and Warren. They all looked across the room at Charlie like a single, three-headed gossip monster.

After a brief bit of bickering that Charlie could likely recite verbatim even though he hadn't heard it, Forester and Penelope started back for him, leaving a sulking Warren to mind the bar. They stopped in the entrance to the alcove, Forester smirking and Penelope bouncing on the balls of her feet.

Charlie tapped the ash off the end of his cigar. "I absolutely hate every last one of you."

"Why didn't you bring him?" Forester asked, crossing his arms over his waistcoat, making candlelight spark off the fine chain of his pocket watch. "I'd like to meet the fellow who got through to Charlie Price at last."

"No one 'got through to me.'" Luckily, the club was as dark as clubs came; the extent of his burning face would be missed. "I can suck a damn cock without having to pay for one of your rooms, Forester. It doesn't mean anything."

At the mention of cock sucking, Penelope squealed so loudly

that a few people looked her way. "Ooooooh, but it *does*! And you *know it*! You've said it yourself."

"What's that supposed to mean?"

Penelope snatched Charlie's drink and brought it close to her mouth. She dropped her voice into a low, swaggering parody of his Northern speech and pointed sharply with one finger off the glass: "'ow *dare* you imply I got a lover? Can you even *imagine* havin' to look at one o' these fools in the *ligh' o' day*? If I can't get *fucked* over the bar, I'll not get *fucked* at all, thank you. Now, For'ster, another round fer'everyone. Put it on *the tab*, will you?" She drained what was left of the drink, shivered as the liquor hit her, then turned to Forester. "How was that? Just like him, don't you think?"

Forester applauded in enthusiastic agreement, but Charlie grabbed the empty glass back. "I never said any of that."

"I'm after the spirit of your words, darling."

He couldn't deny it. "Well… I don't sound like that, anyway."

They both burst out laughing again. Charlie glanced down and realized he was holding his glass close to his mouth with one finger pointing outward from it, just as Penelope had done. He slammed the blasted thing down. "Come off it," he said. "You really think I'm suddenly all gooey-eyed over someone just because I didn't bring him here?"

"No," said Penelope. "I can tell you're all gooey-eyed by the amount of goo in your eyes."

Forester looked a bit smug. "You don't have to be so defensive, Charlie. You're allowed an emotion or two."

"I have an emotion or two," said Charlie. "Contentment, and oftentimes happiness."

"Added a third then, have you?"

"Homicidal?"

"Smitten."

He tried to argue again, but the fight had gone out of him. He was defeated. Next thing he knew, he'd been flanked on either side by Penelope and Forester, and was spilling the details of his first night with Miles. It was a particular version of the story, of course. The bonds were tighter in this telling, and Miles had left pages of filth out on the desk rather than stuffing them away. There was considerably less tea, and considerably more choking on impressive anatomy. Still, he knew he was talking himself into a ditch he'd never climb out of; he could tell by the way they kept *looking* at each other that no matter how he embellished the details, all they would hear was that Charlie had found his weakness.

And they were *thrilled*.

"Whoo!" Penelope fanned her face at the end of Charlie's story. "*Dio mio*, no wonder you're a puddle. I say, you must bring him here, mustn't you? Can't keep a man like that to yourself; it simply wouldn't be sporting."

"Even if I wanted to share—" which, now that Charlie considered it, he very much did *not*, not at all "—I couldn't. I told you before, this isn't his kind of place."

Forester's face crinkled with offense. "What's his kind of place, then?"

"Home."

No clever answer could have gotten a better reaction than the truth. Penelope pushed him nearly over, dabbing her eyes before mirthful tears could ruin her face. "You're too much, Charlie."

"I'm serious. He's quite paranoid, and keeps to himself."

"What on earth are *you* doing with someone like that?" asked Forester. "And what's he doing with you?"

Penelope waved her fan again. "I'm pretty sure he told us what they're doing, darling."

"Still, that seems like an awful mismatch." Forester scanned the parlor, then pointed across the room where some of the theater crowd were drunkenly singing. "We could probably do you better. Have you talked to Mr. Ashley over there? Stagehand. Funny as anything. If you were interested, I could—"

"Forgive me, Mr. Forester," snapped Charlie, "but I can match myself up just fine."

Another face popped into the alcove. Miss Jo. "Who are we matching?"

"Charlie and that perverted hermit you introduced him to," Forester said, still looking very skeptical about the whole thing.

She came into the alcove. "Really?" She did not sound nearly surprised enough. She sat on the table facing him, a whiskey in hand. "You mean a successful bloke like him will give you the time of day?"

"What can I say? My charm makes up for all the rest of it."

Charlie felt Forester's hand on his shoulder as the proprietor stood. "Well, Charlie, thank you for taking a break from your little honeymoon to humor me. We were all starting to wonder if we'd seen the last of you."

"You can't get rid of me that easy, Forester."

He crossed his arms and gave Charlie an odd look. "That's not exactly what I meant, but either way, if you don't need a more suitable introduction, then I ought to get back to the bar before I'm left with no one behind it." He nodded toward the bar where Warren was chatting with Annabelle's friend, looking a bit goo-eyed himself as the line for drinks grew longer.

Penelope stood and straightened her skirts. "I'll help you reel him in, Davy."

"Oh, don't worry about it," Forester said. "I can handle him."

Forester yelped and then flushed as his flank became the next victim of Penelope's fan. "I will help you whether you like it or not." She turned to Charlie. "Best of luck with your lover, love. Bring him soon; we don't bite half as hard as it seems he does." She kissed Charlie and Jo on their cheeks, leaving matching pink prints, then caught up with Forester, clinging to his arm on their way to the bar.

"You're having a good time with him, then?" Jo asked with genuine curiosity. She put her glass down on the table beside her, skating a single finger around the rim of it as she waited on Charlie's answer.

"I suppose I am," he said. "I know it wasn't exactly your intention when you got me the name, but it seems we've taken a bit of a liking to each other. I suppose I owe you another six months on the tab for that."

She laughed, but seemed a little serious.

"What is it, Joey?"

Jo put her elbows on her knees and tapped her fingers together. "You're still going through with it then?"

"With what?"

"The wedding."

Charlie was taken aback. "What other choice do I have? I'm in debt to my eyeballs, and not just to Forester. If I don't take care of some of these by the time I promised, I may end up without any eyeballs, if you know what I mean."

"Did you *really* get yourself in trouble with that sort of lender, Charlie? *You?*"

He shrugged and tried to get down to the business of liquor at last, before remembering that Penelope had left him with nothing more than ginny ice water. "Probably not? But really, the only reason I don't have them beating down my door every day is because my pop intervened. I've got at least three blokes itching to take me to court, and they'll do it if I've not paid by Christmas. Maybe I'll keep my eyeballs, maybe not, but I certainly won't get to keep anything else, either."

"What do you even have other than a worthless stash of pornography?"

"Oh, I don't know, Jo. Access to food, clothing, and a roof over my head?"

"Forester has been letting you drink and fuck for free without actually expecting payback. Do you really think he'd let you starve?" Jo peeked through the curtain. Forester was at the bar, with Warren nowhere to be seen. Penelope appeared to be trying to help, and though her deftness was questionable, the two of them seemed to be having fun. "Warren doesn't do shit; go pick up his slack. Pray heartily for your health, hold your nose, and sleep in one of the back beds. Get your new lover to buy you dinner a few times a week. Pawn a few things off to make up the difference. You won't be as prettily dressed or as comfortable, but you won't die."

Charlie watched his friends as they made drinks and took payments. If he called off the engagement, he would lose his position working for Mr. Merriweather, but Jo was right about Forester. While the nosy proprietor loved any excuse for a good old-fashioned "molly house wedding," he certainly didn't require them of his employees. All he really wanted was for his friends and patrons to be safe and happy; if Charlie needed a job, Forester would give him one.

Numbers and dates ran rapidly through his head as he tried to work out the financial logistics of it. He could take extra accounts at the bank for the next week or so to pad his coffers while he could. Between that and a barkeep's wage, maybe a bit of a front payment to make up the difference if Forester could afford it…

Even if it could technically work, the thought of it left him queasy. As with owning versus selling his collection, there was a difference between popping into a place like this on the weekends and taking payment as an employee.

Not to mention, money was more than a means of food, shelter, and fancy hatpins. Should anything go horribly wrong, he'd be back to begging his parents for help. This time, he might be begging, not for debt relief, but for bail money.

Perhaps if he'd been matched with a bore, the risk would seem worthier, but he cared deeply for Alma Merriweather, with her awkwardness and her love of little pleasures. This entire arrangement had seemed like a decent outcome.

Until Miles.

What if he meant what he'd said? What if he really would refuse to see Charlie again, once the vows were final? If he could not be reasoned with, then...

"Have I lost you, mate?"

Jo's hand in front of his face snapped him out of it. "Sorry," he said. "Just thinking."

"Well, stop thinking and start calling off your damned wedding."

"Is it really as bad as all that?"

Now Jo looked taken aback. Her mouth opened slightly, the rest of her frozen solid at the question. "What?"

"Being married. Is it that bad? You keep saying so, and Mr. Montague clearly agrees with you, but it's the way of things for most of us, isn't it? I'm willing to bet twice my debts that at least half the fellows here tonight are married, as are half the girls at your place. So be honest, Joey." He looked into her eyes more seriously than he ever had. "Is it really so bad that you think I should trade it to sleep in a backroom bed, pouring drinks and risking jail until I've paid every last penny on my own?"

She went quiet. Charlie thought she'd never answer. When she did, the swagger had gone out of her.

"I didn't think that before," she said. "But if you've really taken Montague as a lover, then you should recognize what you've found for what it is. It will never be the same if you marry Alma. You'll never have what you want with him while you're sneaking about with a wife at home."

"I met him less than a month ago, Jo. How could I possibly want anything in particular from the poor man?"

"You do. I can tell. You don't do this. You don't act this way. It's something different."

"What do you know about it? Maybe you know me and can tell that *I've* lost my damn head. Alright. But it takes two, and you don't know what he wants. You don't know him." He took in her guilty look. "Do you?"

She paused slightly too long. "I did find his name for you."

"But, Jo, do you *know* him?"

"Not personally."

"Yet you've heard enough to have an opinion of our long-term compatibility as lovers."

"Charlie—"

"Has he said something about me?"

"I told you I don't know him personally."

"How did you get his name, Jo?"

Her eyes went cold. "That's between me and my dark goddess."

"I'm not kidding, Joey."

"Neither am I."

He'd caught her at something. They both knew it. She was lying. Something was wrong, and it prickled the hair on the back of Charlie's neck.

"Joey," he said carefully. "I need you to tell me what's going on."

"I can't."

That was the worst answer possible. It struck him right in the heart, because it meant there was something. He suddenly wished he'd insisted on hearing the source of Miles's paranoia. There was blackmail involved, that's all he really knew. And now here was Jo, whoever Jo really was, knowing Miles but not really knowing him at all, trying to goad Charlie into taking an illegal job so he could call off his wedding. He didn't like the various ways this could all match up. Didn't like them at all.

Charlie took her hands, brought them both briefly to his mouth. "Joey. Love. You must realize that this looks bad."

"I know."

"You don't have to tell me your life story." He squeezed her fingers and tried to soften his look to take the edges off what he had to say next. "But you have to tell me *something*, or I'm going to tell Forester to escort you out."

Jo—hard, humorous, devil-may-care Jo—put her forehead down on their clasped hands, letting her hat fall to the floor. When she looked up, her eyes were wet and her mouth was trembling.

"Joey—"

"I'm sorry." She wiped her eyes, sniffing and clearly trying to gain control. "I'm so sorry, Charlie. You're right. I've been a shit."

"You must know I don't want to accuse you. I wouldn't, unless—"

"I know." She closed her eyes. Charlie picked up her hat and handed it back to her. She held it on her lap like a comforting kitten. "God, it's just the most boring story ever told."

Charlie laughed anxiously. "Good! Bore me, Joey, please."

She rolled her teary eyes to the ceiling. "The fucking Beast knows his publisher. That's all it is. A stupid little connection from some... I don't know, some deck of cards with ladies printed on the back? I recognized the stamp when you showed me the book. He used to sell tripe like that before he got into better trade. Obviously *I'm* not offended by some tits on the back of an ace; he learned early that he didn't have to hide things from me. Anyway, I knew you liked the chap's work quite a lot, so I asked The Beast about it and he came back to me with the name. I didn't do anything interesting. I didn't do any particular investigation. I asked my sodding husband for help, and he did it for me, alright?"

Her obvious shame was a very peculiar thing. "Why didn't you just tell me that, Jo?"

"I don't want to be someone's little wife here, Charlie. I don't want you to see me that way."

"Well, that's a bit silly. Who am I to judge?"

"That's fair, but it bothers me. I'd take it to the damn grave if you'd let me get away with it."

The explanation felt true enough to ease some of his worries, but it created new questions. "You and The Beast can discuss things like that? Dirty packs of cards and your sodomite friend's book collection?"

"I've been very lucky." She went on picking at her hat, but a little warmth had entered voice. "Neither of us quite knew what we wanted in life until we'd marched to the gallows for good. Eventually, our natures caught up with us, but by that point, we'd been through so much together that we could just admit it and find a way that worked for us. In the meantime, we both get to look respectable and have an alibi should things go south."

"Your marriage doesn't sound so terrible."

"It's not," she said. "I'm actually quite happy with my arrangement. I only complain to keep up appearances here, same as I would talk about lace or some shit with my sisters."

"You're a right chameleon, aren't you?"

"It suits me."

"If your arrangement is so blissful, why are you trying to talk me out of mine?"

"Because yours won't be like that," she said simply. "Yours is going to turn you into one of the sad fellows you fuck and then complain about all night."

Something about her words made him think back to the note of regret he'd sent Miles. The careful wording. The lack of signature. The panicked removal and replacement of his wax seal.

"Stop it," he snapped. "You know I would never."

"I suppose not." She rolled her eyes. "You'll stay bloody happy, won't you? Come on out no matter what's happening, drink and fuck and drink again, and wind up in prison or dead in the alley before your first baby's born."

A thrill of fear and anger shot up his spine. He knew just what she was referring to, and he didn't appreciate it. "I'm fine, Jo. I learned my lesson that night, alright?"

"No, you didn't," she said. "You just got too busy to—"

Charlie slammed his empty glass on the table as he realized just what was going on. "You lot keep stealing my bloody drinks on purpose, don't you?"

Jo pursed her lips, unrepentant. "We'd all hate to see you get carried away again, is all."

"Jesus Christ." He thought back. To Forester giving him an awful lot of ice and assuming the worst when he didn't come in. To Annabelle sending her friend to check on him, and Noah bursting in when he shut the curtains. "I don't need a swarm of nannies at the bloody club."

"Then stop pretending that everything is *lovely*," she said. "We've all been watching how *that* goes for months. You want honesty from me? I'll give it. I'm worried this marriage is going to literally kill you, particularly now that you're in love. And I'm not the only one worried."

In love. Charlie found that to be an interesting idea, but Jo said it like it was a condition. "Being in love isn't going to *kill me*, Jo."

"You wouldn't be the first, would you?" she said. "It's bad enough to sneak around behind your wife's back for a lark; it's quite another to do it for love. Whether it's Montague or someone else later on down the line, it won't be *lovely*. It will eat all three of you alive: you, your lover, and Alma too. Isn't that what he writes about, this bloke? Isn't that the whole damned point? Did you read his shit a hundred times, or not?"

Charlie sat back, staring morosely over her shoulder through the crack in the curtains. The revelry continued around them, but within their alcove was something Charlie very much did not like. He wanted to escape from it, but he saw no way out. He could ignore everything Jo had just said, laugh off the concerns of all his friends, and go about his business. But what if they were right? What if it caught him eventually? His debt collectors certainly had.

He'd thought himself safe from this sort of lovestruck foolishness, but by God, even through all this, all he wanted was to be back above the bookshop, asking Miles's opinion on it.

Of course, Jo was right about that too. He knew Miles's opinion. His work spoke for itself on that matter.

"I'll think on it, Joey," he said at last, taking up her hand and giving it a friendly squeeze. "In the meantime, please stop running up my tab. Just in case I'm the one working it off after all."

She laughed. "God, Charlie. You're too much."

"What do you mean?"

"I've been paying for my own shit, you idiot." She passed her own drink over to him, apparently mollified enough to let him have a sip of the undiluted liquor. "Do you think I'd actually demand six months of top-shelf whiskey from you when your very eyeballs are at stake?"

Chapter Sixteen

Miles

Between an increase at work and his demanding in-laws, Charlie was suddenly only able to spare Miles the occasional meal or a quick hello on his way to the bank. It was an uneasy change for Miles, considering how soon they'd part for good, but in those brief moments and a couple of very bland notes, he did what Charlie did best:

He made sure Miles knew the bright side.

Working late. Enjoy your writing time!—C

Writing time indeed.

The real bright side was that the bookshop had never looked better. Every time Miles sat down to write, an irresistible surge of energy would move him to activities that he typically had to talk himself into. He couldn't *possibly* get anything written until he'd dusted and swept or he'd spend more time sneezing than writing. Once that was done, the stack of misplaced volumes he'd been putting off finally seemed worth bothering with. After all, what if someone came looking for... *A History of Roman Dress*...or...er...this *Governess's Guide to Discipline*...? And couldn't find it? Well, they'd walk right out the door without buying anything at all, that's what. He couldn't afford that. So back on the shelves they went, dozens of them. The slow, drizzly days found him sweeping out the hearth, fixing the bell (no, replacing the bell! He simply had to go out in the sodding downpour and buy a new one), wiping the light fixtures, touching up the sign outside...

By Thursday night, he had nothing left but the publisher's catalogue and the cash he'd put off counting. He was onto himself by now, but this time, there was nothing for it. He'd put the deposit off long enough that it was going to start affecting his accounts if he didn't handle it now. Writing really would have to wait this time. Nothing he could do about it.

Once everything was locked and the curtains were drawn, he emptied the safe and settled in behind the counter. He wiped his specs, sighed guiltily in the direction of the staircase, and began sorting the medley of notes and coins.

He'd made a real mess of it. Some nights he'd counted and left himself inscrutable memos about the outcome; others he'd just shoved it all into the safe in an irreverent pile. It was a nightmare. He had no employees and no reason to believe it wouldn't all balance in the end. Even if there was a discrepancy, he was already using his royalties to make up the difference, so it hardly mattered. He could just let the bank sort it all out. But he kept at it. It was the right thing to do.

There was a rap at the window that startled his tired eyes right up to the clock. Only one person would be here knocking at this hour. He leaped up. There was a never-touched rare book cabinet against the back wall, where he stopped to smooth his hair and fix his collar. After a second thought, he unfixed the collar, mussing back up, and put his specs in his pocket.

A quick peek out the curtains to make certain he knew who he was greeting, then he opened the door to a gust of wind that brought Charlie in with it for the first time in days.

"Evening," said Charlie with his perfect, pleasant smile.

He could hardly wait until the door had shut and the curtains had settled to gather him in, shove him against a shelf, and kiss him until neither of them could breathe.

He was a bit dizzy when at last they broke apart. After a few gasping moments, Charlie smoothed out Miles's rumpled collar, warming right through the chill that had sneaked in on his heels. "Missed me, have you?"

Miles was too giddy to be clever. He put his head against Charlie's, breathing in the scent of cigars and sin that clung to his coat. "Yes."

Charlie did not return the sentiment explicitly, but he implied it with a turn of his lips. "I apologize for coming uninvited, but I was passing by."

"Passing by? Really?"

"Yeah, I decided to have tea at that little spot down the street so that I could be sure to pass by."

"That's what I thought."

"Can I come in?" Charlie looked at him with a particular expression he usually gave from a bit closer to the ground. "I won't disrupt your writing. I'll sit quietly in the corner. I'll keep my hands to myself and won't say a word, I promise."

He decided to go along with Charlie's assumption that he'd actually gotten any writing done. "I somehow doubt that, Charlie."

"If you don't trust me, I'm sure there's things you could do to ensure my compliance. If you wanted." Hands still wrapped in kidskin gloves, he crossed his wrists and offered them to Miles.

That had nowhere to go but straight down to Miles's cock. Why, *yes*, Charlie. Now that you mention it, there most certainly *are* things that could be done, aren't there? Things that *will* be done. As soon as possible.

He took Charlie by the hand and started to lead him upstairs, when the sight of his half-counted notes deflated him.

"What is it?" Charlie followed Miles's gaze. "Dear God, what is that mess?"

"I was, er." Miles crossed his arms tight. "Just counting the drawer."

Charlie wandered over to the pile of embarrassment on the counter. He peered at it briefly before turning back to Miles with a sly little grin. "This is far more than one day's worth, isn't it?"

Miles cleared his throat. "Perhaps."

"Love, you should be counting your drawer every night. That's terrible practice."

"Oh, and I should take financial advice from *you*?"

Unfortunately, Charlie did not look offended. "I'm a do-as-I-say-not-as-I-do sort when it comes to finances. And I say, this is an impressive little disaster. What are these scribbles?" He picked up one of Miles's paper scraps. "I didn't realize your penmanship was so dreadful. How am I ever going to nick your draft pages and read them before they hit print?"

"Can't say I've ever worried about that."

Charlie ignored him, examining each little piece of paper. "You counted some nights, it looks like. But not others. There was one deposit in the middle of these dates, but the rest is… Miles, what on earth have you done?" He started laughing, but must have seen a horrified look on Miles's face, because he beckoned gently. "Come on, love. I'll help you sort all this out."

"Oh, it can wait," Miles said, the sentiment coming out much weaker than he'd have liked. It *couldn't* wait, actually, because he had so conveniently put it off until the last possible moment.

Whether Charlie sensed that or not didn't matter, because

he wasn't having it either way. "Absolutely not. You're going to wind up in real trouble if you keep this up." Without further ado, Charlie shucked off his dripping overcoat and hat, rolled up his sleeves, and got to it. He set aside all the little scraps and began to rearrange the piles of money on the counter. "Where's your ledger?"

Miles stared at him before deciding he would never get away with hiding it. "Right over there, under the counter."

Charlie did not seem surprised by the state of the ledger after seeing the state of the "drawer." His dark eyes darted over it with a fascinating concentration. Nodding with some sort of decision, he put the ledger down. He ripped out the pages Miles had done and started fresh, copying the information down in his tidy, blocky script.

"I'm going to try to make sense of what you have here. Then you open a bit late tomorrow so you can deposit it first thing in the morning. When you get back, you can start fresh with proper records." He nudged Miles teasingly. "Or *passable* records. Or at least, you know, *some sort* of records."

"Oh, would you stop it."

There wasn't any room for legitimate protest. Charlie was already at it. He took over the stool behind the counter, counting and arranging bank notes in a posture that resembled a card player more than an accountant. Miles hovered nearby as if he might help, but he was at a loss. Charlie seemed to be doing at least three things at once—counting, reading, and recording—and the pattern of it was inscrutable. While Miles hated having to sit by and watch someone else do his work for him, Charlie seemed rather content. He probably brightened his bank up quite a bit, but no longer seemed like he'd be entirely out of place.

There was an odd familiarity to it. Sitting by while Charlie handled the practicalities triggered old habits he'd been certain were dead and gone. Suddenly, his fingers itched for his own pen. He recalled where he'd left the poor bastards he was writing about, and knew what ought to happen next.

As if reading his mind, Charlie said, "Don't worry about this. You obviously aren't interested in the details, so I'll just whip it into shape and explain to you what to do next." He never looked up, talking even as he counted, as if words and numbers occupied entirely different parts of his mind. "You can do whatever you want. I warn you, though: if you sneak under the counter and start committing unmentionable acts upon me, I may not do as good a job on your books."

"It's tempting, but I'm not sure my books can handle the strain."

"Sadly, I'm inclined to agree. We'll just have to wait." He flashed a grin. "Now quit distracting me."

Very tentatively, Miles took some paper and a second pen out of the drawer. It was strange enough that he'd taken to discussing his work with anyone but Smithy, but to actually put words down while sitting at the same surface as another human being filled his stomach with nerves. He turned his paper a bit so Charlie wouldn't be able to see it. The ideas he jotted came slowly at first, but soon smoothed out as he relaxed into the circumstances.

By all accounts, Charlie should have been an immense distraction. He talked here and there while he worked and kept pretending to glance at Miles's paper to get a reaction out of him. But his ease and apparent happiness amid the swirl of numbers and notes was strangely catching. It had been a very long time since Miles had sat with someone, each at his own task. He slipped into it without trouble, and next thing he knew, he'd gotten the idea down along with a few dialogue snippets and a new way to describe the look of perfect lips on the rim of a glass.

His own task complete, he stopped to watch Charlie's hands and face as he concentrated on fixing the mess. Miles might have been able to get more done, but he decided against it. The important idea was recorded, and this was a moment worth committing to detailed memory.

After all, with the wedding approaching so rapidly, there was a very good chance he'd never see Charlie quite like this again.

It wasn't long before Charlie had the totals written and the money neatly bundled. Finished at last, he moved his stool much closer than necessary, so close their shoulders were touching. How that simple thing could be so marvelous even after their weeks of hedonism was a mystery.

"So, can I show you what you're to do with this?" Charlie brandished the pen he'd borrowed and tapped the ledger dramatically until Miles took the hint and moved his own seat even closer, peering over Charlie's shoulder without quite resisting the urge to nuzzle the curve of his neck.

"Show me," he whispered against smooth-shaven skin.

Charlie tipped his head to the side to allow for Miles's kisses, but went on in a mostly steady voice. "Once you make this deposit, you fill in what you start with for the day and put your transactions here, yeah?" He tapped the page aggressively. "Always here. Do not put them on scrap paper ever again. And when the day is done, you just make sure the total matches your drawer. If you are unable to get it counted—if inspiration, laziness, or some overeager fanatic forces you upstairs early—don't start some inscrutable new tally, for the love of God. Just make a note of the date and keep the total running. It's not ideal, but it will keep you from having all these piles and scattered records to keep track of."

Miles felt no different about the blasted task of accounting, but he was very appreciative, and seeing this side of Charlie had lit a mad glow in his chest. He ran his hand up Charlie's back until he got to the hairline. His pine-scented pomade was failing so late in the day, and the edge had gone soft and feathery.

"Can't I just make you do it?" he growled in Charlie's ear. "Lock you up in the back to handle all this drudgery for me? If you're bad, you'll get the birch, and if you're very good, I'll consider feeding you. How long could you live on nothing but my cock, do you think?"

Charlie shivered happily. "God, how do you come up with this stuff?"

"I'm an endless well of evil." He gripped the back of Charlie's neck harder and leaned in even closer. "Shall we give your new position a test run? If it goes well, I'll reward you by never letting you out. After all, I can't imagine anyone will miss a useless fop like you."

Charlie straightened up just enough that Miles knew he'd gone too far.

"What is it?" asked Miles.

"Nothing."

But he could tell now when Charlie's smiles didn't meet his eyes, so he saw through the one that flashed over his face. "You promised you'd tell me if you weren't having a good time. I can't subject you to all this evil if you can't keep that promise."

"You're too kind, Miles." He raised an eyebrow. "Really. I wish you were as mean as you pretend to be."

"Oh, well, I'm *so* sorry that I don't *actually* consider you a worthless plaything."

"You should be." He took a deep breath and grabbed the pen up again. He doodled a series of parallel lines across a scrap of paper. "It's nothing new or important. The, um, the wedding is just weighing on me. It's really coming up, you know.

Any little word is making me think of it. Dreadfully inconvenient, considering it's the very last thing I want to think of."

It was the last thing Miles wanted to think of as well. "I see. So, you're not upset I called you a useless fop?"

"No, that's just accurate."

"You're upset that someone *would* miss you if I made you into my sums slave?"

"It's most upsetting, isn't it?" More lines on the paper, very tidy. "In fact, I hate to be a bore, but there is something I wanted to run by you."

"Oh?"

"I'm considering calling it all off." Charlie's voice was very light, almost airy, but the heaviness beneath was obvious. "I had a discussion with a friend of mine. She thinks I should call in some favors and work the debt off myself."

Miles had not expected that. He hardly dared believe it, though he very much wanted to. "Can you do that?"

"I think so. I've managed to get a bit of a head start on it by taking an extra account this week. I'd have to work out the details going forward, of course; the favors I'd be calling are big ones. It would also be a miserable undertaking, to be quite honest. But possibly less miserable than the alternative, at least in the long run."

Miles took that in so slowly that he could tell Charlie was about to start talking again. He held up a hand to hold that off until he'd formed his uneasiness into words. "These miserable, big favors: they aren't the sort to make matters worse, are they?"

Charlie laughed. "No, nothing like that. I've been a regular at my club for so long that I'd have no problem asking for a position making drinks. Bat your eyelashes a little and the tips can be quite good, so it will add up. That's a small favor. The bigger ones would be asking the proprietor to front me some pay ahead of time, and for permission to sleep there so I can avoid racking up other bills."

"Sleep there? Where, behind the bar?"

"That might be better than what I had in mind." He stopped doodling to give Miles a curious look. "Have you really never been to one?"

"Of course I haven't."

"Well, Mr. Forester—the proprietor—keeps things comfortable. There's sofas and chaises, as well as a slew of marriage beds in the back."

"Marriage…what, now?"

"Beds for rent. In smaller rooms. They're for fucking, Miles," he added to clear up Miles's obvious confusion. "I suppose if I'm working there, I'll be helping with linens. I can be sure to squirrel myself away a clean set to collapse onto when the night is over."

Miles blinked at him. "You're joking."

"Not a bit."

"Sure you wouldn't rather I chain you up in my storeroom?"

"I wouldn't want to impose."

Miles didn't like this idea at all. "Don't those places get raided by the police?"

"Occasionally," Charlie said, tone terribly light considering the subject. "I've only been present for one raid myself. It was a right good scare, but most of us got away. The few that didn't only got a week or two for disorderly or had it dismissed. Closed the doors for a month, and then we got back at it. The Fox is rather uninteresting compared to some of the other spots in Soho. Mr. Forester only peddles spirits and space—not flesh like some of them—which attracts a, shall we say, less newsworthy clientele. Unless it's a weekend, we're all just playing cards and gossiping about each other, and even when it's busy, we're a handful of middle-class mollies tucked into a nexus of alleys with a lot of places to scatter. There's better ways to put the raiding budget to use, I expect."

The words swirled around in Miles's head in a flurry. The last five years of Miles's and Charlie's lives had certainly looked quite different, hadn't they? Miles got nervous simply walking down Holywell Street to get his money. Yet here was Charlie, spending his evenings in an illegal death trap of a place that he reckoned was safe simply because it didn't provide its own prostitutes.

What on earth was Miles doing with this beautiful lunatic, and when were they going to start fucking, because realizing the extent of Charlie's insanity had whipped his vivid imagination up into a pure frenzy.

"Miles?"

Miles snapped back to the present, reminding himself that he should be concerned about Charlie's risks, not inflamed by them. "If you're living there, won't you be more likely to be present for the next raid?"

"That is a concern of mine, but I'll be honest with you, love. The real reason my friends worry about me is because they know misery comes with its own risks." Charlie looked sharply at him. "If you're about to stare at me and think about what I've said until you come up with some other vague question, don't. I can't take the suspense, right now. I just want your opinion: do you think I should call the wedding off? Yes or no."

"What about Alma?"

"That's another question."

"An important one. You said you care about her."

"I do." He suddenly looked more determined than ever before. "Which is yet another reason to call it off. I've been thinking about it all week. I've been very selfish in regard to her. She deserves better than she'll ever get from me. It will hurt in the moment, but she will be much better off."

"In that case…" Miles felt a bit naughty. Did he really get to say this? "You ought to call it off."

Charlie's eyes widened happily. "You really think so?"

"Yes!" He grabbed Charlie's face and kissed him before catching himself in his unseemly level of excitement. He cleared his throat and tried to bring it down a bit. "Not that it's anything to do with me. But for your sake—"

"Of course it's to do with you."

Miles froze. "I–is it?"

Charlie looked very bashful. It was charming, the way he went red so easily. But he did manage to keep eye contact. "Yes, Miles. It's everything to do with you."

Panic and joy warred in equal measure. He didn't like the thought that Charlie would make such a decision because of him. He especially hated it because he wanted so badly for it to be true. If Charlie kept his bachelorhood, there was no reason they couldn't carry on indefinitely. Forever, if they felt like it. He knew he was getting ahead of himself, but before he could even think to resist it, he pulled them both to their feet and gathered Charlie in tight.

When he could speak, the words that came out surprised them both:

"Stay with me."

Charlie pulled back enough to look at him, confused. "What do you mean?"

"I would offer you safer work here if I could," he said in a rush. "I wish I could, though as you've probably seen…"

"Yes." Charlie glanced sideways at the ledger. "I had wondered if this was a typical month for you."

"If anything, it was a good month. I can't afford an employee, and I certainly don't have any money to give up front, so you'll have to see about the barkeep situation. But don't sleep there, Charlie. I can't stand the thought of it, for about a dozen separate reasons. If you need somewhere to stay, you stay with me."

For once, Charlie was speechless. He stammered incoherently until they both laughed.

"Miles, I don't know what to say."

"Say yes."

"I'll be coming in very late most nights."

"We'll work it out."

"I'll have to bring my things with me. Once my father knows I've called it off, I'll have nowhere in the world to—"

"I'll make room."

Charlie paused. "You really want me?"

"Yes, Charlie. Yes, I do."

"You just want to chain me up in your storeroom, don't you?"

"No. You're a good boy." Miles kissed his forehead. "I'll chain you to my bed."

Until Charlie got things in order, he obviously still had a home to go back to, but neither of them wanted that. After a bit of discussion, they determined that it would be utterly irresponsible not to do a test run of their new arrangement. They ran upstairs like kids on Christmas, and once the door was bolted behind them, they were on each other with fearsome intensity.

Miles couldn't quite believe this was actually happening, right now, in his real life. It was so stupid, so insane, so certainly disastrous, that it was almost dreamlike. He raked his hands all over Charlie, suddenly wildly possessive.

"You going to chain me to that bed, or what?" Charlie challenged in a husky whisper.

Miles looked over at the door to the bedroom. It was closed, as it always was. He and Charlie had never made it that far.

He hesitated. It wasn't just Charlie who hadn't made it that far. He hadn't shared his own bed with anyone since...well, if one wanted to be technical, it had been Ethan's bed first.

A very unwelcome tally started up in his mind. The chairs and the table. Some of the cups. The fireplace tools. Growing up, his mother had put every extra penny toward her son's rather unlikely education, so Miles had never owned much himself aside from his books and his clothing. He might have spent his whole adult life as a boardinghouse bachelor with no furniture at all if Ethan had not offered him a place in that double-wide bed he was threatening to tie Charlie to.

He'd extended this invitation knowing full well that he was bringing his new lover into his deceased lover's home. He did not feel guilty—it was nothing to be guilty over—but he did feel something. He wasn't sure what it was, but it was a very mixed-up and unmoored sort of something.

He didn't realize how hard he'd been gripping Charlie's arms until he felt a gentle hand on one of his own. He tried to relax into the touch, forcing a deep breath into his tight chest.

Charlie took Miles's hand and planted a kiss right in the middle of his palm. "Don't worry," he whispered with one of those lovely smiles of his, "I will treat whatever ghosts you have in here with the utmost respect."

Miles had never fully explained his situation, but Charlie was a smart chap who had certainly puzzled out parts of it by now. He knew there was no escaping the awkwardness of this, and did not try to. Miles squeezed his hand gratefully.

When at last he managed to set his confused feelings aside for later, he leaned in and whispered, "I want you to go in there. Take off all your clothes and sit on the bed. You're forbidden to touch anything but your cock. I'll be right back."

"Where are you going?"

"I don't keep certain things by the bedside anymore," he admitted. "There's only so much pain I'm willing to subject you to, so I'm going to see what I've got to work with."

Charlie's eyes went so wide with shock you'd think he'd never heard anything so scandalous in his whole lecherous life. "Oh."

"Oh, what? Is something the matter?"

"No! No, everything's lovely. I'll just, er, I'll do as you say, then."

Miles watched him go to into the bedroom, a bit perplexed. He decided to complete his errand before pursuing the matter. Alone as he was, he didn't have any supplies dedicated to getting Charlie properly fucked, which had suddenly become a pressing problem. Cold cream seemed so crass, and he wasn't even sure he had enough to get the job done. He went into the kitchen and glared at his cupboards until he found a bit of nice olive oil from Spain. He poured some into a teacup and brought a few towels along.

In his bedroom, Charlie was right where he belonged: completely naked and perched tentatively on the edge of the bed. His clothes were neatly folded on the dresser, and he was smoothing wrinkles on the quilt beside him. When he saw Miles, he guiltily brought his hand to his soft cock, as if he'd just remembered his instructions.

Once they got a good look at each other—Charlie so awkward and Miles with his little teacup—they both laughed.

"You forgot the biscuits," said Charlie.

"Me? You look like you're sitting in the headmaster's office."

"Christ, what kind of school did you go to?"

Miles put the teacup and such down on the bedside table. Charlie looked so terribly cold and uncomfortable that Miles took pity on him and placed a blanket over his shoulders. "Charlie, are you scared?"

"Me? Of course not."

Well, that was a lie if he'd ever heard one. "I suppose I never thought to ask. Do you like this sort of thing? Or maybe you'd prefer to, er…"

"Pour the tea myself?" Charlie laughed nervously. "Don't worry, it's none of that. I told you, I like things any which way."

"I don't believe you right now."

Charlie ran his fingers along the ratty edge of the blanket, combing out the frayed threads until they were tidy as the fringe on a fancy rug. "You're going to think this is awfully silly."

"Life is silly," said Miles. "What is it?"

Charlie pulled the quilt around himself tighter. "It's just that it's usually so much of a bother, you know. I keep things casual. Very casual. I have only made the effort a few times, and when I have…" He ran a finger down the buttons of Miles's trousers, one by one. "It's been with rather more *modest* apparatuses."

Miles couldn't help it; he was delighted. "You're nervous about the size of my cock?"

"One might say I'm easily intimidated in that respect." He glared at Miles. "You look awfully happy about that."

"I hate to break it to you like this, Charlie, but I'm a bit sadistic."

"Oh, dear, that *is* a nasty shock."

Now that he knew Charlie was only suffering from a bit of nerves, Miles toppled him over and pinned him to the bed. "I won't hurt you." He held Charlie's wrists over his head. "Not more than usual, anyway. Now, keep these here; don't make me waste my time tying you up, or you'll regret it."

Charlie's body was still tense beneath Miles, but his eyes had darkened with desire and his prick was perking up. He'd be alright. More than alright. He'd be *fantastic* by the time Miles had his way.

"I admit." Miles shucked off his jacket and waistcoat and threw them to the ground. "I'm looking forward to showing you how all this is properly done."

"I didn't say I'd not properly done it," Charlie protested, but only until Miles shoved a pillow under his hips and took Charlie in his mouth. "Christ."

He certainly had Charlie's full attention, now. God, he loved doing this, sucking and swirling until his beautiful fop, shed of all his finery, started squirming under his touch. Miles raised his head to say, "If you'd properly done it, you'd have done it more often."

Then he went back to his business.

Charlie gasped and brought a hand down to twist in Miles's hair. "Oh and—*oh my God*—and you're an expert are you?"

Miles wasn't sure he'd go *that* far, but he likely knew his way around better than some blighter rushing things along in the back of a molly bar. He pulled Charlie's hand from his hair, sat up, and straddled him. He grabbed him by the jaw and turned his head so their eyes locked. "Charlie."

"Yes?"

"What did I say about your hands?"

"I don't remember."

Miles pushed his free thumb into a tender spot on Charlie's shoulder he'd found last week.

"Ow! God, fine." He put his hands back above his head.

He was struck by how lovely Charlie looked lying on his bed, dazed with pleasure and anticipation. He was too perfect. It was painful. Miles stroked himself a few times, hoping he'd be patient enough to make Charlie truly comfortable before burrowing into him at last.

And after all was said and done, that pleasant smile Charlie always gave him would happen here, on his own pillow. It would be the last thing Miles saw before he fell asleep.

Something washed over him as he realized that. Something unpleasant, something he'd put off, but something he could not ignore anymore. It would not be set aside for later; he had to look it in the face, like it or not.

He had not needed to be so alone all these years. Ethan had not asked that of him. No one had. He'd done it to himself. Day by day, year by year, he'd let himself become terribly—*criminally*—lonely. Grief had turned so slowly and so smoothly into complete isolation that he hadn't realized just how bad it had gotten, not until the gleam of Charlie's eyes woke him up like beams of sunshine through the curtains.

"Alright?" Charlie asked.

"I love you, Charlie," he whispered suddenly.

Charlie stared up at him, silent, for what felt like an age.

Then he smiled—that bright, cocky, intoxicating smile of his—and he said, "Yeah? Well, I'm glad you've caught up with me. I've been desperately in love with you since I watched you eat that stupid pineapple cake."

"Why the pineapple?"

"No idea. Bit confusing, but here we are." He reached down to lovingly grab Miles's arse. "And now that we're here, love—where were we?"

Miles leaned in very close. "I believe I was about to tell you to shut your filthy mouth and let me fuck you already."

"That was it," said Charlie. "How romantic. Do you think—?"

Miles grabbed one of the tea towels and stuffed it in Charlie's mouth. He got a good little glare for that, very cross and amused. Then he deliberately put Charlie's disobedient hands back over his head. He considered tying them at last, but as he looked down at his lover's perfect face, he knew he couldn't spare the time. He wanted to be inside of Charlie so badly it shook him straight down to his soul.

Pinning his wrists with one hand, he dipped two fingers into the teacup. Charlie tensed. Though it took just about every bit of self-control he had, Miles first took the gag out and slipped his slick fingers into Charlie's mouth. The way he sucked the oil off sent shudders through Miles's whole body.

"What is that?" Charlie whispered when his mouth was free.

"Spanish olive oil."

"Tastes good. Bit spicy." He licked the side of Miles's finger like he was seeking out the last drop.

Miles couldn't bear it. He ground slowly against Charlie as he reached over to slick himself back up. Heart thudding so hard it might burst, he pushed Charlie's legs apart with his knees and slid his hand into the irresistible heat at the center of him.

As soon as Miles found his entrance, Charlie flinched and he cried out in a sort of wanton protest. Miles shushed him gently, taking his time to stroke and explore before trying to take things any further. Charlie was shockingly tense. When Miles finally tried to get a finger inside, he was met with muscles so tight he feared he could not keep his promise to avoid pain.

Miles put his lips against Charlie's ear. "We don't have to do this if it's not—"

"No!" Charlie grabbed Miles's wrist and held it right where it was. His prick was like granite and leaking so much that the dark hair on his stomach was slick with it. Yet, his eyes were squeezed closed with something suspiciously like embarrassment. "Please. Miles. I love you. I want to. It just takes some time for me. It's not about the size, not really. It's me. It's…"

"Hard for you to relax with someone?" whispered Miles.

Charlie nodded frantically. "But I can with you. I know I can. You just have to be patient with me. Is that okay? Do you mind?"

The quiet pleas were so utterly different from his usual bratty quips and naughty jokes that for a moment, Miles wanted to gather him up and just hold him until this intense spell of vulnerability passed. It did not seem fair for Miles to demand this sort of fragility from him, not when he knew how carefully Charlie applied layers of everything from humor to hatpins to protect himself.

He opened his pretty eyes, almost perfectly black aside from the reflection of the single candle. He touched Miles's face. "Please."

Miles took steady breaths until he was certain he could speak without either crying or coming. "Of course, love. Let's take all the time you need." He pressed a gentle kiss to Charlie's forehead. "We can spare it now, after all."

Chapter Seventeen

Charlie

Charlie woke up covered in homey little quilts and knit blankets. The surrounding air was much colder than he was used to, his breath misting above him, but it was warm in bed. He blinked up, a bit bleary. Miles was sitting up against the pillows. He'd put on a woolen dressing gown and had a book in his hands. A second teacup, presumably filled with tea, had joined last night's on the bedside table.

Well, *this* was something. He thought back on Miss Penelope's mockery of him: *imagine having to look at one of these fools in the light of day.* He couldn't remember whether he'd actually said that, but he certainly hadn't done it. Not once.

It wasn't so bad.

Miles seemed to notice the change in Charlie's consciousness. He glanced down only for a moment, then placed a heavy hand on Charlie's head, stroking the spot just above his ear with a lazy thumb. The room was very quiet, but the clangs and clamors of a London morning came through the drafty window right along with the daylight and the chill.

"Are you really still reading?" Charlie asked. "Or are you pretending?"

"I'm trying."

"Am I distracting you?"

"The answer to that is nearly always yes." He put the book down and came under the covers so they were looking at each other across the pillow. He didn't look like a fool in the light of day at all. His always unruly hair was even wilder, and his dark blue eyes seemed somehow fresh when he slipped his specs off. "Good morning."

"Good morning." Charlie knew the sappy smile on his face probably looked ridiculous, but there was no taming it. "Have you been up a while?"

"I thought I'd let you sleep," said Miles. "You looked like you needed it."

"That's your fault, you know. You exhausted me."

Charlie had gone into last night's lovemaking fully prepared to grit his teeth and take it for the sake of Miles's pleasure, but it hadn't been like that at all. He apparently *hadn't* ever done it properly. It took an awful lot of patience, but Miles didn't seem to mind in the slightest. In fact, by the time Miles finally clambered on top, it was clear that he very much liked the process of using his hands and his mouth to get his lover good and ready. He'd been trembling, his sweet reassurances giving way to half-coherent growls about how hard he was, how badly he needed it, how much he adored Charlie and *please, please can we try now, I'll be careful, I swear I will.* Miles, always the one to control their encounters, had seemed almost helpless. Though Charlie had been flat on his back with a rather big fellow begging to push a rather big cock into him, the look of absolute ecstasy on Miles's face when he said yes had made him feel strangely powerful.

"Are you feeling alright?" Miles asked. He reached across the pillow and brushed some hair out of Charlie's eyes. "Anything hurt?"

"No, actually. I feel marvelous."

"Told you I'd do it right." He looked smug. "Are you hungry?"

"My stomach thinks my throat's been cut."

Miles kissed him. "I'll put the kettle back on."

Imagine. Not just looking at your beloved fool in the daylight, but cooking breakfast with him over a crackling fire. Imagine him putting slightly too much sugar in your tea, but drinking it anyway. Imagine taking turns in the washroom and smoothing that bit of graying hair that won't stay flat on his head while he teases you for taking too long on your own. Imagine—just imagine—following him down creaky stairs to his shop to see what his mornings look like, and offering to run the deposit to the bank for him, dragging your sleepy arse into the cold and wind, just so he doesn't have to open late after all.

It was far beyond Charlie's trite little imagination. When he returned to find that Miles was writing behind the counter while waiting for customers, he found himself horribly torn between his desire to never leave, and his new desperation to go talk Forester into giving him work as soon as possible. He'd clean glasses and backroom floors until his fingers bled. He'd feign interest in the most horrid of patrons to squeeze every shilling he could from them. He'd handle all the things that Warren had neglected, and he'd do the books while he was at it. If it meant he could come back here when he was finished and warm up Miles's chilly little flat until morning, he'd do *anything*.

No one had come in the shop yet. It was still just the two of them. The curtains were open, though, and the door unlocked, so he stayed on the other side of the counter, not certain he could keep his hands to himself if he got too close.

"Do you have to be at the bank today?" Miles asked.

Charlie thought about it. "They wouldn't miss me, but I

suppose I should show up for a few hours. I need the money, after all."

"Don't let me keep you. I think I can handle this rush all on my own."

Charlie laughed a bit, but he couldn't sustain it. "Miles?"

He glanced up from his writing, peering over the tops of his frames. "Yes?"

"If your shop isn't making any money, why aren't you selling it?"

Miles tapped his pen on his paper in an anxious rhythm, looking anywhere but at Charlie.

"I thought I understood the situation," Charlie went on. "But that was before you admitted that it's losing money. It's one thing to hold on to a business that's barely hanging on, if you love it enough. But if it's *not* hanging on at all, how can you justify it to yourself? *I'm* fool enough to do something like that and assume it will shake out; you're far too smart for it."

The pen went on tapping. Miles's mouth had grown tight. He looked like he'd never speak again.

"Obviously, you don't have to tell me," said Charlie.

"Of course, I don't," Miles muttered. *Tap, tap, tap.* "But I suppose I ought to, oughtn't I? If you're going to be stuck with me?"

Miles stood up. He put his papers facedown behind the counter with the pen on top like a toppled sentry. He went into the little hallway that led to the back and beckoned Charlie over. There were a few framed articles and photographs. Charlie had never noticed them before, too eager to have a door closed behind them to pay attention to the path.

Miles leaned back on the wall right across from a photograph of the front of the shop. Though the photograph was low quality, the Morgan & Murray's sign was obviously new. There was a young man with close-cropped, light hair standing in front of the doors. He wore almost absurdly bookish clothes and looked proud as anything as he squinted in the poor light.

"Ethan Murray." Miles's voice was so low as to hardly be audible. "I hadn't met him yet, when this was taken. I started coming in here a few years later, when I took lodgings on this side of town. My writing wasn't going as well back then; I was trying to be like Dickens or someone, you know. It was profoundly ridiculous. Ethan noticed me coming in all the time, and we'd talk about books. Argue about them, sometimes. He thought I was *very* snobbish." Miles paused, smiling at some memory. "When he learned I was struggling to get published, he offered me a job at the counter. And, well, I suppose it went from there."

Charlie stared at the blurry image of the man. "He looks like a lovely chap."

"He was."

"What happened to him?"

Miles tipped his head back against the wall, eyes drifting over the ceiling. "I'm sure you can guess. A couple very nice years went by, us living together upstairs, him working down here, me writing while I pretended to work. But eventually his family heard that he'd moved a man into his flat. When he wouldn't turn me out, they got very angry. I wasn't the first suspicious character in his life, you see, but they were determined I'd be the last. He didn't tell me about the trouble until it was too late to do anything about it. If he'd told me... He was like that, though. Thought if he ignored people aggressively enough, they'd give up and vanish. It had worked for him before, but not this time. His cousin got in touch with a former lover. That's when the blackmail started."

Charlie was starting to wish he hadn't asked, could not

imagine this story ended in a way he wanted to hear. For once, he was quiet so long that Miles went on talking.

"By the time I understood what was happening, Ethan had paid off his cousin three times. He said it would be fine. That once the money was truly gone, the bastard would get bored, and go away. He did not. I told Ethan we had to sell the shop, run off to France, start over. I begged him. But the shop was like his own child, and he'd not hear a word about leaving it. Literally. He'd pretend he couldn't hear me when I said it, the stubborn arse.

"I was scared, so I rented a room down the street to stay out of the way. A few days later, they arrested him. They tried to get him on buggery and put him away forever, but that horrible, sniveling thing he'd made the mistake of trusting didn't provide quite enough evidence."

"What sort of evidence was even available?" Charlie looked at Miles. "Did they drag you into it?"

"No. His cousin bought a stack of incriminating letters off the lover, things they were both supposed to burn after reading." Miles sighed. "Ethan had destroyed the bloke's responses years ago. Didn't occur to him that his trust would come back to haunt him. The judge seemed to think the whole thing was a bit stupid, reduced the sodomy charge to assault with intent and sentenced him to just one year out of a possible ten. Seemed like a blessing at the time. I agreed to run the shop until he came back."

It was awful enough. Charlie wished it ended there, but obviously there was more, because it did not appear that Ethan Murray ever made it back.

Miles glanced sideways at him. "You look a bit ill."

"More than a bit."

"There's not much left. Scarlet fever got into the prison halfway through his sentence. He didn't make it. His solicitor had kept a copy of his will so no one could steal it, so that's who I heard it from, along with the news that he'd left me everything, including the shop. I thought that might get his family after me, but they didn't give a damn. They'd gotten what they wanted, I suppose. Didn't even bury him themselves; it fell to the jail. I didn't get to see him off. He just left one day, we exchanged some letters, and then a few months later, he was gone." He looked over at Charlie. "Are you really so surprised?"

"I shouldn't be."

Miles pulled him in and kissed the side of his head. "I hate this shop, you know. I always have."

Charlie was startled out of his sadness. "*What?*"

"He knew it too. I'm entirely unsuited to shopkeeping. I don't like thinking about what sells, I don't like ordering and organizing, and I don't like people. He only let me work here because I liked books, and he liked me; I was never any good at any of it. I only keep it going because he loved it so much."

Charlie stared at the happy man in the picture. "He died for it, yeah? In a way."

Miles caught Charlie's eye, looking surprised. He squeezed Charlie's hand tight. "That's right. That's just how I see it. We could have escaped, you know? It didn't have to be like this, it didn't. But it is like this, and... God, I just can't bear to shut it down or hand it off to a stranger. It's been five years. Longer than I knew him for. Long enough to become ridiculous. I can't seem to help it, though."

"Why did he leave it to you? If he knew you didn't like it?"

Miles shrugged. "What else was he going to do?"

"Where was Mr. Morgan through all this?"

"Mr...." Miles threw his head back in laughter. "Lady Morgana was the name of his cat. She stuck around to keep me company for the first few years."

Of all the awful things Charlie had just heard, this might have been the worst of it. "His cat?" he echoed. "Do you mean to say, it was really just you and him? In the whole world, just the two of you and a bloody cat?"

"Think about it. His family preferred him dead; mine *is* all dead or estranged. We couldn't have close friends, because how do you know who to trust? So yeah. For all intents and purposes, I was the only person he had for the last three years of his life. And when he died, I suppose I had no one."

Charlie couldn't stand it. He thought of his friends, of Jo and Forester, Noah and Warren. His own family was a real bother, but they certainly wouldn't refuse to *bury* him, for God's sake, no matter what he'd done. Even sweet Alma had been a good friend to him through their engagement, and her father—miserable creature that he was—had still given him work when he'd needed it.

It was not so hard to imagine blackmail and jail and death; there was a reason he was guarded with most everyone he met. It was, however, extremely painful to consider facing those things in a state of near-isolation.

Charlie took Miles by the tie and turned both their attention away from the photograph. "Thank you for telling me," he said. "I sort of wish you hadn't, but I suppose it was inevitable."

"I didn't want you living with ghosts you hadn't been introduced to, to use your metaphor."

"*You're* using *my* metaphors?"

"Don't get used to it."

"Miles." He broke off as he tried to collect the words he wanted to say. "I need to go to the bank for a few hours. Just long enough to say I did. When we're both done for the day, I want to take you somewhere."

Miles looked at him sideways, like he knew just where this was going. "Do you?"

"I have to talk to Forester about working the bar for a bit. I want you to come along."

"To your molly house?"

"To meet my friends, Miles."

He looked uncomfortably at the floor. "Charlie, I'm a dreadful bore. I hate crowds. You don't really want to bring me out to meet anyone."

"We'll be there early. You can leave before it gets busy."

"I don't know."

"You do know." Charlie leaned up to plant a kiss on his forehead, just above the bridge of his specs. "You know perfectly well that you don't want to go under any circumstances. I know that too. But you trusted me in your home. You trusted me with your past. You even trusted me with your deposit, and I can't say that's the sort of compliment I get every day. You need to trust me on this."

Miles gave a scolding look, but Charlie could tell he was winning him over. He grinned for good measure, a cheery smile that worked on everyone, Miles especially.

"I don't want to embarrass you in front of your friends," Miles said.

"I'll be much more embarrassed if they spread rumors that I've made you up."

Miles sighed very heavily. "Fine. But only for a bit."

Charlie applauded his bravery. "Thank you, love. You won't regret it… Well, you might, actually, but it will make *me* very happy. And if you hate it, you can punish me in whatever manner you see fit."

"I'll start thinking through my options now, then. Perhaps I'll read back over some of my old work for ideas."

They kissed goodbye, and Charlie got his coat. Just as he

reached the door, Miles called his name and he turned back. "What is it, love?"

Miles had retreated back behind the counter, his hands flat upon it as he looked at Charlie carefully. "Are you going home to change first?"

"Change what?"

"Your clothes. Before the…outing."

"Of course. Why do you ask?"

"I don't know what one, you know, *wears* to this sort of place." He looked self-consciously down at his bookish tweed jacket.

Charlie positively lit up with laughter. "Oh, love. One wears whatever one wants to The Curious Fox."

"But—"

At that moment, Charlie was nudged out of the way by the door as it opened from the other side. The first customer of the day had arrived.

"Welcome," Miles said to the customer, standing up a little straighter. He turned rather gruffly to Charlie. "I'll figure it out. Have a lovely afternoon, sir."

Charlie tipped his hat, tickled half to death by the thought of what this evening would bring. "You too, old boy."

Charlie should have felt guilty showing his face at George Merriweather's bank when hidden in his mind were plans to call off his union with Alma. But he couldn't manage. He had already moved on to tonight, to showing Miles what life could be like if he got out into the world a bit. And anyway, Alma would be so much better off. No use fretting about it.

As promised, he stuck around only as long as strictly necessary, then went back to his own home to put on "whatever one wears to this sort of place." He'd try not to go overboard, so as not to make Miles more uncomfortable than he had to be.

He went up the front steps and nearly died of shock when Quincy opened the door before he'd grabbed the handle.

"Alive, are you?" the butler drawled.

Blast. The tiny staff were used to him coming in late, but he hadn't stayed out *all* night since they came into service.

"Yes." He pushed past the old man and started right up the staircase.

"Sir—"

"I'm fine, Mr. Quincy. Don't fret about me."

"Sir, please." His voice was harsh enough that Charlie stopped on the steps, looking down at him. "Miss Merriweather came by this morning."

"D-did she?"

"I told her you'd gone early to the bank."

"Yeah," Charlie said. "That's, er, that's exactly where I've been."

"At the bank," said Quincy, dry as a crackling desert road. "Stayed all night and through to the morning, did you? Should have known. After all, you're such a hard-working man."

"Why thank you, Mr. Quincy."

"Sir—"

"Please!" Charlie snapped. He immediately wished he hadn't, but the man was so leathery that he didn't wince anyway. "I appreciate your dedication. I'm certain that in my absence, you and the rest have tended to the house beautifully. But my business is my own."

"For now."

"What's that supposed to mean?"

"It means Miss Merriweather was rather put out even hearing you'd left early. Apparently, you told her she could join you for breakfast any time?"

"D-did I?"

"Please forgive my boldness, sir, but I would be remiss if I did not assist you in all the ways I can. And the best assistance I have now is a bit of advice: if you want a happy home, I suggest you tell your mistress that you'll need to be a bit more discreet in the future."

Charlie tapped his fingers on the banister. Perhaps the tale of Ethan Murray had made him paranoid, but he wasn't sure he liked the way Quincy said *mistress*. He'd be very glad to see the back of this man. The back of this gloomy house. Damn all of it right to hell, actually.

"Thank you, Mr. Quincy," he said curtly. "However, seeing as I still have a week or two of freedom, perhaps don't expect to see me much between now and then."

"Planning to be out all night again, sir?"

"I plan to do exactly as I please tonight. Perhaps that will lead me home. Perhaps not. It's nothing to do with you. If something's to do with you, I promise, I'll let you know straightaway. Until then, I suggest you do as you please as well. Then we'll all be happy, yeah?"

Quincy's posture changed. He crossed his arms and looked like he was considering something difficult. "Mr. Price," he said at last, very carefully. "I want you to know something. Your father, when he hired me on, made me promise I'd tell him if you started doing this."

Charlie gripped the banister tightly. "Started doing what?"

"Staying out very late. Coming home drunk. Acquiring finery. I wouldn't know about that last one, seeing as you don't let anyone touch your clothes except to clean them, but that laundry always seems to smell of smoke and perfume."

God bless Penelope and her perfume. He'd have to buy her a good one tonight. "Pop's always been a right killjoy," said Charlie, trying and failing to lighten the tone of this exchange. Quincy didn't budge. "So, er, are you going to tell him?"

Quincy didn't answer right away. "I thought it was a bit

silly, that he'd asked that of me. You're a grown man, after all, even if you don't act like it. What business is it of his at your age? But now that I'm seeing it for myself, I think I understand."

"Understand what?"

"I won't tell him of your habits, Mr. Price." He raised a severely disdainful eyebrow. "I still think it's silly. But if you turn up in a gutter somewhere, because you've wandered down the wrong alley or taken the wrong pipe with your gin, I *would* have to tell him that. Your mother too. And soon enough, your wife and brats. I don't think any of us will be 'happy' then."

He gave Charlie that grim, judging expression that had probably gotten him hired in the first place. He looked ready for an argument, a contradiction, an eye roll.

And so he was satisfyingly surprised when Charlie nodded.

"You couldn't be more right, Quincy," he said brightly. In all the distraction, Charlie still had his hat, which he lifted politely. "You can go ahead and report to my father that you and he are absolutely right."

Charlie hadn't realized Quincy's eyebrows were capable of such heights.

"We are?" said the butler.

"Yes. My habits have grown dangerous and unsustainable. I thank the both of you very much for your concern. Please know, however, that I've been made aware of my weaknesses, and am on the path to correct them once and for all."

"I see." Quincy blinked a few times, like he wasn't quite sure where he was. "Jolly good then. Shall I have the cook prepare supper for you? Or perhaps I could draw a bath?"

"Don't be silly. I'm going out."

"Out? But— When will you be back?"

Charlie put his bowler back on at an excessive angle. "If you don't hear from me by Monday afternoon, you may assume that my remediation has failed and start checking the gutters."

He left Quincy to stare after him as he went up the stairs to get ready for his evening out.

His notion of toning it down for Miles's sake vanished as soon as his wardrobe was open. Why should he, tonight of all nights? He still thought everyone's worries had been a little overblown, but either way, they were irrelevant now. There'd be no wedding, no sneaking around, no preference for blackout drunkenness to his daily existence, and absolutely no bloody *gutters*. As of tonight, he was free of that fate, and anyone who did not think he should celebrate it could go choke himself with a starched collar.

He got the stud out and got his own collar off first, replacing it and his shirtsleeves with more sumptuous counterparts, cream colored with lacy cuffs and all of it put together with glossy opal studs. He rummaged in the wardrobe until he found the burgundy waistcoat he wanted, pairing it with a rose-embroidered tie and plush black jacket. He spent a good deal of time getting his hair right, slicked and shiny and perfectly shaped. Let's see… A red ribbon around his hat, but that wasn't quite enough, so he added a lovely gold-and-peacock-feather pin that had contributed handsomely to his financial ruin. He slipped rings onto as many fingers as he could stand. The finest kidskin gloves he owned, the handsomest coat, the glossiest black shoes… What else? At some point, the maid had put some carnations in a vase on his nightstand, so he plucked a pink one out for his buttonhole and checked his reflection.

Not bad. Maybe he'd let Noah put a little kohl and lipstick on him; he'd get a kick out of that, and Charlie felt determined to appear as the epitome of a disappointing, gutter-bound Mary Ann tonight.

And then he—unlike poor Ethan Murray—would survive

it and return to collapse in Miles's bed to get fucked silly before sleeping off his hangover, calling off his wedding, and telling them all to shove it.

Except Alma, of course. He couldn't marry her, but he genuinely wished her a better life than the one he'd have been able to provide.

Charlie went back to the shop after close and tapped on the door until Miles arrived to rush him inside.

When he did, he gaped at Charlie like he'd never seen anything quite like him.

"I think I might be underdressed," he said.

"You're perfect." Charlie straightened the lapels of his black evening jacket. It was a soft velvet. He was charmed beyond all reason to see that grumpy Miles had gone out of his way to clean up for their adventure. His hair still looked like someone had gone at it with fork and knife, but he did look lovely. "You're going to leave before anyone even arrives, right? So, what difference does it make?"

Charlie could imagine for a thrilling second that the wink he gave might get him smacked right in the face. They'd not explored that one, though he had a sudden feeling that they'd both like it quite a bit...

"I did look back over the books for ideas of what to do with you if I hate this," Miles grumbled.

"Which books?"

"I believe I'm going to make you guess. I want to test your knowledge of my work. Pray you get nothing wrong."

They went out together into the bitter night. The icy air was chokingly thick with soot and fog. They shivered their way to a hackney, which Charlie directed to the club in Oxford Street that he used as cover. He paid and ushered Miles out.

"Alright, now stand and look pretty until the driver turns the corner."

"You're utterly ridiculous," said Miles.

Once the cab was out of sight, they walked away from the respectable place, slipping through one dark, damp alley and then another. Charlie thought nothing of them, familiar as they were, but Miles kept looking about and back behind them, holding his coat tighter against his chest.

"Charlie, where in blazes are you taking me? We're going to get bloody mugged back here."

"Nah, to get mugged, there'd have to be someone about. These are well deserted."

"That doesn't make me feel better."

It made Charlie feel better. In fact, Charlie wasn't sure he'd *ever* felt better. He was positively giddy, floating along, invincible. When they ducked down into a particularly narrow little ginnel that hardly had room for them to walk side by side, he pushed Miles against the dirty brick and pressed himself up tight to his jumpy lover.

"I'm telling you, Miles, there's nothing back here." He danced his fingers over Miles's trouser buttons. "We could get away with anything."

"Charlie—"

But Charlie felt like the devil himself. He dropped to his knees on the freezing, filthy ground and ran his hands up and down Miles's legs a few times before parting the bottom of his wool coat. "Oh, *my*. Already, love? Looks like dark alleys get *someone's* imagination fired up." He leaned in to press his lips against Miles's surprisingly intense excitement, the intimate and familiar scent of him cutting through the cold air. "Have you done it before? In an alley? I bet you have. I bet you love it." He kept his mouth whispering against the warm cock while he talked. "Do you ever think about shoving me against a brick wall, Miles? You want to spit on your fingers and fuck me like an animal right here?" He licked the hard ridge right through the dry, scratchy wool of Miles's trousers, base to tip. It twitched under his tongue.

"Stop it, Charlie. Please."

Miles looked delicious up there, aroused and terrified out of his mind, biting his lip as he glanced around guiltily. Charlie knew he could bring him off right here in the shadows and sleet, and Miles would do nothing to stop him. Miles *couldn't* stop him—the sheer danger and wickedness of the moment seemed to have gotten him mostly there already.

But Charlie took pity on him. He stood up, the knees of his own trousers wet and mucky. He didn't know what with. He didn't particularly care.

Miles looked a bit unsteady, his eyes glazed. "Good God," he whispered.

Charlie put a gloved finger to Miles's lips. Miles closed his eyes and kissed it like he had no choice. Charlie took his time tracing his way down to Miles's hand, which he took briefly before setting back off toward the Fox.

Chapter Eighteen

Miles

Miles followed Charlie down that horrible street as if hypnotized. Watching him waltz between filthy, stained walls, all done up like that in feathers and lace...he would risk obliteration if only Charlie would get back on his knees and finish what he'd started. He was fevered. Lured as if by dark magic through a maze of alleys that he would never step foot in himself.

He realized why this happened to all his characters the way it did. Their helplessness was simply a reflection of his own. He'd known, somewhere deep down, that he could be utterly destroyed with desire under the right circumstances. Well, here it was. He would follow that peacock-feathered hat straight into hell. In a way, that's just what he was doing.

At last, Charlie stopped in front of a door so gray and pathetic that Miles hardly noticed it. "Welcome to The Curious Fox," he said with a flourish.

Miles looked at the doorknob. When he squinted carefully, he saw a little image scratched into the metal. Three triangles, three dots, arranged into the vague suggestion of a fox's face. He took a deep breath, trying to calm himself. "Charlie, I don't know if I can go in yet."

Charlie glanced down smugly at Miles's obvious condition.

"We're not going to church, love. You'll fit right in. Though, if you'd like, perhaps…" He licked his lips slowly, and that very nearly took care of the problem all on its own. He looked wildly happy about what he'd done to Miles. "Oh, I love this. I think I'll make you wait, actually. Goodness knows, you deserve to suffer a bit after all you've put me through."

As Miles breathed deep and struggled to get it together, Charlie rapped on the door in a peculiar pattern. After a few moments, someone knocked back from the other side. Charlie replied with another few, and then the little fox on the handle flipped over.

A fellow opened the door. His complexion was dark, probably Indian, and he wore a topaz in one of his ears. He smirked and crossed his arms over an amber waistcoat, looking Charlie up and down. He opened his mouth, but before he could say anything, he seemed to notice Miles and gasped instead.

"*Charlie!*" he hissed.

"Love, I'm pleased—or something like that—to introduce Mr. Warren Bakshi, our barkeep. Now, make yourself useful for once, Warren, and let us in, would you?"

"Not so fast. Got to follow proper protocol with guests, don't we?" Mr. Bakshi leaned comfortably against the door frame. He held a leather ledger in his hand, the other poised with an ostentatious feathered pen. "You think you're above the rules, Price? Now tell me. Who's your lovely friend? And are you willing to take full responsibility for his bad, bad behavior?"

It was rather dark back here, but Miles thought he saw a very devious spark in Mr. Bakshi's wink.

"Would you cut it out?" said Charlie.

"State his name, Charlie, or no one goes in. Them's the rules."

Charlie rolled his eyes. They'd discussed this on the way

over, but it still made Miles very anxious to see his full name and occupation put down on paper in a place like this. Mr. Bakshi finished his records, snapped the ledger shut, and touched the feathered end of the pen to the tip of Charlie's nose. "That'll do. In you get."

Miles followed Charlie through a dark hall while Mr. Bakshi locked up behind them. They passed through not one but two sets of curtains that were studded with tinkling little bells, and then the narrow passage opened up into a slightly cramped parlor with a bar along one side and a series of curtained alcoves along the other. The middle was filled with an eclectic but pretty assortment of tables and chairs, velvet sofas set with beaded pillows, and a good deal of overlapping rugs. The ceiling was hung with more fabric, purple and blue swaths that suggested twilight while the crystals dripping from the chandeliers served as stars. The air smelled of flowery perfume, incense, and cigar smoke, a scent he immediately recognized as the one that clung to Charlie's coat. That was uncanny, but the smell was so familiar that he couldn't help feeling more at ease.

As promised, there was nearly no one inside. All the alcoves were empty, the curtains drawn back tidily. A piano sat to the side of a little stage along the back wall, unoccupied and silent. Each seat and barstool stood straightened and waiting. The only people in the place were a bearded beauty who carried himself like he was in charge and a lithe little fellow dressed tidily in black and purple who'd perched right on top of the bar, legs crossed, sipping something from a tumbler.

When that man spotted Charlie and Miles, he slammed his drink down on the bar and smacked his friend on the shoulder. Miles was quite sure he'd never had so many ecstatic eyes on him at once. Three pairs, Mr. Bakshi and now these other two. Perhaps not much for someone like Charlie, but to Miles it felt like being onstage in a concert hall.

The fellow on the bar beckoned to them with a single finger. Miles stayed a step behind Charlie as they approached.

"My beautiful butterfly." Charlie held his hands out. The fellow slipped down off the bar like he was made from liquid and scurried into Charlie's arms. They hugged. They *kissed*, right on the mouth.

That threw Miles for a moment, until the fellow made a happy little high-pitched noise and the next thing Miles knew, *he'd* been hugged and kissed on the mouth by this complete stranger.

"*Ciao, bello,*" he purred. His voice was very quiet, yet somehow impossible to miss. He put a hand in the center of Miles's chest. The nails on it were painted red. He glanced at Charlie and lowered his voice further. "This is *your* lover? He's so butch."

"That's him," Charlie said with a little flash of pride on his face. "Love, meet Mr. Noah Clarke, resident butterfly."

Mr. Clarke stood back to get a better look with his rather intense and appraising set of eyes. Miles might have felt like a specimen, but he was staring just as intently back. Mr. Clarke appeared to be just what the rest of the world thought they all were; he had a smooth, youthful face with brows and lashes a lady would envy. His hair was long enough to tuck behind his ears, both of which had little sparkling studs in them. His wrists and neck were draped with pearls and black lace.

Charlie came over to stand beside his pretty friend and admire Miles a bit. In context, Charlie was looking rather pretty himself. Together, they were positively breathtaking. Miles had never seen anything quite like them, and was shocked at how much he appreciated the sight.

"Not bad, eh?" said Charlie.

Mr. Clarke ignored Charlie's question. "It's lovely to meet you at last. Charlie's told us very little about you, but certainly enough to pique our interest." He turned to Charlie. "What am I to call him?"

Miles was surprised by the question. "Call me?"

"Shall we give your real name, love?" said Charlie. "Or something else?"

He hadn't considered it. It seemed very polite of Mr. Clarke to ask. "Erm. I—I'm not sure."

"How about Mr. Cox?" Charlie suggested.

"Ah, that's right. Mr. Reginald *Cox*," Mr. Clarke repeated with relish.

"Y-yes. I suppose that is me." Miles cleared his throat awkwardly. "Wh-what should I call you?"

"You'll find we're most improper here, seeing as we don't all like our family names floating about, you know. When you see me like this, you may call me Noah, if you'd like." He batted those ridiculously long lashes. "You won't see me like this for much longer, however."

"Noah's something like a caterpillar." Charlie slid an arm around his friend's shoulders. "He arrives early, fattens himself up with a few drinks, then goes into his chrysalis in the back to transform into the beautiful butterfly known as Miss Penelope Primrose."

"I…" Miles found himself without any words. "What?"

The third man, the sort of swaggering one, leaned over the bar with an eyebrow cocked. "He dresses up in women's clothes and plays the part for the night."

Miles blinked. "Women's clothes?"

"Knickers and all."

"God, Forester." Noah rolled his eyes. "You make everything sound so vulgar. Why can't you be more like Charlie and call me nice things like butterfly?"

He kissed the tips of his fingers and pressed them to Charlie's cheek, then he whipped around, grabbed his drink, and took off for the mysterious "back."

The other bloke—Forester—stared after him with a long-suffering expression. "I've known him too long to have not seen that coming."

"Yes," agreed Charlie.

"Well, hopefully his *sensibilities* can handle my *vulgarity*. I wasn't going to let you two keep confusing Mr. Cox all night long."

"I appreciate that," said Miles. "I'm sorry if I caused trouble."

"Don't be sorry, love," Charlie said. "Noah's a moody chap. He'll have forgotten all about it by the time he's gotten his face on. Anyway. Forester. There's something I need to discuss with you."

"If you and Warren can add up to at least one whole, functioning employee, I'll happily take you."

"'Scuse me!" protested Mr. Bakshi. He'd come behind the bar while everyone else was talking. He snapped a cloth toward Mr. Forester's backside, which was expertly dodged.

"I implied that you're at least half an employee, Warren. I think that's generous considering how long you actually stay up here before your legs give out and you're off on your knees somewhere." He pretended to stumble, gripping the bar for support.

"Wait." Charlie held up a hand. "How did you know I was going to ask you for a job?"

Forester shrugged, his bony shoulders looking like they'd been crafted specially to fit a barrel of subtext into the gesture. "Miss Jo."

"Oh, goddamn her."

Her. "Another butterfly?" Miles asked.

"Opposite of that," Charlie said. "A wolf. A tribade. *Palone-omi*. A damn meddling Sapphist. Doesn't even belong over here, and yet somehow, she's always in my business."

"You shouldn't have taken that bet, Charlie. You didn't belong over at their place, either," said Forester.

"Warren implied I could be out-drunk by a few girls in suits. I couldn't let such an insult to my masculinity stand." He haughtily adjusted the lace at his cuffs.

Mr. Bakshi smiled deviously at Miles and muttered, "I can get him to do the most ridiculous things if I insinuate that he's being a bore."

"Alright," said Charlie forcefully. "I'm not done, Forester. I don't just need a job. I need—"

"I can front you something. You weren't fool enough to tell Jo the exact numbers, so we'll have to talk. But I'd feel awful if you wound up married on the count of my tight pocket. I'll do what I can to help." Mr. Forester leaned his elbows on the bar again. His eyes were warm and amused, even indulgent. "I can't believe you didn't ask earlier. It seems obvious, now that Jo's mentioned it."

Charlie looked uncharacteristically humble, peering guiltily out from under the brim of his hat. "I already owe you for about a year's worth of drinks."

"Charlie, I stopped bothering with your tab almost as soon as you stopped paying it off at the end of the night."

"You're too generous. You really shouldn't have done that."

"Most of the money comes from the rooms, and the owner keeps me comfortable." Mr. Forester gave another weighty shrug. "I can afford to keep one pet freeloader, so long as he's amusing enough."

Charlie seemed to consider that. "What about when I buy rounds for everyone?"

Mr. Bakshi leaned on the bar beside the proprietor, the two

of them looking at Charlie like they were the parents of some amusingly naughty child.

"Forester told me to start ignoring your calls for rounds a long time ago," he said. "You never do seem to check back in to make sure I've done it."

"You mean no one is getting the drinks I buy for them?"

"You aren't buying them, though," said Mr. Bakshi. "That's the whole problem."

"Anyway, Charlie," said Mr. Forester. "Would you like to give it a go tonight? If you can learn the way of it quickly, I'll still have someone pouring even after Warren's legs grow too weary to go on."

Miles was interested in how pleased Mr. Bakshi seemed by this goading, grinning to himself as he started shelving cleaned glasses. Everything between these fellows seemed all in good fun. Miles felt sharply outside of it, but it was rather lovely to watch.

Charlie turned to him. "Love, would you mind that? I don't want to abandon you."

"Don't worry about me," said Miles. "I'll just, er, I'll be perfectly happy right over here at the bar."

"You don't have to stay, if you don't want to. I know it's not your sort of place, though I do really appreciate that you've come out to meet everyone."

Miles thought about it. "Do you want me to leave?"

"Don't be silly."

"I think I'd actually like to stay, then. I'm curious."

Charlie brightened like a beautiful chandelier. "You've come to the right place then."

While Mr. Forester went to hang up their coats, Miles settled in on a high seat at the very end of the line. Charlie, meanwhile, hopped right up on the bar, spun round on his bottom, and landed on the other side next to Mr. Bakshi.

"You and me, then, eh?" he said. "Where shall we begin?"

The barkeep wandered over to Miles. "Pouring's easy. We'll get to that as the night goes on. Let me teach you the important bit first: getting your tips."

He rolled his sleeves up to show off rather lovely forearms. He loosened his cravat a little and leaned languidly over the bar in front of Miles. He batted his lashes so brazenly that Miles half expected officers to start swarming out of every alcove.

"Evening, beautiful," he said sweetly. "Don't believe I've seen you here before. Please, call me Warren. I'll be here for you all night. What do you like? To drink? Anything you want." He ran a finger over the back of Miles's hand.

Mr. Bakshi—Warren—had gone from being a slightly silly object of mockery into an intriguing and sensual creature in the course of about twenty seconds. Miles felt heat rise to his face. "Um, er, I don't know."

Charlie grabbed Warren by the buckle of his waistcoat and yanked him away. "Stop that," he snapped. "I don't like that."

"Charlie, are you *jealous*?" Warren looked thrilled.

"No," Charlie lied. He slid into the space Warren had just occupied, rolling up his own sleeves and loosening his own collar. "What will it be, love? You do look like you could use a drink to calm you down a bit." He threw a glare over his shoulder.

Miles laughed. He glanced at the lines of bottles. He doubted very much that any wine they had here would be up to his tastes, but he didn't drink a lot of liquor. Mr. Forester returned as he was trying to decide and started asking him questions that could lead to recommendations.

Behind him, though, Miles caught Warren's eye. The fellow began to pantomime pouring bottle after bottle into a glass, then pointed at Charlie.

"Give me," Miles said slowly, "the most complicated thing you lot can think of to get the new barkeep started off right."

Charlie glared between him and Warren. "I should have known better than to bring you here. These hags are going to be a terrible influence on you."

Miles couldn't help but smile. "Come on, Charlie. Don't be a bore."

Warren and Mr. Forester were pleased as punch. Charlie pretended not to be, batting Miles's hat down over his eyes before sauntering off to the bottles and glasses, muttering something about poison.

It was the strangest and most wonderful night Miles could remember.

Well supplied with much stronger drinks than he was used to, things were swimming nicely by the time the club began to fill up. Miles started things off watching Charlie and Warren answer the door and make cocktails for a trickle of fellows. Then a proper doorman and the pianist arrived. Once the post-performance theater crowd showed up, things began to look more like what he'd expected. By the numbers, it couldn't have been more than a few dozen chaps, but the size and arrangement of the place made it feel like a crowded ballroom.

Noah completed his transformation and returned looking like an absolute vision in gauzy skirts and satiny ribbons. It was hard to believe this was the same person; if he saw Noah on the street like this, he didn't think he'd suspect a thing. A few others had put on similar getups in the meantime, but none nearly so intricate. Much to Miles's surprise, Charlie took a break from mixing to ask Noah (Miss Penelope now, and he'd best not forget it, or that fan was coming for him) for a bit of eye and lip stuff, which she applied to him with great joy. Miles declined an offer for similar treatment, but he did tell Miss Penelope that her transformation was true art.

"Oh, you're too sweet, Mr. Cox!"

That was how Miles wound up with a scarf of feathers around his neck and a lipstick print on his cheek. Three prints, actually, because Charlie got jealous again and came around to leave his own marks on the other side.

As the night went on, he grew bewilderingly happy. He left the feathers to save his seat and took a little stroll about the place. There were a lot of beautiful things at The Curious Fox. Penelope and the other butterflies. Laughing dandies chattering away with groups of friends. Lovers sneaking into alcoves. He understood that the most illegal of activities had to take place in the back, with high fees and a stricter check-in procedure that kept Forester busy. But he noticed that they were all rather loose with less risky affections, the curtains only half-heartedly drawn.

It was a lovely little turn. He declined two offers to have his cock sucked, the first because he was too shocked to even consider it, and the second because it would be a shame for Charlie to poison someone his first night on the job. He did accept another drink from the pianist, who'd heard that he was an erotic novelist and could relate to a life of providing entertainment to a pack of ungrateful heathens. Miles liked him quite a bit. They were interrupted by the return of Miss Penelope, who dragged him off for a cigar and a game of cards.

The game was confusing, with an explanation that seemed to require a strange amount of poorly accented Italian. ("Certain ideas can't be translated, but don't worry, *amore*, it will all make sense once we start.") One lady convinced him to bet his jacket a few hands in, which he promptly lost to Miss Penelope. He eventually won it back somehow, along with a few pounds, which he brought back to tuck into the front of Charlie's trousers for a tip.

"What's happened to *you*?" Charlie asked.

Miles settled back in at the bar, accepting the fresh cocktail Charlie slipped to him before he could consider whether it was a good idea to have another. "Not sure." He slid a brandy-soaked cherry from the toothpick and into his mouth. "I think I might be having fun."

Charlie leaned over the bar to wrap the feathers back around his neck and give him a sloppy sort of kiss. He felt and tasted like he'd been dipping into the bottles while he worked, against Mr. Forester's explicit recommendation. It was so unsurprising that it was a wonder Mr. Forester had even bothered trying.

"Charlie!" An exasperated Warren dragged them apart. "Come on, mate."

Charlie blew another kiss, stole the second cherry off Miles's drink, and skipped off down the bar.

So many lovely things, and yet Charlie remained the most captivating by far. He bounced about happily from customer to customer, chatting with everyone, ruining drink orders with such charm that everyone accepted his questionable creations with a smile. The paint had added a wickedness to him that Miles found completely irresistible. Maybe he should have gotten his cock sucked after all. He couldn't even look at Charlie without getting painfully stiff; he might just spend the second he touched that delicious devil.

Miles wasn't the only one suffering as the night went on. Charlie was clearly just as worked up, sneaking him kisses and caresses between tasks and walking away with tented trousers. He also started spilling things around one o'clock; no one was quite sure how much he'd drunk, but it was clearly catching up to him. It annoyed Warren half to death, but Charlie was so amusing about his failings that no one else complained and sometimes even tipped him more generously.

When things finally slowed down a bit, Charlie wasted no time. Before Miles knew what had hit him, Charlie grabbed him by the collar, thrust his tongue into his mouth right in front of everyone, and then dragged him off to one of the alcoves.

He threw the curtain back to reveal two suddenly terrified-looking patrons who had been sweet-talking each other on a flowery chaise.

"This is my spot," Charlie barked. "Go find another one."

They did not need telling twice.

Once they were gone, Charlie yanked the curtain closed.

It was unstoppable, the way they grabbed hold of each other. There were no words, only a desperate, open-mouthed kiss and an immediate scramble for the other's buttons. Miles was spinning drunk, and Charlie didn't seem any better. They nearly tripped over the low table as they grasped at each other with hours' worth of pent-up wanting. Miles couldn't get his tingling fingers to free Charlie's cock even half fast enough, and when he did, it was like hot iron in his hand. Miles stroked him at the mad pace he was craving himself, and when Charlie got him out and matched it, they both came just as quickly as Miles had feared, clinging tight so they did not end up in a spasming puddle on the floor.

The harsh waves of pleasure seemed to last an age, but when they finally returned to earth, they smiled another kiss and laughed at themselves. Miles wasn't quite sure how they could return to a respectable state, but Charlie had apparently planned for something like this. He put a finger to his lips and clumsily reached under the chaise cushion for a towel. They did the best they could.

"Shh." Charlie folded the ruined square and hid it back

where he'd found it. "I'll put it with the sheets'n whatever later. Don' tell For'ster, though. We oughta done tha' in the back."

He was slurring horribly and too drunk to hide his Northern speech even as poorly as he usually did. He leaned against Miles, seeming unable to stay entirely upright.

Miles eased him down onto the chaise. He hadn't realized quite how far gone Charlie was. "Are you alright?"

"I'm good!" said Charlie. "I'm *so* good. I take back er'ything I ever said about Warren, though. I dunno 'ow he lasts as long as he does, everyone flirtin' like that, and slippin' money in me clothes, tellin' me the filthiest things on their minds. An' you sittin' there watchin' me like you fuckin' *own* me... I was worried I'd bump the counter wrong an' embarrass myself righ' there while pourin' gin."

Miles laughed. "God, I love you."

"I love you!" Charlie sprang up, steadied himself on Miles's arms. "And Miles. I'm gonna do this, yeah? I'm callin' it all off. All of it." He put a hand on Miles's face, and though he was drunk off his bloody rocker, his dark, made-up eyes were utterly sincere. "And then I'm gonna make you 'appy, yeah? Yeah, Miles? I'm gonna pay off my debts, and I'm gonna help you get your shop makin' money again. And then I'm gonna make the rest of your life so 'appy you won't hardly be able to stand it."

They settled in together in Charlie's spot, basking in each other's presence as they listened to the piano and some suggestive sounds coming from the wall behind them.

The curtain pulled back. Miles jumped a bit, but Charlie stayed put, his head heavy on Miles's chest. It was Warren and another fellow in a dapper suit.

No. Not a fellow. A woman. Everything here was such a dream that he questioned whether it was perhaps a man who'd dressed as a lady in a suit, but he realized that he recognized her heart-shaped face. Her dark, somewhat devious eyes. He couldn't place it, but he'd definitely met her before.

"Would you look at him?" Warren said to the woman, incredulous. "He's bloody asleep!"

And so he was. Miles looked down to see that Charlie's eyes had closed and his breathing had evened out.

"I'm sorry," said Miles. "That's my fault."

"No, it's not," said Warren. "It's the fault of the entire fifth of gin he's nipped through the night."

Mr. Forester appeared, putting his scruffy chin on Warren's shoulder to peer into the alcove. "How sweet," he said. "Our kid's taking a little nap."

"What do you have to say to that, eh?" Warren demanded.

"He's done better than I expected," Forester said. "He'll either learn to pace himself, or barkeeping will kill him. Either way, we won't have to keep listening to him pretend he's alright with that wedding. Now, come on, you." He slapped Warren's bottom. "Back at it."

"Why doesn't he have to get back at it?"

"We all know what happens when he wakes up, Warren. When he gets sick, do you want to be the one to deal with it, or would you rather leave it to his beloved?"

Warren wrinkled his nose. "Fair point. Best of luck with that, Mr. Cox."

"Er, thank you."

They left him with Charlie in his arms and the familiar woman in the opening of the alcove.

"You must be the writer," she said. Her eyes were warm and happy, but Miles still felt uneasy beneath them.

"I suppose I am," said Miles. "Who are you?"

"You can call me Miss Jo." She extended a hand. He did not take it.

"Who are you really?" he pressed. "We've met, haven't we?"

Reluctantly, she returned her hand to the safety of her pocket. "No, can't say we have."

But Miles knew they had. She had a distinctive shape to her eyes and cheekbones, things that couldn't be hidden by a bowler and a bowtie. He didn't like that she was lying about it. "You're the one who gave him my name, aren't you?"

She paused, considering him carefully before she answered. "That's me."

"How did you know who I am? Particularly if we've never met?" When she hesitated to answer, he went on. "You must forgive me, but I'm particularly careful about my identity. The whole thing is a bit disconcerting."

She rolled her eyes to the gauzy ceiling. "I suppose it would be." She collapsed onto the chaise on the other side of Charlie. For a quiet moment, she just looked at him, then she stroked his hair gently and snorted out a bit of laughter. "He's drooling on you."

Miles was not to be distracted. "Who are you, Miss Jo? How do you know me, and how do I know you?"

She breathed deep and bit her lip. When she spoke, she kept her eyes on Charlie. "Does he seem alright?"

"Yes?" Miles didn't understand the question. "He's drunk, is all."

"I'm going to tell you something, Mr. Montague. It's not what you want to know, but it is something you need to know." She put a hand on Charlie's back as if to assure herself that he was breathing. "We thought we'd lost him, a few months back. Right after he got engaged. Burst in here like a force of nature, saying he was getting married, and we all ought to celebrate it. He was obviously barking, but wouldn't hear a single bad word about anything because *it was going to be lovely*. Well, anyway, he went ahead and 'celebrated' himself into half a coma. We couldn't wake him. Scared us all half to death. Poor Noah thought he'd, you know, done it on purpose. Broke character and everything, checking him all over for an empty opium bottle. But that assumes more self-awareness than Charlie has, I think. Anyway, he did come around eventually, but it was a dreadfully long time.

"We thought that might make him realize how miserable he was, but no. He just keeps saying how lovely Alma is, and how happy they'll be. He'll have it all, won't he? A wife and a house and five fucking Charlie Juniors biting his ankles, yet he'll still be the life of the party, nothing will change. Meanwhile, the weeks go on and he's blacking out all the time, trying any funny substance anyone hands him, acting like such an unbearable prick that the fellows fool enough to take up with him either wind up crying or threatening to deck him. And I'm just thinking: Christ, Charlie, have you even noticed you're trying to kill yourself yet? Fortunately, the Merriweathers got him that job and started expecting him at dinner, so he couldn't carry that pace on to its logical conclusion."

Miles looked down at Charlie's sleeping face. Charlie was endlessly surprising, but at last, Miles wasn't surprised at all. There'd been a missing piece to what he'd shown Miles, and this was the one. He could see it, now. Like Jo, however, he wasn't convinced that Charlie could see it in himself.

"You must understand, Mr. Montague," Jo went on, her voice just barely loud enough to cut through the clinks and chatter of the club beyond the curtain. "He's one of my dearest friends. I had to help him, somehow. I knew from conversations we'd had just how much your work meant to him. It seems a bit backward, doesn't it? Cheery bloke like him, fascinated by such horrific tragedies? But it gets him here." She patted Charlie's chest, over his heart. "And he's fairly allergic to all that, normally. I'm not sure what it is about you that gets through to him, but he certainly wasn't listening to anyone else. I pulled every string I had to uncover your identity. I didn't expect it would end with you here, letting him slobber all over you, but I hoped that even just a talk with someone who understood his soul like you did would set him right."

Miles could tell that this was mostly true. He didn't doubt the sincerity of her love for Charlie. And he was very moved by the reason she decided to find Miles in the first place. He was still bothered, though, by how much was left out of the story. "But who gave you my name?"

"I promised I wouldn't tell."

"See, I don't like that."

"Of course, you don't. Who would? But if you knew the details, a lot of things might become unpleasant for everyone. So forgive me, but I'm staying mum for now, for your good as much as anyone else's."

As she kissed Charlie's head and took her leave, Miles wracked his poor, intoxicated brain for any hint of who she could be, who his revealer could be. There were so few people who knew the identity of Reginald Cox.

Or so he'd thought.

Chapter Nineteen

Charlie

It had proven impossible to even get out of bed the day after his first go as a barkeep. Unfortunately, the plan to call off his wedding right away was replaced with a morning spent humiliating himself in front of poor Miles, who was quite sick himself, but slightly more dignified about it. He was a good sport, but by the time Charlie started to feel better in the early evening, he got the impression that making a habit of this would wear quickly on their cohabitation. Miles wasn't a natural caretaker and kept making dark little quips about death by drink that made him wonder what his friends had said while he was unconscious.

All in all, he supposed it was as good a time as any to take things a bit easier.

"I am sorry for all this, love," Charlie said as they took a brew by the fire, a bit of food in both their bellies and the worst of the situation well past. "I hope I didn't ruin things."

Miles sipped his tea, which did not quite hide a suppressed smile. "Can I admit something?"

"Anything."

"The whole ordeal, start to finish, has been an adventure. I've never had a single fellow put me through anything quite like this."

Charlie leaned back in his chair. "You've clearly not met the sort of fellows I have. Speaking of which: my friends. Do you think you'd like to see them again? I know they'd be happy if you came back. They liked you."

"I liked them too." Miles seemed very surprised to be reporting such a thing. "Most of them."

"Yeah, Warren's a twit."

"I'm not talking about Warren. Warren was lovely. If not for you, I'd have invited him to give me a tour of the back."

Charlie fumbled his teacup. Then he saw how Miles was laughing under his breath, and he nearly threw it at his head. "Stop it, will you? My constitution is still delicate."

"It's funny how jealous you get. I wouldn't have expected it."

Crossly, Charlie knelt in front of the grate, picked up the poker, and started jabbing at the logs in the hearth to wake them up. "To be fair, Warren gets it going in me a bit more than others. We've been known to compete."

Miles leaned his elbows on his knees, fascinated. "For men?"

Heat rose to Charlie's face, not entirely due to the increased flames. "We don't have to talk about that if you don't want to."

"Unlike you, I don't get jealous." He grabbed the back of Charlie's waistcoat and tugged at it until Charlie turned around and came over to the chair, still on his knees. The poker fell to the hearthrug with a dull clang, and Charlie looked up at a wolfish grin. "I get excited. I want to hear all about what a bad boy you've been. Spare me nothing."

"Are you really looking at me like that? After the day I've put you through?"

Miles leaned down to kiss the top of Charlie's head. "Also unlike you, I don't consider a fellow all used up the second he annoys me. I don't reject my lovers for being human."

"Damn, you were talking to my friends, weren't you?"

"Yes, though they did not give me nearly enough of the fun details." He grabbed one of Charlie's hands, kissed it, then placed it on his inner thigh, along the hard evidence of his excitement. Charlie's breath caught. "I've given you enough stories to toss off to; it's your turn."

"You're just saying that because you have writer's block. Ow!"

Miles had grabbed him hard by the hair. "Go on then, my darling," he said, the sweetness in his voice at odds with his rough treatment.

Charlie shook him off and glared upward. The glare turned into a smirk rather quickly, though, as he considered his options. He had a lot to choose from. "Alright," he said. "I'll tell you one. It's not the wildest, but it involves a character you'll appreciate."

"Oh? And who's that?"

"Warren Bakshi."

"You and him?" A low growl rumbled Miles's chest and his prick twitched under Charlie's palm. "I confess, I am *quite* appreciative of that notion."

"There were extenuating circumstances. We were interested in the same chap, you see." Charlie glanced at the door as he trailed his fingers lightly over Miles's swelling excitement, half expecting Miss Penelope's ladies to burst in for the details; he and Warren complained about each other too much for either of them to live this little debacle down. "Our normal rivalry wasn't getting us anywhere, so we decided to put it all aside for the night, sneak into one of the rooms, and split the winnings."

Next day, Charlie was much better in almost every way imaginable. He'd survived his hangover and got the front money from Forester. He had a job to go to, a place to sleep, and—by the end of the day—a bit of extra cash from what he'd been willing to part with at the pawnbroker's. On top of it all, he was positively floating along with the purest, most blinding love he'd ever experienced. Miles Montague was sun, moon, and stars as far as Charlie was concerned, and he was so absorbed in dreams of all the wonderful things they could do together that he could hardly think of anything else.

Just one last little end to tie up.

Later in the week, he was scheduled for his usual dinner with the in-laws. Afterward, he was often afforded some time alone with his fiancée. He was tempted to just send a letter to her parents and then disappear into the mist, never to be seen again, but Alma did not deserve that. Instead, since it was a milder night than it had been, he'd take her for a turn about the garden and break the news to her first, as privately and gently as possible.

The thought of calling off his wedding had been a real thrill for a while. He associated the act with the harder but freer life he'd planned out with Miles.

That excitement lasted right up until the moment he arrived on the Merriweathers' tidy suburban doorstep. The instant he rang the bell, it burst like a balloon. Far from thrilled, he was actually very clammy by the time the footman let him inside.

Dinner was torture. He was determined not to drink too much wine, for Alma's sake, but his unfortunate sobriety made the whole thing almost unbearable. George Merriweather asked him about the bank until, simply *famished*, Charlie couldn't carry on the conversation *with his mouth so full of this delicious meal, Mrs. Merriweather, my God your cook's outdone herself tonight!* Then Alma and her mother talked about nothing but the wedding, with Charlie trying to make all the right sounds when he was addressed. George Merriweather seemed to sense Charlie's discomfort. He did not attribute it to planned abandonment, however. Instead, he insisted that the women save all that talk about flowers and face paint until they were by themselves. We *men* don't care about such things, eh, Charlie? And Charlie had made some vague gesture with his water glass that hopefully didn't offend anyone, praying no one had noticed that he hadn't got all the traces of kohl off his eyes yet.

By the time they'd finished dessert, he was madly trying to figure out how he could escape this wedding without Alma having to find out about it.

"A game of chess, perhaps, my darling?"

Alma's sweet, earnest voice scraped across his eardrums so painfully that he jumped.

She laughed and put a hand on his arm. The staff were clearing the plates and her parents were in a conversation of their own, now. "Everything alright, Charlie? You seem distracted today."

He cleared his throat and smoothed out the napkin he'd folded neatly on the table when he was finished with it. "The rain has stopped at last," he said. Another crease vanished under his finger. "Perhaps we get our coats on for a bit and have a stroll before it gets miserable again?"

Alma clapped her hands together. "Lovely idea. I can't believe I didn't think of it. You always have the very best ideas. Mother, Father, Charlie and I are going to take a turn in the garden."

Mrs. Merriweather looked suspiciously over her coffee cup. "Awfully dark out there isn't it?"

"Oh, let them have it, Pru," Mr. Merriweather said, looking irritated but resigned. "There's no harm. Do bring a lantern, though. There are a few lights lit, but she has a point."

Bundled up and outfitted with a lantern that Charlie held out before them, they went out into the Merriweathers' back garden. It was subdued this time of year, most everything pruned back and covered in preparation for what promised to be a tough winter. The paths were clear, though, and as promised, a few lights led their way along winding paths that ended at a tidy gazebo near the back wall.

Alma clung to his arm, warm and happy beside him, chattering on about one of the adventure novels he'd bought for her from Miles's shop. Her mittens were fluffy and pale blue, so innocent and girlish that Charlie felt tears well up in his eyes at the sight of them on his coat. This was going to kill her, wasn't it? By God, how had he thought he could look her in the eyes and hurt her like this? He should have sent the letter. What an awful mistake.

"That sounds most amusing, dear," Charlie said when she paused for breath. He'd only been half listening, but it seemed to be the right response.

"Have you read anything interesting lately?" she asked, squeezing closer to him.

Her poor little mind would melt if she knew the answer to that. *Indeed, my dove. I sneaked a peek over the shoulder of an erotic novelist, and the characters were committing the most* interesting *crimes against nature you could imagine!*

"Not in particular," he said lightly. "My best recommendations come from you. What do you think I ought to tackle next?"

And she was at it again, talking on and on about what might suit him.

He somehow managed to carry on a conversation about these things without hearing a word out of either of their mouths until they reached the gazebo. They sat together, their heads covered by white metal entwined with the soggy brown remainders of summer's flowered vines.

Charlie set the lantern beside them and let Alma snuggle

in under his arm. He closed his eyes and tried to capture this last moment with her. She was small and soft, such a comfortable little thing. He really did care for her. In theory, he'd have liked to be married to her. He wanted the abstract idea of their children. It wasn't just the debts that had brought him here. If it were, he'd have done this months ago.

As he blinked his eyes open and looked up at the house, sitting so pretty under the moonlight, he couldn't help but envy his proper, healthy brothers. Life was awfully easy for them. They could just have this and enjoy it all on its own. He rarely wished to be like them, but he felt a wisp of it now.

He took her mittened hand in his own. He wore the same glove that Miles had kissed in the alley.

Being married would not make him happy. The part he really wanted was to wake up next to someone who loved him. *That* he could have.

And Alma could too, if he set her free to find it.

"Alma," he said quietly. "My sweet pet, I have to discuss something with you."

She didn't move at all. Charlie had never spoken to her in such a serious tone the entire time they'd known each other. "Oh?"

He burrowed his face in her hair. "I can't marry you."

She sat as if frozen, as if the chill had turned her right to ice in his arms.

"Yes, you can," she said.

A choked little laugh escaped his throat. "I love you, Alma. I do. And that's why I can't marry you. I'm not suited. I'll be a terrible husband."

"No," she said. "You'll be lovely, Charlie."

"If you had any idea what a terrible fiancé I've been, you wouldn't say that."

She breathed deeply, as if she'd forgotten for a few moments and had to catch up. "Have you been unfaithful?"

"Horribly so."

With a resolute nod, she turned to face him. She took his hands and looked up at him. Her eyes were a little wet, but determined. "I forgive you, Charlie."

"What?" He shook his head in a way he hoped was firm and final with no hint of the panic her words kicked up in him. "No. You mustn't forgive me."

"But I do."

"Stop," he snapped. "Tell me I'm awful. Slap me in the face and run inside and find someone better. Please, Alma. *Please*."

"I can't do that."

Why couldn't she let it be easy? "I'm trying to put this as gently as I can. I'm not marrying you, Alma. I will not be at the church. I will not give vows. There's no wedding. There's no marriage. I'm calling it off. I just wanted to tell you first. I wanted you to know...oh, darling, please, please don't cry."

One of those fuzzy mittens had gone up to her mouth while the rest of her face collapsed into tears. He tried to hold her, but she slapped him away.

"It's nothing to do with you, Alma," he went on, desperate to somehow make this better. "You're delightful. I love you so. You're going to make a man so happy, *so happy*, I know it. It's everything to do with me. I'm not suited to marriage. I've tried my very best, but I'll not subject you to my weakness. It's not right."

"I don't care."

"Alma, don't make me do this!" he said through gritted teeth. "I'm in love with someone else. Alright? I can't marry you, because I'm in love with someone else."

"You can keep him—her. You can keep her. Your mistress."

A numb cold, nothing to do with the chill, shot straight through Charlie's whole body.

"What did you say?" he whispered.

"I said you can keep your mistress."

"Before that." She tried to shake her head, but he grabbed her shoulder and made her look at him. "What did you say?"

The sadness on her face warped further into a tragic sort of amusement. In a voice very unlike the bubbly one he was used to, she said, "Goodness, Charlie. Didn't your parents bother telling you what this marriage is for?"

Apparently, they had not. "What are you talking about?"

She put her face in her hands. When at last she spoke, she spoke to the ground. "It's to save us both. If you've decided you don't want saving, alright, but you'll be leaving me in a very bad spot."

"I don't know what you mean."

"They really didn't tell you?"

"What bad spot?" Charlie stared at Alma, suddenly trying to envision her dressed up like Jo. That didn't feel right, so what on earth…?

So quietly he could hardly hear it, she whispered, "I'm ruined."

Charlie sat back, stunned silent. Alma? *This* Alma? Sweet and innocent and bubbling like the shiniest little virgin on the planet? *Ruined*?

He instantly thought the worst, wondered who had done it to her and whether anyone had killed the fucker yet.

He asked her as much.

Alma wiped her wet cheeks, shaking her head miserably. "It wasn't like that."

"What do you mean? What was it like, then?"

Much to his surprise, Alma laughed through her tears, batting his shoulder with her mittened hand. "What do you think, Charlie? He was handsome and charming, much more so than I thought possible for an awkward girl like me. We weren't formally courting, but we found our excuses, some aboveboard and others a bit...sneakier."

"Sneaky?" A chuckle escaped Charlie's throat. "Like sneaking out of your house at night?"

She looked sideways at him, a gleam in her eye like the one she'd had after the shot of brandy. "Or sneaking him in."

"Alma!"

"It's dreadful, I know, but he kept saying he would marry me when the time was right. I had no reason to doubt it. We talked about it in such detail: a house in the country, children, horses, a lovely library packed to bursting with books. It seemed like a technicality, that we hadn't gotten around to the formalities yet. I loved him, and he loved me, and as I say he was...handsome."

She looked a little nervous, so Charlie kissed the side of her head and squeezed her hand. "Handsomeness really ought to be more tightly regulated, I think. Very dangerous stuff."

"Oh, Charlie, you're wicked." She smiled, but Charlie recognized the type. He used it so much, that eventually even his friends had seen through it. It was the sort of smile that covered terror. "You really don't hate me? Hearing this?"

"Hate you?" He considered that for a moment. It certainly changed his perception of her, but that likely said more about him than it did about her. "Alma, I've never cared for you more."

"Stop it."

"I mean it." He wanted to smile too, to make some joke about their shared hedonism, but for once he resisted. He softened his face so that she could too. "So, what happened, dove?"

"Well, it turned out not to be a technicality," she whispered. "It was reality, as I found out when I told him I'd missed my courses. I was so foolish. I thought he'd be as happy as I was about it. You see, I didn't realize what a disaster it was. I thought it was just the excuse we needed to run to the altar. I half expected to elope that very night. But instead he went home, and I literally never heard from him again." She squeezed her eyes shut, voice wavering. "I was in more trouble than I knew what to do with. I ran away, to one of those places the bluestockings run to keep girls in my situation off the street. It was very strict, but before I could decide whether it was better than the alternatives, my parents found me and brought me back. They sent me to a convent until my little girl came and then… Oh, I know it was for the best, Charlie. She's better off with the couple she went to than she would have been with me. It was selfish for me to have even considered keeping her. I know this is the best outcome for everyone, I know it."

Perhaps her words knew it, but her eyes didn't. She started crying again, and this time Charlie gathered her up tight, shushing and muttering comforts that seemed as thin as the mist of breath they came on.

When she'd calmed down, she went on.

"My parents wanted to pretend it had never happened, which, I suppose, is a more generous treatment than I deserved. But the labor was very difficult. There's no hiding my condition, none at all. I nearly died. It's a shame I didn't; that's what my mother says."

Charlie's heart cracked right in two and before he knew it, he was biting his lip to keep it from trembling. "Alma, please don't talk like that."

She shrugged, her body seeming a bit limp and tired from this telling. "In any case, we knew if I got married, I'd be found out straightaway." She looked up at him. Her eyes were red and wet, but admiring. She took his hand again. "That's where you came in. Our fathers knew each other from business. I don't know how on earth they got to talking about such humiliating things, but my parents sat me down one night and said they'd found me a husband, someone who had to get married to clear a nasty debt. They said it was suspected that he might not be…familiar enough with the female form to appreciate the difference."

It was so vulgar and strange that neither could help cutting the tension with a nervous burst of shared laughter.

When they'd recovered, Charlie said, "Alma, what was meant by that, exactly? Was my father explicit?"

"I'm not sure how the conversation went between the parents. Your father was just worried, I think, and wanted to get you settled down before you got yourself in trouble."

Charlie stared off into the cold, dead garden beds. His parents knew? And not only that, *they'd told the Merriweathers*? He thought back to Mr. Merriweather's comments about how men ought to respond to wedding talk. His father's unshakable faith that he wouldn't touch Alma before the wedding. His mother's assumption that, if he had, it would be a good thing, because then he'd be proper and healthy, and a girl like Alma would lose nothing in the bargain.

He suddenly felt quite ill.

"It's alright, Charlie." Alma squeezed his hand and looked up at him. "As you said before, handsomeness is dangerous business."

"It really is, isn't it?" he said weakly. "So, what did they tell you, exactly?"

"They told me that after what I'd done, a sodomite was the best I could hope for. That even if you did notice my condition, between the debts and the rumors, you were in a bad spot too. They said you wouldn't dare complain."

Charlie took all that in. It was bewildering. Dizzying. "Why didn't *you* complain?"

"I tried. I admit, I was very scared of you at first. I'd never met a sodomite, and had heard only the most dreadful things. But they insisted, and then…and then I met you!" She reached out to touch his face, but seemed to think better of it. "Charlie, I don't think you understand how difficult things were for me. To suddenly have someone like you in my life, with your colors, and your jokes, and your cakes… Who cares if you don't desire me? Desire got me into this mess in the first place. So long as you keep your vices discreet, we can have a happy little home. We'll have fun together like we always do. That's all. That's all that matters. You can keep me off the street, and I can keep you safe as well. If anyone ever gives you trouble, I'll attest to your upright character as your loving wife. It's perfect."

It was, wasn't it?

It was so bloody perfect that Charlie felt right dead inside just thinking about it.

"Please don't call it off, Charlie," she whispered desperately. "I understand that you want to, but you won't suffer as my husband. I promise."

"But Alma," he said quietly. "What makes you so sure you won't suffer as my wife?"

She didn't answer for so long that Charlie finally looked over at her. Her face, so blotchy and pink from crying and cold, had gone a little blank. "It's my best option," she said simply, as if his question were completely daft.

"Is it?" She looked like he'd gone mad, but he pressed on anyway. "Yes, we have fun together, but I don't think you really understand what you're getting into."

"Charlie—"

"I'm very bad with money, Alma," he said, surprising himself with the vehemence of his admission. "I stay out too late, too often. I drink a lot more than you think I do. While I like spending time with my brothers' children, I don't know the first thing about raising my own. Assuming, of course, that—"

"Assuming I can even give you a child," she said miserably.

"*Assuming* I agree to try, considering the last one nearly killed you," he snapped. He could hardly believe he was talking to her like this, so seriously, but now that he'd started, he couldn't seem to stop. "I mean really, Alma. Would you even consider taking all that on if you weren't desperate?"

"Charlie." Her eyes went serious too, deadly so. Such friends they'd become, and yet right now, they seemed like strangers. "I planned to live out my life with the man who loved me, my baby girl, and a library up to the ceiling. I thought I was getting that. Instead, I got this. And I thank God for it, because my alternatives are to spend my days wearing black and praying for my soul, or selling myself in the city center until I die. I don't think you understand. I have no other choices." She clutched at the front of his coat and came closer, so their foreheads were nearly touching. Her voice lowered to a foggy whisper. "Maybe you don't love me. Maybe we won't have children. But at least you've promised me control of your pathetic little library, and that will just have to do, Charlie." She swallowed hard. "If, of course, you'll have me. Whether I like it or not, the outcome is up to you."

The facts of it weighed about a ton around his shoulders. He'd agreed to this marriage to shirk his responsibilities. Somehow, that had twisted up until he was sitting here, shivering and on the verge of tears, having found himself completely responsible for the life of this sweet woman, his friend, whom he had used terribly for his own, selfish ends.

Maybe if Alma knew, if it wasn't all lies all the time, it wouldn't be as awful as Jo had suggested. Perhaps all the orchestrators of this union were right. Perhaps it could work out. Like Jo and The Beast, he supposed.

In the end, as he pulled her head tight against his chest, he blamed Miles for what he had to do. Well, not Miles, exactly. Just the grief-addled part of himself he called Reginald Cox. It seemed Charlie had read one too many of his tragedies over the years, seen one too many characters ripped and stomped and destroyed for their desires. The consequences of a little heat and misplaced trust should not be so steep. Not for Alma, not for Ethan, not for all those poor sods so heavy-handedly represented in the overused pages locked up in his trunk.

If he could save one person from an ending like that, he had no choice.

He kissed the top of Alma's head. "I won't leave you, little dove," he whispered. "We'll make it work. I promise."

Chapter Twenty

Miles

The new bell above the door tinkled its tune, a bit lower than the last one.

Miles did not look up straightaway. He was in the middle of *proper accounting* in the ledger. That it was covered in Charlie's crystal-clear print was thrilling, but also distracting. His mind kept wandering off to the story of the "split winnings," wondering if he could work it into the new book or—better yet—if he could convince Charlie to let him organize a real-life sequel.

A shadow fell over his page. "That doesn't look like my next sensation, Reg."

"Smithy!" Miles slammed the lot down so hard ink splashed from the pen. He looked up into the snide, smirking face of his publisher. "How many times do I have to say it? You. Can't. Be. Here."

"And yet…" Smithy raised both his hands and his face to heaven. "Nothing smites me when I come in. I do not burst into flames. Harpies and demons do not swarm from the rafters with their eyes full of lightning and their hands full of pitchforks. I simply walk in like anyone else. Imagine that."

Miles impatiently watched him turn a full circle. "What do you want?"

"Have you looked over the offer?"

"Yes."

"And?"

"I burned it."

Smithy draped himself dramatically over the counter, dead.

"Stop being dead," said Miles.

"How can I when you're killing me?"

With as disgusted a sound as he could manage, Miles paced off in the opposite direction, arms crossed.

Smithy came back to life, just enough to grab the ledger when Miles turned his back. "That's not your chicken scratch. Who'd you hire?"

"None of your business." He took the ledger back.

"I can't believe I'm saying this, but you seem to be in better spirits than I'm used to. Are you finally getting fucked?"

Miles threw his hands in the air. "And how is *that* your business, either?"

"How lovely for you, Miles. I'm *thrilled*. I do hope this cheeriness it's inspired will last."

"Go away."

But no. Smithy was sitting on the counter now, the heel of his well-shined shoe thudding irritatingly into the wall of it. "Look. I told O'Donnell that you weren't selling. I was very clear. Firm, even." He pantomimed spanking someone over his lap. "But the man is insistent. I told you, he's very motivated for both personal and professional reasons. He sent me back to plead with you."

"Why doesn't he come himself?"

"Because he's as bloody bad as you are. Sodding hermits. I don't know why I'm surrounded by them all the time, but I suppose that's the literary life."

Miles peered at Smithy. His irritation was waning a bit as he realized he might be able to get some information out of the man. Miss Jo had said her husband was friends with Smithy. O'Donnell was a friend. Perhaps there was a connection. "Hermit or not, do you think you could tell me a little more about him?"

"He's rolling in money and wants your little hovel. What more is there?"

"I don't know. Is he married, by chance?"

"Not sure he swings in your direction, Reg, but there's always exceptions."

Miles could not believe he'd expected a better answer. "Never mind."

"Really. I'm sorry. What is it?"

Miles came over to the counter, leaning his elbows on it and trying to decide what to divulge. "Someone's figured out Cox's identity. It's a rather long story, but I was curious if there's any connection with O'Donnell."

Smithy suddenly looked almost serious. "Haven't gotten any threats, have you? I'll take care of them, if you do."

"Nothing like that. It's just troubling."

"Well, I can tell you with absolute certainty that O'Donnell means you no harm. Should you really refuse to sell, should you really, *really* decide that's the idiotic choice you want to live with the rest of your life, he'll not make things difficult for you. I promise."

Something dawned on Miles, slowly and somehow all at once. "It's you."

"What?"

Miles looked at him incredulously. "There's no bloody O'Donnell. You want my shop."

Smithy smiled, very winning. "It's such a lovely location."

"You bloody idiot." Miles hit him on the shoulder with the ledger. "Why didn't you just ask me honest?"

"Your dark imagination keeps me up at night, Reg. If you

were angry, I didn't want to be on the receiving end of whatever you do to your enemies."

"Well, I don't know!" Miles came around to the back of the counter, tapping his pen on it while his mind ran circles. "Maybe it would have changed things."

Smithy sat very still, as if afraid to spook a barely calmed stallion. "You think so? I thought you'd prefer the place go to someone as *wholesome* as yourself. That's why I really bothered with the ruse."

"I don't want it to go to anyone, but, if it were *you*, I could…"

It was strange, how peaceful the notion made him feel. Selling the shop to a stranger was impossible. Who knew what they'd do with it? But Smithy was a damned good businessman. While Miles struggled to keep this thing afloat, Smithy could turn it around and have it doing Ethan proud in no time flat. And Miles could see to it that things were done properly, that Ethan's memory was preserved and respected while his shop saw success again for the first time in years.

Meanwhile, he could name his price. His *price*. He could pay off Charlie's debts, couldn't he? Or help, at least? If Charlie would accept such a thing (which Miles suspected he would) then Charlie wouldn't have to test his poor impulse control by working a bar every night. With that sort of help, he'd have time to start fresh in an accounting position that wasn't dependent on Mr. Merriweather.

And they could be together. Him and Charlie. Upstairs… or not. They could live wherever they wanted to live, do whatever they wanted to do. They could travel. They could go anywhere, everywhere. They'd be free of all the things they'd been dragging about with them. They would be free. The both of them.

"Reginald Cox, are you *smiling*?"

He was, wasn't he? Right at Smithy. "I suppose I am."

"I can't believe I came up with an alias when it was me you've wanted all this time." He put one dainty hand to his forehead and the other out as if Miles should kiss it.

And fuck it. That's just what he did.

"I'm not one-hundred-percent, now," Miles warned him. "We need to discuss it thoroughly, and then you need to give me time to think."

"Splendid. Just to ease you mind at the get-go, it will be well cared for. I know how much it means to you. I've got one fellow lined up to run it already, quite under whatever orders I give, and you can help me with all that. We'll likely need to hire one more once things get going, but I can even give you a say in that too, if you want. Only thing, of course, is that the respectable storefront won't be the entirety of the enterprise."

"Trying to make the next Holywell?"

"Trying to make sure I have something *off* of Holywell. Things are going to shit down there, worse than usual."

"Have you been caught?"

"Not personally, but there's been a few more raids than I'm comfy with, these past few months. I won't be going the way Dugdale did, I'll tell you that much. I'm just not that dedicated. I need a clean space going forward, somewhere to hide my hide if things start going down. That said, you lot—my writers—I want to make sure I have somewhere your books are available to the right people. I know that makes you nervous, but you know perfectly well how successfully I run my illegal enterprises; there will be no bother about it. And exclusive as access will be, we're going to get a damned lot of money per volume, I'm sure of it."

"I do trust you on that, believe it or not. Now, as for the sum, I need to check on a particular—"

The bell rang above the door. It was Charlie.

"Just who I wanted to see," said Miles. "Smithy, this is Charlie Price. Charlie, my publisher, Paul Smith. Mr. Price is a great fan of our particular line of literature. Might want your autograph, in fact, before you go."

"Lovely to meet you, Mr. Price. Are you the one responsible for Miles's sunny disposition? If so, I'd like to thank you personally."

Charlie opened his mouth, but nothing came out. Miles realized that something was quite wrong. Charlie looked pale. His eyes were red, cheeks a bit blotchy. His hands were so tight in his pockets that it looked like they might shake, should he take them out.

"Charlie?" Miles took him aside toward the staircase, hands on the tops of his arms as he tried to read into that shocking expression. He looked like someone had died. "Charlie, what is it?"

Charlie tried to talk, though his lips trembled so badly he could hardly get it out.

"You're crying," said Miles, incredulous. He'd never seen Charlie cry. He might not have realized it was possible.

Charlie wiped his face and shook his head. "No, I'm not. I don't... I don't do that."

"What the devil is going on?"

"I'm sorry. I'm so, so sorry, my love." His voice was a shaking little rasp, a horrible shadow of his usual banter. "The wedding is on. Ten days from now, I'll be married."

Next thing Miles knew, his happy, smiling, devilish Charlie had dissolved into a heap of tears in his arms.

And Miles felt nothing.

If he was very lucky, that nothingness would last a good, long time.

Smithy quickly took his cue and left.

Upstairs, Miles and Charlie shared a particularly good bottle in the flat for the telling of it. Something to busy their hands and the backs of their minds while Charlie explained how their well-laid plans had become a miserable failure.

"I can't leave her to that. Can I?" He took a long drink of his wine. He looked far worse than the rough morning after the Fox. Miles might actually prefer to have him retching again. "It would make me a terrible monster if I left her, wouldn't it? Or am I mental?"

Miles wanted to say that yes, it was mental. That her lack of virtue wasn't his responsibility. But that sounded cruel, so he rephrased it. "You aren't technically bound to go through with it. You're not the rake, after all. It's him who should have married the poor thing."

"But in his absence, I've made a promise to her. A very real promise, that will have very real consequences if I break it. A broken engagement could be the thing that gets her turned out. In *November*. It's bloody cold out there already, Miles, and wet and… You know just what it means if they turn her out, don't you?"

Miles did. He'd written those tales too. His fallen girls did not fare any better than his sodomites. He poured himself a steeper glass while Charlie got up to pace around the flat.

"And I keep thinking: what else could I do? How else could I get her out of this? And all I can come up with is to give her a place to stay…which I can only do if I marry her. It's a damn circle I can't find my way out of."

It was hard to watch, but Miles had to admire Charlie's chivalry. Miles wouldn't bother with the circles, if he were in this situation. He'd have packed his bags already.

He wished Charlie would do the same. But that wasn't looking likely.

"Do you see anything?" Charlie begged. "Anything at all.

What am I missing? How do I get out of this without having this lovely girl's downfall on my conscience?"

"I'm not sure you can, love. Looks to me like someone's getting hurt no matter what happens."

Charlie collapsed onto the desk chair, head in his hands. "Are you writing the story of my life, Miles? Am I in some twisted moral struggle that's going to leave me well-fucked and dead?" He got a very dark look in his eye that Miles did not like, but it passed. "I can't believe this is happening. Everything was working out so well."

Miles didn't have the heart to tell him how close they'd come to having it even better.

"But there's a bright side." Charlie looked up. Something desperate had come over his face. "It's right good protection, it is. A wife who knows the situation, and is alright with it. Jo's in a similar boat. She and The Beast protect each other. I, um." He took a paper out of his pocket. "I haven't shown this to you yet. It's mad, really, but we realized that once our wedding night is passed, her purity won't be expected anymore. So to keep it fair, she's written out this confession. I'm to hang on to it. You know, like...like the calling card. When we met. Even-like."

Miles stared at the wine in his glass. He could not look at Charlie. A single glimpse of the beautiful mouth that had kissed him so rudely that night would undo him entirely.

Charlie went on in a rush. "So, it's not perfect. It's not like we wanted. But it won't be so bad. I can still see you. I'm sure I can stay here, sometimes. I'll get out to the Fox when I can. It will be lovely. Maybe it *will* be perfect, actually." He began to sound a bit hysterical. "You don't want me here all the time anyway, do you? It's bad for your writing. I distract you. Yeah? So it will be better, actually. I don't know why I didn't see that before. It's—"

"Charlie." Miles held a hand out, faintly sick. "Please stop."

He fell silent, but seemed to vibrate in place, like a thousand words were jittering around inside him.

Miles, on the other hand, only had a few. Bad words. Very bad ones. But true.

"Charlie, I told you before. I can't carry on with a married man."

Charlie rolled his eyes so hard his whole head went toward the ceiling. "Right, yeah, but you didn't really *mean* that."

Miles froze. "What?"

"You were just stressed about the visit from my parents," Charlie said, steady as anything, like he really believed what he was saying. "You said it, sure, but it was the fear talking."

"Are you serious?" said Miles slowly, hardly able to believe his ears. "Of course I meant it. Do you honestly think I would say something like that if I didn't mean it?"

Charlie faltered, but scraped himself up enough to snap, "Well, that was before!"

Miles couldn't deny that. He'd had no idea, then, what Charlie might come to mean to him. Still. He examined the notion again and found that it was still true. Maybe truer. The thought of some shadowy half-thing with this man he adored so desperately was excruciating. "I'm sorry, Charlie."

"Bollocks!" Charlie was on his feet. "Don't you give me that, Miles. I'm not a 'married man.' I'm Charlie. *Your* Charlie. You've wrapped me round your damn finger too tight to just shake me off now, mate. And you know it. You love me. You said you did."

"Oh, and are you sure I *meant it?*"

"Come on, Miles."

It was incredible that not an hour ago, he wanted nothing more than to see Charlie's face. Now, he still couldn't bring himself to look. Even what he could see at the fringes was too much. He took his specs off and pressed his hands to his eyes.

"I do love you, Charlie. Of course I do."

"Then drop all this nonsense. We'll carry on. We have to." He rushed over. He took Miles's wrists, guided his hands down. Miles kept his eyes closed. "Look at me, love. Please. I can't bear this. What's your alternative anyway? You break it off with me over some stupid little rule you made up, and then what? Back to your bookshop? *Alone?*"

"I'm selling the bloody bookshop!" Miles stood sharply, nearly toppling his chair. He felt he towered over poor Charlie, especially as the words sank in. "That's what Smithy and I were talking about, you stupid idiot. It was him who wanted it all along. My own publisher. I decided I could live with that. Had to live with that, if I wanted a life worth going on with. I trust him, and I had you, so was going to make Smithy pay it all off for you. Tack whatever you owe onto a reasonable price for the place. Start fresh."

"M-Miles—"

"But no. You've gone and traded out my beautiful devil for a knight of the sodding Round Table now, saving your swooning little maiden and telling me that everything is going to be perfect. Well, it's not. It's not perfect. It's not even alright. It's bloody terrible, is what it is." Miles put his hands on either side of Charlie's face, finally looking into eyes so scared and despairing that he might not have recognized them if those things hadn't been hiding behind the light this whole time. "And you know it, Charlie. You knew it before you even met me."

"Piss off," Charlie hissed. But he didn't storm away. Didn't move at all except to reach up and clutch one of Miles's wrists.

Miles squeezed his eyes shut again and brought his mouth down to Charlie's. He did not expect a response, but he got one. A ferocious one. Charlie kissed him like he intended to solve everything with his tongue; if his words couldn't do it, surely this would.

When they came apart, Miles said, "I understand why you have to do this. I really do."

"Then why are you punishing me for it?"

"Christ, Charlie."

"I mean it. I'm trying to save a girl's life."

"Then save it. It's a noble thing, it really is. But you can't go back to pretending it's not at your own expense. If you don't come to grips with what you're giving up, then by the time reality catches you, it's going to have grown into a terrifying beast."

Miles could see by the way Charlie's shoulders dropped that he knew full well what Miles meant. But he wouldn't give it up. He ran his hands down Miles's body until he clung to the band of his trousers with his fingertips. "See me sometimes, then," he whispered. "Just every so often. You can remind me what I'm missing."

He dipped a hand lower, but Miles caught his wrist and stopped him. "I will not be party to your destruction, Charlie. Not more than I already have." It looked like Charlie would keep arguing until sunrise, so Miles kissed him before he could get another word in and bowled right over whatever he might say next. "Can we please just enjoy the time we have left? Ten days. That's something."

Charlie broke at last. It was horrible to watch. He wrapped his arms around his stomach and looked at the floor in horror, like he could at last see all the shattered bits of himself that crunched under his feet. The silence lasted an age. Then he shook his head. "If it's done, it's done. I can't bear to drag it out."

Miles should have taken his awful victory and run with it,

but he wasn't that strong. He pulled Charlie in close. "One night, then."

"No. I'm leaving, and I never want to see you again. Never."

The sentiment must have been as hollow as the words themselves, because Charlie didn't move.

Miles went over to the table. He downed the rest of his wine in one go. It wasn't enough, so he took another pull right from the bottle. He passed it to Charlie, who did the same. They finished it off that way, back and forth a few times. It was a lovely and expensive vintage. Miles didn't taste a drop of it. It served only to help him get Charlie into the bedroom without completely falling to pieces.

Chapter Twenty-One

Charlie

Charlie would have submitted to absolutely anything Miles wanted. Anything. He didn't care. He was ready to be thrown on the bed, birched and bitten until he bled, tied down and done over with nothing but spit and a prayer. He was headed for a Reginald Cox ending, after all; he at least ought to get a Reginald Cox fucking, first.

But Miles was so much crueler than that.

All he did was lie down beside Charlie on the bed, face-to-face, and begin undoing his clothes with unbearable slowness. One button and then another. A kiss. And then another button. Just like that, on and on. Charlie wanted to scream. His waistcoat came off, but there were more bloody buttons on his shirt. One by one. As his skin was revealed, Miles pressed his mouth to him, tasting inch by inch. When he'd finally gotten Charlie out of his shirt, he grabbed his hands and put them on his own buttons. *Your turn.*

Wishing he was ripping the fabric to shreds instead, Charlie mimicked what Miles had done.

By the time he was running his tongue toward Miles's navel, the resentment was fading. He finally understood what they were doing. They were supposed to spend their lives together. Since they had just one night, now, they'd have to make it last the rest of their lives. Miles was right. It had to be like this. It was this or nothing. This or...he couldn't even think about it. Instead, he slowly slid his hands along Miles's warm skin, his chest and belly, shoulders and back, memorizing every inch. Or so he hoped.

Miles coaxed him upward. Face-to-face again, pressed together. Miles stared into his eyes. This gruff, lonely creature who'd been so closed off was wide open now, his expression of adoration unguarded and honest. No one would ever look at Charlie like that again. He knew it. Who else could? Circumstance had shaped them for each other, each chipped and bent in just the right spots for the other to fit perfectly. Parting wouldn't change that; instead, all those empty bits would just stay empty.

They tangled themselves in each other so tightly that Charlie began to lose track of where he ended and Miles began. For some indefinable, pulsing span of time, they just hovered like that, kissing, moving gently against each other as if in a dream. All the bad began to fade, replaced with a hazy sort of pleasure that did not confine itself to any one part of him. His fingertips digging into Miles's back, his tongue sliding slowly into Miles's warm and responsive mouth, every searing spot where his love's lips pressed against him. The longer they went on, the more unbearably delicious each little bit of contact became. He did not even wonder if Miles felt the same. He could see it on his face. He could feel it in every movement. They were deep in this dream together.

There was little urgency, because they didn't want it to end. It built and moved along of its own accord. They slid the rest of their clothes off and clung still more tightly, every lazy little stroke starting to feel like lightning. Everything else had melted away, was gone forever, and thank God for that.

At some point, Miles got into his nightstand for the oil

he'd started keeping in there again with the expectation that his bed would be occupied. He spread Charlie's legs and carefully coaxed him open, every slicked movement just as surreal as everything else. Once the sensations were both inside and out, Charlie finally forgot. He forgot it was the last time, because there was no time. Time had died. They could be here forever, Miles could hide away inside of him, perfectly still, and they'd never have to face anything ever again. Miles started moving, rocking into him more slowly even than the buttons, and it felt like they'd die together, didn't it? Right to heaven, both of them.

Very suddenly, Miles's fingers dug into Charlie's shoulders. Charlie stilled his own hips, tried to keep it from happening, but Miles had had all the heaven he could handle. His kiss lost its rhythm, his eyes rolled back, and he came apart while Charlie held all the little pieces of him together as tightly as he could.

Miles did not insist that Charlie return to earth with him. He kept it going. He went on stroking and sucking and saying nothing, nothing at all. But reality was coming closer. If it really were the heaven it promised to be, he'd dive in, but it wasn't. He knew what was on the other side and wanted nothing to do with it.

He held back as long as he could, but there was nothing for it. He came to a soul-wrenching crisis in Miles's mouth. It was painful. It was beautiful. It was heaven after all.

And then it was over.

They lay together for a while. Neither could bring himself to speak. Charlie was not convinced he'd ever want to speak again. Eventually, Miles got up and brought Charlie a towel, because life went on, didn't it? In his other hand was something Charlie had never seen Miles use before: a bottle of laudanum. He put a good number of drops on his tongue, then left the bottle on the bedside and came back under the covers.

Charlie didn't blame him, but didn't take any himself. Miles soon drifted off, mumbling incoherently about all the stars he could see in Charlie's eyes.

Soon after, Charlie dressed and tucked the quilts around Miles nice and tight. It was cold in here again. Hopefully he'd take better rooms when the shop was sold. He closed the bedroom door quietly behind him.

As he got his coat off the chair he'd flung it on, his eyes fell to the desk. After a moment's hesitation, he carefully opened the drawer to find pages covered in Miles's scrawl.

The new manuscript was coming along better than Miles had insinuated. It was a nice, thick stack by now, every page covered in script and scratch-outs. Knowing that Miles was well off in dreamland, he lit the candles and put the pages on the desk.

And he'd have sat reading it if he hadn't discovered something under the manuscript. A button. It was Charlie's. The one that had popped off, weeks ago now. Miles must have found it. He must have kept it. Because Miles was Miles, he must have hidden it away and never mentioned it. A stupid little button, not even anything pretty or interesting. Not a peacock feather. Not a jeweled ring or a silk ribbon. The plainest little shirt button, usually covered by the rest of his clothes, now sharing space with something as private and beloved as a manuscript, simply because it had once been Charlie's.

He put the button and the pages back and blew out the candles. He couldn't read it. Not here. No. He couldn't stay here another moment.

He closed the drawer, then changed his mind and opened it again. He did not take all the pages, but he did fold a few up.

When he returned home, he climbed the deserted stairs to

the second floor. He didn't encounter Quincy. He encountered nothing he cared about at all, in fact. The runner in the hallway he hadn't chosen. A few paintings and sconces on the walls that meant nothing to him. He felt like an intruder here, in his own silent, perfectly kept home. He walked on tiptoes, though he wasn't sure why. There was no one to hear him. Not even a single ghost in this soulless place.

In the library, he lit a few candles and took out the trunk that held his collection. Inside, he found everything stacked just the way he'd left it, the books, the artwork, the woodprints.

He opened the book he'd left right on top. The signature on the cover page was surreal. He swirled his finger across the ugly curves of it. He took the pages he'd stolen out of his pocket and spread them out over the signed one. Between the dim light, the terrible penmanship, and the sudden blurriness in his own eyes, he could hardly read it. He pushed on, though, through a lengthy description of the beautiful aristocrat, the nervous knots in the main character's chest, the gnawing lust for the man that he mistook for lust to climb beyond his status. It was very Cox. It was very Miles. And the last paragraph was very ruined by a series of drops that escaped Charlie's lashes to splash against the blue ink and melt it.

Charlie closed the book with the handwritten pages inside. He closed the trunk and locked it. He put his forehead down on the wooden top.

He could go back. It wasn't too late. Miles hadn't turned him out, after all; Charlie had chosen this. This misery was of his own making. If he could just convince himself that Alma would be alright. Or that he didn't care either way. If he could convince himself that he really was the devil he wanted to be, the devil the world thought him to be anyway, then he could be it.

But it had gotten all tangled in his mind, now. All Alma had done was trust the wrong person. Same as Ethan Murray. If he'd abandon Alma, who's to say he wouldn't have abandoned Ethan too? If he were the sort to do that, what would he do to Miles, should things go wrong? And things could go wrong. Things did go wrong, and there wasn't always an escape alley big enough for everyone.

He wanted Miles to be with someone who'd rather start desperately digging a new route than leave him behind. If Charlie left Alma, he wouldn't be that person. He wouldn't trust himself do to right by Miles, either. Or anyone.

Another circle. No way out.

No way out, but he knew the way through. Life marched ever forward, as Pop always said. Forward was the only way, even if it took him around and around and around. Anything was better than sitting down in the middle of the hoop and giving up.

He sat up. He ran a hand over the smooth wooden top of the trunk. His lovely collection. He still had that, at least, and better than ever with the addition of stolen draft pages. In fact, with his wife in the know and so determinedly in charge of the library, perhaps he wouldn't have to put it out of the house after all. Maybe someday, years from now, she'd even want to read them. They'd find their little pleasures together.

They'd make the best of it.

From that moment on, time remained very wonky. The rest of the night lasted about ten years, while the next ten days lasted only a minute.

Fortunately, he was kept busy. The wedding was to be held at the Merriweathers' parish just outside of London, so his entire family came down from Manchester to visit for the week ahead of it. Charlie and Alma's little house wasn't large enough for the lot of them, so they stayed with the Merriweathers. Charlie stayed as well, because his mother begged him to, and because if he had to live in his own house alone with Quincy for a week, he'd set the whole thing on fire.

So, he passed his last few days of freedom surrounded by people in very high spirits. He bought about a hundred toys for the children, and spent hours doing whatever odd games and tasks they requested, happy to let them do the thinking for him. His sisters-in-law laughed and said he ought to save it for when his own came along soon enough. In the evenings, his brothers were more than happy to get him good and drunk on their own dime. They could be a little tiresome, and Charlie did not always understand their humor, but it wasn't nearly so bad as he would have guessed. He ate chocolates with his mother and played chess with Alma. He stayed busy, distracted, facing forward, forward, forward.

Until, two nights before the wedding, Pop had one of the footmen call him into the parlor for a cigar.

He didn't appreciate the interruption. He, Alma, and the kids were in the nursery that the Merriweathers kept nice for their legitimate grandchildren, putting the finishing touches on a block castle that had so many windows and doorways to let the light in that it was a wonder it could stand at all.

Charlie, who was on his belly on the woven rug, placing a tricky arch on one of the walls, glanced up at the footman. He hesitated long enough that the children decided they were within their rights to protest his departure, giving off a disharmonious chorus of complaint that Alma tried to shush.

"Go on, Charlie." She rubbed his back, giving him a half smile of encouragement. "We'll get it finished."

He strongly considered refusal. Men, however, could not put off summonses from their fathers so they could build block castles, a fact that was very apparent on the footman's face when Charlie did not jump directly to his feet.

"You lot won't knock it down without me?" he said.

The two older ones reassured him, though the youngest seemed to get excited to hear the words *knock it down*. Alma pulled him into her lap just in time. "I'll stand guard. Don't worry."

Charlie got up and stepped carefully around the castle, anger bubbling up in him as he followed the footman to the parlor. When he got there, he found his father sitting by the fire in his waistcoat with a brandy decanter and a box of those cigars that Warren liked.

Pop seemed to guess his mood. He cut and lit one for Charlie and passed it over without a word. Charlie took it just as silently, turned his back, and stood puffing it near the fireplace tools.

After a while, Pop cleared his throat. "You could sit down."

"And you could let me enjoy the enjoyable parts of my circumstances here." He spun around, glaring daggers. "Tell me, Pop. Did you call me in here to admit what you've done to me and Alma? Because if not, I'm not interested in what you have to say." He blew a mouthful of smoke out slowly. "Even if you did, I think it might be too little too late."

He wasn't sure what he'd been expecting from the outburst, mostly because he hadn't meant to say it at all. Whatever he'd expected, his father surprised him by leaning over and putting his head in his hands.

"I'm sorry, Charlie," he said to the floor. "I know this isn't what you want, but—"

"Isn't what I want?" Charlie repeated with an eyebrow up. "Pop, it's *blackmail*."

Pop's face went very sharp. "Stop being ridiculous."

"I'm not being ridiculous. You and the Merriweathers have

bloody blackmailed each other, and somehow turned me and Alma into both your victims and your conspirators." He went to the table beside his father and tapped ash into the ceramic tray. "Please, at least promise me it didn't have anything to do with business. That no one's profiting off this sham."

"Is that really what you think of me?" Pop sounded genuinely wounded.

Charlie tapped a little more ash even though there was hardly any left. "No," he muttered. "No, I suppose not."

"We were worried about you," Pop went on. "You were getting yourself in trouble again and again. I didn't know what else to do."

"You could have tried talking to me."

"I might have," he said evenly, taking a sip of brandy to buy a little time. The crackles and snaps of the fire seemed very loud in the silent gathering of thoughts. "Perhaps I should have. But I didn't know how. I suspected there were things you wouldn't want to tell me, and that, quite frankly, I wouldn't want to know."

"Of course. So instead of talking to me, you shared those suspicions with *George Merriweather*. How sensible of you."

"He can't hurt you, Charlie. I made sure of that."

"Yeah, by blackmailing his daughter."

Pop leaned his head back on his chair and closed his eyes. He did not do well with unpleasantness. None of them did. It was how they'd gotten rich, in fact, turning pennies into pounds through optimistic speculation, forward thinking, and a habit of squeezing every ounce of goodness from whatever was in their pockets. The Prices simply didn't dwell on past failures. They put on a smile and marched forward, confident that they could make the most of what they had.

But Charlie couldn't smile his way through this anymore. Not when *what he had* no longer included Miles Montague.

"It's not an even arrangement, you know," Pop whispered, his light eyes almost desperate for Charlie to understand his intentions. "I have no proof you've done anything wrong. Merriweather thinks I do, but I don't. If I did, I would have destroyed it immediately. I have no interest in seeing my own son dragged through the mud over stupid follies, Charlie. You have to believe me. I wouldn't have taken the risk of this if her shame weren't so much greater and more apparent. Does that make you feel any better about what I did to protect you?"

Charlie felt his face twist unpleasantly. He stubbed out his cigar and left it on the tray.

"It might make some blokes feel better, I suppose." As for himself, it made him feel like he'd swallowed hot coals. "And I can see that it makes you and Mum feel better. Forgive me if I don't thank you, but I can admit that I understand your rationale."

"Charlie—"

"I think I'd like to go change for dinner."

With that, he opened the cigar box and scooped out a handful. He turned and started toward the door.

"Charlie, what are you doing with those?" Pop asked. "The Merriweathers will pitch a fit if you smoke outside the parlor."

"Oh, these?" Charlie held them out. "I thought I'd go ahead and have you pay off *all* my debts while we're at it. I've been nicking this same kind from my chum at the molly house for months."

Pop stared. "Are you just saying that to get a reaction out of me?"

"Oh," Charlie said slowly. "So *now* you want to talk."

He put one of the cigars between his teeth, raised his eyebrows, and walked out.

He knew he was lucky to be able to do that. Alma couldn't. Ethan had failed miserably at it. But Charlie could, and so he did. His father would move forward from it. He'd probably even find the bright side of it by Christmas.

The first thing he did was return to his room. He tucked the cigars away for the next time he saw Warren, then found Alma's letter of confession hidden among his things. He felt like an arse for having brought it along *just in case*, but was suddenly glad he had. He glanced at the damning evidence of her ruin one more time, then ripped it to shreds and scattered the pieces in with the fireplace ashes. Charlie had never been and would never be a blackmailer. Ever. If Alma decided to do him in, he'd simply have to hope scarlet fever stayed out of the jail.

Once that was complete, he went back to the nursery, where the children and their nurse were putting the blocks back in the box.

For a moment, he didn't see Alma among them, but then he found her. She was sitting in the rocking chair, looking wistful and a little red-faced as she watched the littlest one toddling about.

When she spotted Charlie, she wiped her eyes quickly, got up, and joined him in the hallway.

"They knocked it down," she said lightly. "I tried my very best to secure the walls, but it was to no avail."

"Thanks, dove," he said, voice a little weaker and quieter than he'd have liked.

She took his hand, smiling sadly as if she knew just how his conversation must have gone. He gave her one back, for the child who was missing from this nursery.

"So," Alma said at last. "I heard that Cook has made some incredible little honey cakes for after dinner. Shall we go see if we can steal a few ahead of time?"

He couldn't seem to speak, but he did squeeze her hand and kiss her cheek before setting off with her down the corridor.

★ ★ ★

The morning of the wedding, Charlie woke with dread claw-ing at the very pit of his stomach that did not let up enough for him to eat anything at all.

Time still wasn't quite right. Though he woke with hours to go before the ceremony, the clock seemed to spin madly. Before he could blink, friends and close family members had begun to arrive at the Merriweathers' house to get the wed-ding party prettied up and well plied with champagne before they all went over to the church to finish the job.

He got dressed in a daze with some help from a valet and very unhelpful ribbing from his brothers. Champagne with no food to soak it up was turning his stomach, well at odds with the dapper suit his mother had helped him select. His reflec-tion looked very good by the time all was said and done—simple and a bit somber—but handsome. Within the costume, though, he was shaking and could hardly breathe.

Once he'd been deemed suitable for the altar, his brothers patted him on the shoulder and gave him a moment to collect himself, vanishing in search of more champagne.

He fell into a chair the second he was alone.

He glanced at the clock. Jo should be here soon. He'd got-ten in touch with her through Forester early in the week, and she promised to come visit him before it was done, to hold a basin for him, should he need it.

He might.

At last, there came a quiet knock. Charlie leaped up. Thank God.

Behind the door, however, he did not find Jo.

It was Miles.

Charlie's heart stopped. He thought for a moment that it must be a hallucination; his brothers must have slipped some-thing mad into his champagne flute.

Miles had tried to tame his hair, and wore formal clothes, all black and white. He held a narrow package in his hands. He looked like a dream.

"What are you doing here?" Charlie whispered. "Who let you in?"

Miles held out the package. It was obviously a bottle of wine. "I simply wanted to send my regards to the happy couple. And check on, you know, the wine delivery. As your sommelier. Mrs. Merriweather had a few complaints, which I will be sure to take up with the suppliers, but I wanted to speak with the groom as well. Has everything gone as anticipated?"

Charlie dragged him inside, then shut and locked the door behind them. He whipped around, tails flying about his knees. "Everything is lovely, thank you. Now will you please go? I thought you wanted nothing to do with a married man."

"I've still got an hour, haven't I? Open your present."

Charlie glared, then did as directed. "Surprise," he said dully as the bottle was revealed.

"It's the same one I taught you tasting from. You seemed to like it."

He would not be charmed. He would *not* be. "Thanks, mate. This will help me out tonight, that's for sure."

Miles looked surprised. "Oh. Are you going to...? Considering the circumstances, I wasn't—"

"Yeah, I don't know." Charlie shrugged like nothing mattered and set the bottle down on the dresser. He adjusted it so it was facing perfectly outward. "We thought it might be a bit of a lark to give it a go. Might as well. I've never finished the job in a cunny, but I do know my way around a bit better than my father gives me credit for. I assume you have, haven't you?"

"Charlie."

"Yes?"

"I absolutely did not drag my arse over here to have this conversation."

"My apologies. I've been with my brothers all week."

Charlie watched him out of the corner of his eye. There was an unbearable silence.

Miles was the one to break it.

"You have to call this off, Charlie." His eyes were wide, voice low. "I'm sorry. I'm sorry to come here and do this, but you can't go through with it, love. You can't."

Charlie stepped back a few panicked paces. "It's too late for that."

"Charlie, please." He reached out, but seemed to think better of it. "I love you. I know it's selfish, but I'm going to hell anyway, aren't I? Leave her to it. I'll give her some money, that will start her off right. I got plenty from Smithy. I'll give it all to her, if you want. Every penny. Just…" He dropped off, his entire demeanor deflating as he realized that Charlie was not relaxing into his pleas. Was not swayed. Was, in fact, growing tenser with every word. "I'm leaving, Charlie."

That was not what he'd expected. He swayed a bit, those blasted bubbles rolling about in his belly again. "Where?"

"Anywhere?" He laughed anxiously. "I've sold the shop, love. It's in good hands now, better than mine. I can go anywhere, and I find I very much don't want to go back to the flat. Ethan isn't actually haunting it, after all; he's moved on. I have to as well. I've got a good deal of money, two books in the pipe, and nothing holding me here. So, I'm leaving."

Charlie had never felt more trapped in his life, hearing him say that. The words clanged and clicked like another padlock. "I'm, uh, glad Smithy could do that for you."

"Smithy didn't do it," Miles growled, like it was the most obvious thing in the world. "Two months ago, I'd have told him to fuck himself silly if he tried to buy the shop off me. I agreed because I had something to look forward to for once. I could *see* the future, really look at it for the first time in… And when you left, I considered calling the whole thing off, but it seems you didn't take that future with you. I can still see it. And I'm going to go for it. I've wanted to go back to Paris for a while now. Thought I'd start there. Maybe stay until I finish this book, and then… I don't know. All I know is that the future looks much better with you in it than without. I want you to come with me, Charlie. Today. Now."

Chapter Twenty-Two

Miles

Charlie couldn't seem to stay upright. He fell back into his chair, head in his hands.

Miles approached him carefully. He hated to do this, wished almost that he hadn't. But he'd spent the morning finalizing things in Smithy's office, getting the transfer of the shop all together under the watchful eyes of the ladies on his walls. It was done. And it was glorious, to be free after all this time. To let some of the past rest peacefully, while he did what Ethan would have wanted him to do years ago.

But he didn't want to do it alone. He would. He certainly would. But if he didn't have to…

"Charlie?"

"I can't, Miles!" His teeth clenched tight around his hissing words as he turned back to stare daggers right into Miles's heart. "My God, why don't you understand that yet?"

"You don't have to, though. No one can force you—"

"I'm sorry that I've got more principles than you do!" Charlie caught his voice rising, and looked nervously at the door before continuing at a lower pitch. "I'm not being sarcastic. I'm actually sorry. Principles are shit, aren't they? I want to be your devil more than anything, but you don't really want a devil. You only think you do. If I walk away now, you'll

never unsee it. You'll know forever what sort I am. Fact is…"
He squeezed his beautiful eyes shut, hiding them from view.
"The fact is, I shouldn't have agreed to marry her. I shouldn't
have asked my father for help. I shouldn't have gotten into
the situation in the first place, because I'd been in it before,
and I knew better, and I still did it again. I've made this bed,
Miles. I've made it up nice and smooth with the best linens I
can't afford. And then I let my parents drag this innocent girl
into it. If I go with you now, if I leave her there, then it will
be you who gets dragged into my next mess. And left there."

Miles didn't care. He didn't care about messes. He didn't
care about principles or regrets. All he wanted was to pull
Charlie to him and *take him*. Just take him. Like the monsters
who lived in his head did, when they couldn't get who they
wanted in any other way.

But obviously, that would work out about as well as it did
in the books.

And that's just what Charlie was saying, wasn't it? If he had
to be a monster to get what he wanted, then he wasn't worth
what he wanted to begin with.

From the moment he'd accepted that Charlie was a fan of
his work, he'd questioned what a man like him could get out
of books like those. No longer. He understood them deeply,
maybe deeper than Miles himself did. He'd written the damn
things word by word, and yet somehow, he'd unquestioningly
assumed it was the desire itself that started the characters on
their path to monstrosity. But that was moralist bollocks, wasn't
it? The desire was incidental. It was what they did to get it
that ruined them in the end. Each and every one.

"You did read them, didn't you?" said Miles.

"Until the spines needed regluing."

Charlie couldn't seem to muster the smile, but he was so
irresistible that he hardly had to. Miles desperately wanted

to take everything back. To stay. To say they could carry on after all, in whatever form they could. Give him anything he wanted.

But Miles had tasted the future, now. He didn't have it in him to keep clinging to things that had ended, however beloved they were.

He put his hands in his pockets, defeated. He had Charlie's lost button in one of them, which he flipped over and over. Seemed that was all he got to keep. "I wish you and Alma the best, Charlie."

"Thank you," Charlie said into his hands. "Now will you leave?"

"I have one more question."

"Always one more sodding question."

Miles kept running his fingers over the button to avoid touching its former owner. He wouldn't be doing that again. But perhaps there was something… "My pages—"

"You can have them back. I'm sorry."

"I don't want them back. I want to know if that's the last you want of my work. Or will you keep reading my books, when I put them out?"

Charlie was quiet for a long moment. At last, he nodded.

And so did Miles, quietly resolving himself to this disappointing farewell. "I'll write them to you, then. Just remember that, alright? When you read them. They're for you. Every depraved word. Forever."

"That seems a bit dangerous," Charlie muttered. "What about Ethan? I don't want a jealous ghost after me."

"Stop projecting your own jealousy onto the dearly departed," said Miles. "Ethan already got my Dickens phase. Trust me, he won't be wanting anything else after that."

Charlie laughed, such a rough sound that it might have been half sob.

And then there was nothing. Charlie did not move or speak again. Practically a statue of a groom, perfect but for his defeated posture.

Miles carefully left. He leaned against the door when he shut it behind him. He had to gather himself up to be the unconcerned sommelier until he could escape this place. This country. This entire phase of his life. Starting fresh. That was it. He'd go off, wherever he wanted.

And he'd find someone to share it with eventually. Someone happy, with brown eyes and a lovely, filthy mouth. He might be spoiled for anything less.

"Didn't expect to see you here. You actually care for this prat, don't you?"

Miles's eyes shot open. A woman stood before him, a brunette with a heart-shaped face.

He knew her. Twice over, he knew her.

"*Miss Jo?*"

She put a finger to his lips, then patted his cheek. "It's Jenny today."

He stared. She was dressed as a lady. Her hair was long, her gloves dainty.

And yet.

"I know where I've seen you," he said slowly, as the recognition finally took shape.

"Is that so?"

He thought back…yes. Yes, that was it. He'd just seen her again today, hadn't he? All morning those eyes had watched his negotiations. "The picture. There's a picture of you in Smithy's office. A big one. Dressed…" He waved his hand up and down. "Not like this. Or like you were at the Fox. Dressed…not a lot."

She smiled wistfully, eyes drifting to the ceiling like she was reliving some highly interesting memory. "Yes, I've had some silly times in this life, I admit. That was a particularly embarrassing phase."

"Smithy calls you his—"

"Wifey?" She groaned. "Awful, isn't it? Don't you just want to strangle him sometimes?"

"*Are you*? Married to *Smithy*? *He's* The Beast?"

"Under God, I suppose," she admitted with a hearty roll of the eyes. "If you care about that sort of thing."

Miles reeled. He hadn't realized Smithy was married at all. What girl in her right mind would marry *him*?

Jo (or Jenny Smith?) seemed to read his mind. "What can I say, Mr. Montague? We all make mistakes. Mine's worked out for me fairly well, though, all things considered."

Something else occurred to him. "Luck of the Irish?"

Her grin was wicked. "On me dad's side only."

"O'Donnell, perhaps? Jenny O'Donnell. J.O."

"Hush that whore mouth, that's between you and me. Even Charlie doesn't know my full name."

"Are you the 'man' Smithy put in charge of the shop? The one he had me write up guidelines for this morning?"

"He said he put a man in charge? Bugger him! Can't admit he's put a woman up to something even when it's his own wife. That fuckster. Don't worry, I'll kill him. I have to kill him at least twice a week anyway."

"What are you doing here? Mrs. Smith?" Miles asked. The name felt wrong. Jo seemed to like how awkward it sounded.

"Charlie invited me. I never wanted him to see me like this, but I couldn't tell him no. How could his best mate miss the happiest fucking day of his life?" Her demeanor grew a bit more serious. "How is he?"

"Just awful."

"Yeah, that's what I thought." She glanced around him down the hall. "Now, if you'll excuse me. I need to go talk some sense into someone. Do you know where the bride might be?"

Confused, Miles pointed back at the door he'd just come through.

"You silly bugger; you're so cute." Jo laughed and patted his cheek again, rather harder than necessary. "I meant the other bride."

Chapter Twenty-Three

Charlie

The organ music in the church was very expertly played. Everyone was beautifully outfitted, from Charlie's lovely mother in the very front row all the way back to the most distant acquaintances of the Merriweathers. The flower arrangements and ribbons on the sides of the pews were also very prettily crafted and smelled perfectly wonderful...

Charlie stood in his place at the front of the church while the priest went on about something or other. There were a lot of lovely things, but his usual habit of noticing and counting them was of no interest. He couldn't focus on any of that, because he was not really here, in the church, standing in front of his entire family; he was still in the Merriweathers' spare bedroom, listening to Miles tell him over and over that he was leaving England.

The reading or whatever it was finished, and the music swelled dramatically. The sound of it shook him into the present. Alma was about to walk down that aisle. She would be smiling, but she would know full well what she was getting into. He hoped he would be able to find a smile for her in return.

The moment lasted a painfully long time, the music going

on, everyone up and staring expectantly at the back door of the church.

It kept going, those seconds of waiting. Time really hadn't come back to itself since his last night with Miles. Miles who was leaving England. Who'd been able to sort out his own joys and miseries so that he could now live however he pleased.

Miles Montague, whom he would go back to knowing only through the well-worn pages of Reginald Cox.

He wanted to put it from his mind, but he would not. He would think about what he'd just given up. He'd chosen this. And just because he could make the most of it didn't mean nothing had been lost. He would go into this with his eyes open, even if it felt like staring into the bloody sun. Once Alma came out, he would continue staring into it with every little step she took down that aisle.

On and on the moment went, as everyone waited for Alma.

And on.

And…on?

Whispers began to break out among the pews. The music was growing repetitive. He felt a hand on his shoulder, his eldest brother, whose usually jolly face was now stark with concern. In the front row, there was quite a lot of hissing between all the parents. Charlie's mother and Mrs. Merriweather all but raced one another to the back door, while the whispers around them became louder mutterings and a few nervous titters. One of his little nieces said, full voiced, "Where's Miss Alma?" and was quickly hushed.

It occurred to Charlie to worry about Alma, but they'd all arrived at the church. What harm could have befallen her in that time?

With the mothers still gone, some people began to sit back down. It was all very awkward and embarrassing, standing up there while everyone looked from the back door to Charlie's face and whispered on, their tone fading from confusion to pity.

The music became quieter. The priest said something to calm the families down, and might have even said something to Charlie, but he didn't hear it.

Where was she?

The back door opened. Every face in the church whipped around, but it was just Charlie's mother. She crooked a single finger at him.

He was frozen to the spot, but his brother took him around the shoulders and led him toward her. Everyone watched the groom walking up the aisle, rather than the bride walking down it.

It was chaos behind that closed door. Mrs. Merriweather was screaming at one of Alma's handmaidens, while another of her daughters tried to calm her down. The other girls Alma had along with her were hurriedly comparing their searches of the church, all with the same conclusion: *I can't find her anywhere.*

"Charlie!" Mum, who was dressed in a violet as shocking as Charlie had threatened for his own suit, came up and took his hands. Her dark eyes were horrified, at odds with a tug of clearly inappropriate amusement at the corner of her mouth. "Charlie, she's left."

"Left?" Charlie echoed. He didn't know what to make of that. He was not as pleased as he might have been. Alma didn't have any option but to marry him. How could she leave? Where had she gone?

His bewilderment was interrupted by a small explosion as Mrs. Merriweather rounded on him.

"You!" She pointed her angry finger at his nose. She was red-faced and more miserable than ever. "What did you do?"

"Nothing!" His response was automatic, but he did start

running back through their last interactions. *Had* he done something? "Last I spoke to her, everything was fine."

"Well, it's obviously not fine! You...you..." She imploded, eyes full of fire. Her voice was a harsh whisper when she spoke again. "I told George this was a bad idea. That you both ought to be done with properly, instead of this ridiculous—"

Charlie's mother stepped right in front of him. "Done with properly?" she said loudly enough to catch everyone else's attention. "Care to elaborate on that, Prudence? Do you have something you want to share with us about Alma? Or perhaps you'd like to slander the good name of the Manchester Prices? Go on. What was it you wanted to say? Because I'm not sure I've caught on yet."

Mrs. Merriweather looked fit to burst. As they went on arguing, Charlie felt his brother's hand on his shoulder again, steering him firmly away. "Let's get a bit of air, yeah?"

They went out to the front of the church. The air they got was thick and chilly. Charlie was just in his suit with no coat or scarf to catch the snowflakes that the cold had made of the morning's rain.

As they came down the wide steps, which were all twisted around with green boughs and pink ribbons like it was Christmastime already, a slim, handsomely dressed man approached Charlie and his brother with a friendly wave.

"Hello there!" the fellow said. As he got closer, Charlie recognized him.

It was Miles's publisher. Mr. Smith.

"Who are you?" Charlie's brother asked.

"A humble neighbor," Mr. Smith said with a little bow. "It's up and down the street that someone's misplaced their blushing bride. That's you, I expect?" He gestured sweepingly toward Charlie. "I happen to be in possession of a very fine coach, with a coachman who knows every nook and cranny of the neighborhood. I'd be happy to share this blessing of mine with the groom, should he wish to move as quickly as possible to search the streets for his beloved."

He gestured to the curb, where a fine coach indeed had joined the others.

"Yes," Charlie said in a rush. "Yes, let's find her."

His brother looked confused. "Charlie, perhaps we should check with—"

"She could be in trouble." He embraced his brother and patted him on the back. "Thank you, for everything. But I have to find her. Tell everyone I've gone to look for her, and that I'll send word just as soon as I can."

Leaving his confused brother in the swirling snow, he got into the coach with Mr. Smith. The inside was ostentatiously lined in the most ridiculous fabrics and ornaments. They started off down the slushy street, in silence until they'd turned the corner.

"Mr. Smith," said Charlie, "what on earth—?"

"Call me Smithy." Though the smirk never seemed to leave his face, it could apparently still grow wider. "You may also know me as 'The Beast.'"

Charlie was fairly certain that his mind was going to melt out from under his top hat.

"The what?" he whispered. "You're...you... What the devil is going on?"

"All will be explained shortly. Though you must promise me something, Mr. Price."

"What's that?"

Smithy looked sideways at him. "When all is said and done, you must not think differently of Jo. It was very against her nature to forsake her alias to save your silly arse, but she's done it. If you make her regret it, I'll make you regret it. I'd hate that, seeing as my best author loves you so dearly, but that's business. Do we understand each other?"

Charlie wasn't sure he'd go quite that far, but he did understand that it would be a very poor choice to admit that. He nodded, and Smithy-The-Beast seemed very pleased to be making Charlie piss himself.

The coach took them back into London. As they made their way through the city, Charlie began to recognize the route.

They were headed to Morgan & Murray's.

Miles's lonely little flat didn't seem so lonely anymore. It was quite populated, in fact, once Charlie and Smithy arrived. Charlie saw Jo first, sitting near the fire with one of Miles's old books in her lap. She wore a dress, jewelry, and a most girlish sort of hairstyle.

"If you call me butterfly," she said when she saw him, "I'll bloody kill you."

At the table, he found an even stranger sight. Alma sat on one of the dining chairs, dressed full-on in her bridal frock, a perfectly lovely little dream of a girl. He'd dreaded seeing her like this in the church, but he found it rather nice here, in the familiarity of Miles's flat.

Miles... Miles was here too, pouring her a glass of one of his fancy wines, explaining to her where it had come from. "Do be careful," he added in his usual growl. "I recall that your tolerance is quite low, so take very slow sips."

When he turned to hand it to her and saw Charlie in the doorway, he fell silent.

Charlie's heart twisted right up into a knot. He had not expected to see that face again.

"Charlie," Miles said, like he couldn't quite believe it.

Smithy barreled in and stole the glass right out of Miles's hand. "I told you I'd get him, Reg. You really must trust me."

"Can someone please tell me what's happening?" Charlie's voice came out a bit weak.

Alma patted the chair beside her and he gladly took it. "I'm so sorry to have left you standing there, Charlie. I hope it wasn't too dreadful for you."

He still felt very unmoored. "Why did you leave? I thought we had to do it."

"We did," she said. "But just before we left for the church, I was given another opportunity. I should have taken it straightaway to save you the embarrassment, but I couldn't think it through that quickly. I'm sorry."

"What kind of opportunity?"

Jo came over, then. It was surreal to see her dressed this way. To know her husband was in the room with them. She had a whole other self he'd not known about…

No. No, she hadn't. It was all the same Jo. That's what he'd promised to remember, and he would.

Miles took his usual chair by the fire. "I'm rather antsy for the whole story as well. I've only gotten bits and pieces."

He seemed to be trying very hard not to look at Charlie. Charlie, on the other hand, couldn't keep his eyes on anything but Miles. By now, Charlie should have been married. That he was here instead was a dream he kept expecting to wake up from.

"Alright," said Jo. "The jig is up, Paul. We're going to have to tell these poor fools what we've done to them."

Smithy sighed dramatically. "Our conspiracy could not last forever."

"What conspiracy?" Miles snapped.

"To save our friends and acquire a lovely bookshop in the process, of course." Smithy languidly draped himself on the second armchair and sipped the wine with great relish. "Good stuff, this. Anyway, I've been watching you squander your money and spirit away on this place for years, cringing all the while at how poorly you managed it. When my wifey—"

"Business partner," Jo corrected.

"My business partner. When we determined it was a good time to open a storefront in a better neighborhood, I knew I had to have yours. Not only is it a lovely place, but it was for your own good as well. Imagine how much more filth you could write for me if you didn't have this shop eating up your time and energy! It was perfect!"

He waited for Miles to say something, but Miles was doing his impression of a boulder again.

Smithy gave up and went on. "I should say, it *would* have been perfect. If not for you being so unbearably gruff and depressing all the time. You refused to even talk to me about it; I knew you'd never sell it to me if I didn't get a little sunshine into your life. But how? You're too private for me to simply introduce you to someone. I wasn't even entirely sure what sort of someone was *your* sort, though of course I had my suspicions. At a loss, I did what I am never supposed to do: I asked my wifey for a favor. She runs with the Sapphists and the sodomites, after all. Did she know anyone who we might be able to send your way? Perhaps someone appreciative of the illustrious Reginald Cox, so as to have a proper excuse for speaking to you?"

"I told him to bugger himself at first," Jo said. She stood up and crossed the room, stopping to lean on the wall just behind Alma's chair. "Charlie, I knew you liked this writer quite a lot. But I wasn't about to put your name out there. Until the engagement. Once you started scaring me half to death, I decided it might be for the best to see if you two couldn't set each other right."

Smithy lifted his glass. "Cheers to that! It all worked quite a lot better than we expected. Miles was selling me the shop,

Charlie was getting his act together, and it looked like it would all be peachy for everyone. We were feeling like very talented little matchmakers, until I overheard Charlie's unfortunate meltdown."

Charlie's face warmed. "Very sorry about that, Smithy."

"Don't apologize. It's the price I pay for working near artists. We thought the whole sunshine thing was over. We'd still gotten the shop, which was lovely, but it felt rather sad to see you lot end this way. Then a final opportunity presented itself."

Jo turned to Charlie. "You invited me to the Merriweathers' house to see you before the wedding."

"Sure, I did," said Charlie slowly, amazed at how little time had passed since that dreadful hour spent waiting for her in the spare room. "But you never made it. I assumed—"

"If you assumed that the Merriweathers wouldn't allow a strange woman to be seen entering the groom's boudoir, you'd be correct. But that didn't matter. It wasn't you I needed to see anyway. It was Alma."

Alma went very pink indeed as everyone turned to look at her.

One thing about this story still didn't make sense. "Alma, my sweet dove," said Charlie. "What on earth could Joey have said to make you run from the altar?"

Alma glanced at Jo, but Jo nodded her on. "Tell him, pretty thing."

She took a very deep breath. "Well, you see, Charlie, I told you before that when I discovered the sort of man I was to marry, I was terrified. Once we met, I liked you quite a bit, but I still had misgivings. I didn't really understand what I was getting into. So I found the little place where Jo and the other girls go. I stopped in one night, just to take a look around. I knew it wasn't quite the same, but it felt safer than, you know." She lowered her voice to a whisper. "The molly places?"

"You can imagine, she stood out a bit," Jo said. "I was about to turn her out, when she burst into tears and told me why she was there. I sat and talked with her a bit, since I obviously knew just who she was within a few words. At first, I tried to tell her that you're a monster, Charlie. So she'd call it off herself. But she'd had a few to drink by then, which she doesn't handle well. She spilled her whole situation to me. I took back all the monster talk and assured her that you were a lovely man. However, I also told her that life didn't have to be a choice between you, a habit, or a whorehouse. With the right friends, even a ruined girl can have a lovely life. I swore I'd be the right friend to her, if she needed it."

"I told her I'd think about it," Alma squeaked.

Charlie could hardly believe all this, but everyone looked so very sincere. "Jo, why didn't you tell me you'd met Alma?"

"Our discussion was in confidence. I swore I wouldn't, so I didn't. Just as I didn't tell you and Miles who my husband is until the shop was handed over, even if it made me look bad. I'm not Noah, for God's sake; I can keep a secret if I'm asked."

"Anyway, Charlie," said Alma. She took his hand sweetly. "Jo came to me as I was getting dressed. I told everyone she was a dear old friend, and asked for a moment alone. She said she had a place for me, should I choose not to go through with it. A flat. This flat." She waved her other hand around. "She was very honest that it was your lover's flat, and that he was leaving England and would never, ever see you again after the wedding. I wasn't so sure about it, but then she said I could work the bookshop as well. It needs curating and up-keep. And the shelves, well, they're up to the ceiling, aren't they? Like I always wanted."

Charlie put a hand over his mouth so that, perhaps, no one would see how his lips trembled. When he'd pushed all that back, he said, "My library is a bit pathetic, isn't it?"

She laughed. "It was a better option than I ever could have dreamed up for myself. It won't fix everything, but it's safe and..." She glanced at Smithy with an uncharacteristically sly look on her face. "Well, maybe not *entirely* respectable, but what it lacks there, it makes up for by being a lot more fun than a bluestocking home. Besides that, Jo also said you were willing to give up everything to protect me. After she left, I just kept thinking about that. About how good of you it was. And I knew then that it was the best option for you as well. So I left the church with her just as soon as I got a moment to myself. And here we are."

It was almost too much. Charlie was entirely overcome with some jumble of emotions that couldn't possibly be sorted out. "So, Alma," he said. "Are you telling me that you've called the wedding off? For good?"

"Yes, Charlie. I know our families will be disappointed, but yours can't blame you for my actions. And as for mine?" She sighed so heavily that it was nearly a grunt, backed by what must have been years' worth of pent-up rage and frustration. "Who cares what they think, honestly?"

If Charlie had not been so overwhelmed, he might have full-on cheered. "That's the spirit, dove."

"As for me," she went on. "I'm going to be a bookseller, I suppose. Who'd have guessed? You may be whatever you wish. But I do hope we can still be friends. I love you dearly, after all."

He brought her hand to his lips. "I'd be honored to remain in your acquaintance."

His own words made him very suddenly wonder if Miles would want to remain in his. Miles was still a stone on his armchair, silent and unmoving, his eyes deep into the fire. Charlie's mouth went very dry.

Jo reached out a hand and helped Alma to her feet. "Come

on. Shall we tour the shop a bit? Let you see where you'll start your life anew? Paul, you too."

"Me? But I'm so enjoying nipping all of Miles's wine."

Jo looked meaningfully at Charlie and Miles. "Come on."

With rolling eyes and a fresh splash of wine that nearly reached the top of his glass, he joined Jo. Husband and wifey gave each other an interesting little look before following Alma down the stairs.

Once they were gone, Charlie watched Miles watch the fire. It was very quiet, nothing but the crackle of flames and the occasional joyful little word from the shop below.

"Well," said Charlie. "I, er, I suppose I'm not a married man after all."

Miles finally moved, just his eyes, just enough to look at Charlie. "I suppose you aren't."

Charlie couldn't stand it another second. He rushed to Miles and slid right down onto his knees on the hearthrug, his hands gripping Miles's thighs. It was one of his very favorite places, right here, just like this. More home than the entirety of the town house. "I'm sorry. Miles, my darling, I'm so sorry to have put you through all this, I—"

Miles shushed him with a finger. He didn't say anything at all. Just looked back into the flames.

Charlie's soul dropped straight through the floor. "Yeah," he said. "I suppose I ought to leave you be to...to think things through."

He started to stand, but Miles's hand darted out, grabbing the front of his jacket. Finally, Miles looked him right in the eyes. "Charlie."

The breath was knocked right out of him, gripped so tightly, looked at so intensely. "Yes, Miles?"

"If you so much as try to walk out that door," Miles said

slowly, "I swear to God, you won't be able to sit down for a week."

Slowly, as the words soaked in like a sip of tea after a snowstorm, Charlie smiled.

Grin in place, he shook Miles off and stood up. With a cocky wink, he turned toward the door.

He hardly made it a step before Miles bolted up and wrapped his arms around him tight, knocking him off balance but catching him before they stumbled. Kisses spotted the side of his neck, and he leaned his head back against Miles's shoulder, melting into a bliss he'd thought was forever out of reach.

"You've asked for it, you know," Miles growled into his ear. Miles's lips turned up into a smile as he gave Charlie's arse a solid smack to get things started off right. "You can't be angry with me when I give you what you've asked for."

"Miles?" Charlie was so relieved, so completely ecstatic. "Does that mean I can come with you? Wherever it is you're going?"

Miles started undoing the knot around Charlie's neck. "If that's what you want, the invitation is certainly still open."

"It is." Charlie spun around and kissed Miles, grateful for every tiny point of contact. "That's what I want. I want to go with you. Anywhere. Everywhere."

Miles's hands crept up to either side of Charlie's face. No one had ever looked at him before like he was so very precious. And no one ever would again. And that was just fine. In fact, it warmed him to his toes, though he shivered when a kiss was pressed to his forehead.

"Then that's what we'll do, Charlie. You know I can't bear to tell you no."

"Paris first?"

"Naturally. I'll get you appreciating wine yet, just you wait."

"And then where? Spain? Italy? I do love Tuscany, you know. And have you ever been to America? I've not, but I've always wanted to see New York City. And when we eventually come back to England, perhaps we could take a room in—"

He was cut off with a kiss. "That's all lovely. But let's get your debts paid first, shall we? See what we have left before we go spending what we don't have."

Charlie laughed, feeling his face redden. "Fair point. Um. Assuming you still want to help with all that. I'd understand if you've changed your mind. I don't exactly deserve it."

"I will do it once." He put a single finger to Charlie's lips. "But I have no more shops to sell to indulgent publishers, Charlie. I will not be able to do it again."

Charlie nodded, a bit more seriously. "Yeah. Yeah, I've got some habits to break. And I think I'll have to find a new accounting position, whenever we get settled in somewhere." He thought about it a bit. "At least I'll get all the best erotica for free. And you won't make me lock it up." He looked a bit suspicious. "Will you? You won't be too paranoid to let me keep it all around, will you?"

Miles looked like he was struggling a bit, but a moment of consideration and a coaxing look from Charlie made him soften. "You can keep it around. There's probably not any harm in it. Not really."

With a smile so wide he thought it might be permanent, Charlie threw his arms around Miles's neck and held him tight. "I'm so happy," he whispered. "I thought I was happy before, but I think I was wrong."

"You were definitely wrong," said Miles with a little chuckle. "But I'm glad you're happy now."

Charlie leaned back to look him in the eyes, those warm, beautiful eyes that he wanted to see every single day until the sun exploded. "Are you happy, Miles?"

"Yes, Charlie." Miles smiled. Anyone who didn't know him might think he was a sweet, innocent fellow who never tied anyone to anything. "I'm so happy I can hardly stand it."

Epilogue

"Well, well, well. Look what the cat dragged in."

"Shut up, Warren."

It was an early night at The Curious Fox, very much like the first night Miles had been there. It was similarly deserted, with just Forester, Warren, and pre-transformation Noah in the whole place. There were differences, though. The curtains were new. One incense seemed to have been changed out for another, a bit cinnamonlike. Aside from that, it was pleasantly familiar.

Miles watched Charlie's face transform when they came in. They'd had lovely travels, but it was really something to see, for the first time, what Charlie looked like when he'd arrived at home.

They were squashed by hugs and peppered with kisses before Noah made them sit down at his card table and barked drink orders for them.

Noah slid onto Charlie's lap, arms around his neck. "I've missed you so terribly! I can't believe you abandoned us for nearly an entire year."

"I'm tethered to nothing and no one, not even you lot."

"That's a lie if I ever heard one," Warren said. He placed icy drinks on the table and smirked. "I hear Mr. Cox keeps you tethered to his bedpost at all times."

Miles picked up a glass and clinked it against Warren's.

"Stop liking him!" Charlie commanded. His face softened quickly, however. "Open the bag, love. Give these menaces their presents before I change my mind and keep it all myself."

"Presents!" Noah squealed. "Me first. Ladies first, always."

Miles reached into the bag and pulled out a small wrapped box. Noah ripped into it, and took out the dangly, pearl-encrusted earrings. "From Paris," Miles said.

"They're stunning!" He switched out his studs at once. "I can't believe you two managed to do so well. I wouldn't have guessed you had a single ounce of style between you."

"I resent that," said Charlie.

"Davy, darling," Noah said to Mr. Forester, preening himself a bit. "What do you think? Do they fit my face?"

Forester smiled indulgently. "They're almost as pretty as you."

As Noah pretended to blush and blew his friend a kiss across the table, Miles thought he caught a little something in their interaction that perhaps he'd missed before.

"You two—" he started, but was cut off quite abruptly as they turned disconcertingly similar nothing-to-see-here looks his way.

"*Us two* what?" Noah asked innocently.

"Nothing." Miles shook it off. He should know better than to read much into any given show of affection around here. "Anyway. It's your turn, Forester. Just a little something we thought you might like."

"Stop it." The proprietor crossed his arms, looking a little bashfully out from behind a stray strand of hair. "You didn't have to get me anything."

Charlie passed over a bottle of very fine limoncello. "Are you kidding? Of course I did. I should have got you more, actually, but I confess, I'm just not as thoughtful as you are."

Forester peered curiously at the bright yellow liquor. "This looks interesting."

"Oh!" Noah bounced up and down a bit, one of the new earrings nearly hitting Charlie in the eye. "I had that in Milan. It's fantastic stuff, darling, and you'll be drunk before you know what hit you."

Forester looked a bit skeptical, but thanked them with sincere kisses on their cheeks.

"What about me, then?" said Warren.

"Something very special for you," said Charlie. He took out a little box of Italian cigars, along with another bottle.

"Two presents? Why, Charlie Price, I should have known I was your favorite all along. Now, let's see what we've got." Warren set aside the cigars and removed the tissue paper from the bottle. "Olive oil?"

"From Spain."

"That's… I don't really cook, Charlie."

"Oh, I know that!" He swatted Warren in the middle of his chest. "It's not for cooking, for God's sake. I do apologize that it's not a bigger bottle, but hopefully this will last you, what, a whole weekend?"

Everyone laughed, even Warren, though he did pretend like he was going to break the bottle over Charlie's head.

"How's the shop?" Forester asked. "Have you been to see Joey and the rest of them yet?"

Miles sat comfortably back in his seat. "We have. They're all doing very well. The shop is humming, and Jo and Alma seem quite happy with the running of it. They've done what I never could."

"And Miles was able to hand over his next manuscript," Charlie added with a devious smile. "I like to think I had something to do with how depraved it becomes in the second half."

"The fun sort of depravity?" Noah asked from his place on Charlie's lap, still tapping at one of the dangling earrings. "Or the other sort?"

"Both, I assume," said Forester. He fixed Miles with a knowing sort of grimace. "Didn't you say that's the way of it, Mr. Cox? The more fun they have in the beginning, the worse it's got to be for them in the end? So you have a bit of deniability if the law comes calling?"

"I wish I could say you were wrong," Miles muttered into his glass, thinking about the pages he'd sent, the arguments he'd had, his final acquiescence to Smithy's insistence that the happy ending he'd put into the first draft would certainly see both of them locked up. "The original draft ended a bit differently, but in the end, it's the tragedy that has to go to print. No way around it."

"No one blames you." Forester reached across the table to pat his hand, a friendly sort of gesture that Miles was starting to get used to. "Do you have any idea of the knots I have to tie myself into to keep *this* place running?" He shook that lock of hair out of his eyes and chuckled with a twinge of cynicism that seemed beyond his years. "I mean, *shit*."

"Thank you," Miles said, genuinely appreciative. It was lovely, but still strange, to speak honestly with people who could commiserate with his constraints. "I imagine it's—"

He broke off, noticing suddenly that everyone's attention had shifted from him to Charlie, who was grinning so wide and blushing so red that it was impossible to ignore the sense of joy that emanated from him for a moment longer.

"What is it, love?" Miles asked.

"Well, they don't all end in tragedy, do they?" That grin grew bigger as he rested his chin on Noah's shoulder, staring across the table at Miles with unmatched adoration. "Aren't you going to tell them about the collector's edition?"

Miles's stomach flipped pleasantly and—in a most rare oc-currence—he felt his own cheeks start to burn a bit. There was no getting that past the rest of them, who started right in on a chorus of snickers, squeals, and nudges.

"Found a place for that happy ending after all, didn't you, Cox?" said Forester, so earnest and sappy that Warren pre-tended to gag, Charlie looked like Noah had dipped his head in a vat of rouge, and Miles could only laugh wordlessly, hardly able to believe that one begrudging signature had set him on the path that led *here*. To freedom, and friends, and a love that he'd never even dared to imagine.

Warren topped off their drinks, and they all toasted mer-rily, a lovely start to a lovely night. Miles and Charlie talked a while more about their travels and were filled in on what they'd missed here in London. Then predictably, Noah went to change, Warren and Forester went to work, and patrons began filling the Fox.

When the crowd became a little much, Miles leaned in to Charlie's ear. "Shall we see what we can get away with before Forester makes us take a room?"

"Absolutely." Charlie took his hand. They pulled the cur-tain back to find a kissing couple who all but leaped out of their suits. "Get out of the way, chaps. I'm back, and this is…" He paused, then snaked a hand around Miles's waist and pos-sessively into his trouser pocket. "This is our spot."

★ ★ ★ ★ ★

Acknowledgments

My path to publication has been a long and winding one. While the transition from isolated scribblings to finally getting a book out into the world could have been stressful, I have received such incredible support along the way that I can safely say it has been a dream come true.

My first shout-out is to my first reader, first fan, and my all-around first-favorite Michael Rauh. While this whole experience has been wonderful, sharing my work with you remains the most exciting part of my creative process, time and time again.

The team at Carina has been amazing every step of the way. Thanks so much to Ronan Sadler for starting this project off with such enthusiasm and understanding, and to Alissa Davis, who jumped in the middle with wonderful insight and contagious confidence. Thank you, Kerri Buckley, for handling all the behind-the-scenes details and keeping this project running so smoothly. Also to Stephanie Doig, Lee Tipton, and the rest of the Carina team who had a hand in bringing this book into the world—thank you!

To my agent, Laura Zats, thanks for keeping me sane, well-informed, and supported. You are awesome! I don't know what I'd have done without you through this first foray into publishing.

Particular thanks to my beta readers Garrett Hutson, Perry

Lloyd, and Ashley Alford for sharing comments that helped get this book into shape, and to Monica Newcomb and Anna Langford for brainstorming and early-stage cheerleading. Thanks and much love to all my other friends from the North Columbus SFF critique group, the Midwest Writers Conference, Great Lakes Fiction Writers, and anyone else who has supported my growth as a writer over the years.

And finally, a special thanks to my wonderfully supportive friends and family, particularly Suzy Murphy (who will never look at me the same), and Nana and Grandpa Russ (who make me feel like a rock star for every writerly win, big or small).

Their differences made them enemies. One summer tied them together forever. Keep reading for an excerpt from All the Way Happy *by Kit Coltrane.*

Prologue

He was thirty-seven. Fuck. He was thirty-seven.

When he ran away from everything—from Baltimore, from his family, from blue eyes and guilt and casual schoolboy violence—he ran far. He got his first shitty apartment in Cork, Ireland, and he tried to live on the razor edge of a knife, in the dangerous dance of his own self-destruction.

He had a dodgy upstairs neighbor, Cathal, and windows which didn't shut all the way, and the water wasn't ever quite warm enough, but it was—it was his.

He'd cashed out the small trust fund that hadn't been impacted by what his father—what had happened, and the first thing he bought was an old record player and a stack of LPs. Music was what kept him going. The kind of music that his parents had never let him listen to, ugly and wailing and wild, soft and heartbreaking, stupid and silly and utterly perfect.

Led Zeppelin blared out when he smoked his first spliff (courtesy of that same upstairs neighbor, who was quite sketchy indeed, but with an apartment full of exotic birds and a too-kind heart). Tiffany sang about being alone, and he danced in front of the bathroom's cracked mirror while he cut his own hair. Long locks shorn, revealing an angular, violent beauty.

He listened to the Clash and thought about his father, about imposing his own brand of anarchy on his stilted and tight-fisted childhood, that man he had worshipped and the man who had hated him. He threw things and threw up at two in the morning, the fast food he'd grabbed after a night at the clubs coming up looking not all that dissimilar from the way it went down.

Stevie Wonder sang about falling in love and he tried, he really did, not to think about sky blue eyes and black hair.

And then there was David Bowie.

The feeling of sunrise in Cork—the way the air was damp and fresh, shaking, all too aware of the panic of nighttime, liminal and lined with edges of gold—went best with Bowie. Some mornings he listened to "Heroes," and he thought about what he had never been. On other mornings, he put on "Let's Dance" and drank cup after cup of shitty instant coffee before heading down across Saint Patrick Street to scrub the sticky floors of the club he'd been writhing in four hours before.

Rainy days and it was "Bring Me the Disco King," and he thought about taking a knife to the inside of his arm. When the flat was freezing with cold in a wet way which felt like falling into the sea, he played "My Death," which was Jacques Brel, but Bowie lived and died it. And "Wild Eyed Boy From Freecloud" was what he played when he first took another man into himself and wanted to scream out to his father and his past and those blue eyes.

He'd had enough of silence.

But most of all, that first year was marked by an almost or-giastic adherence to Bowie's sepulchral warning—the desired brevity of his life, an anticipated early end by twenty-five.

He didn't think he would make it, not even that far. He figured there was nothing much to live for at eighteen, any-way, other than one more drink, one more fuck, a few more cups of coffee, trad nights with American exchange students grinding in the corners, balancing on the rock wall across from The Thirsty Scholar at three in the morning and itching, always, to jump into the water and melt the fuck away.

And now, at thirty-seven, he was still very much alive—his blood pumped through him, and his brain was sparking in manic fury and discontent, and his skin felt like ice. He had a job, a respectable one, and he had a smooth face which no one could read. He had an ex-wife and a child, an aging mother who had never really loved him but who was maybe trying her best now. He was usually sober. He played music at an acceptable volume.

He was back in his childhood home. Managing it, and his money, and making it all look good.

As the Beaumonts had always done. At least until his father had fleeced half of Baltimore. But he was reclaiming that name, that heritage, even as he hated it.

And every little part of him, the broken bits, the whole bits—every breath which reminded him of cigarettes at midnight—every time his mother looked at him with a vague, muted disappointment—every time he saw blue eyes in the street or in a bar or the Gwynns Academy alumni newsletter—every morning when he didn't wake up in that shitty flat with Cathal and the parakeets upstairs and the old record player and the LPs which skipped—

Every single cell in his body longed, desperately.

Silently.

He was thirty-seven.

He wanted to burn the world down.

Chapter One

The first time Jack Gardner met Theodore Beaumont, he was staring at a rack of blue blazers, knowing that his mother could never afford them, and doubting every decision which had led him here, to Gwynns Academy, the most exclusive—and expensive—preparatory school in Baltimore.

All Jack had ever worn were hand-me-downs, clothing used by others, and the crisp lines of the Gwynns uniforms were foreign to him, nearly strange. The stitching was impeccable, the cloth a deep navy blue, and the school's crest was in gold and red embroidery, and he had never had anything so fine, so costly, so clean. Starched white shirts and pleated trousers and striped gold ties were the other elements of his soon-to-be school's uniform, and he wondered if this—this outfit, this costume, this mask—could ever hide the little boy who'd never really had enough to eat.

The school shop bustled with other students and their perfect families—ice-blonde mothers with pearls, and fathers with platinum tie tacks, and kids who looked like their copies, utterly at ease, expectant of nothing other than this, the chore, the way the world was, spending money without a thought. Jack was already out of place—school hadn't even started yet.

He caught a glimpse of himself in the full-length mirror and wanted to look away, but he couldn't. He saw his skinny frame, knobby knees covered by too-large shorts, a collarbone as thin and delicate as a bird's wing exposed by the stretched-out neck of his black T-shirt. His hair was thick and messy, impossible to tame. The only feature which might have been attractive were his blue eyes, piercing. He tried not to worry so much about how he looked. That wasn't why he was here.

He could see the rest of the school shop behind him in the mirror, crammed tight with the uniforms and notebooks, lacrosse gear, Shakespeare and Yeats and mathematical texts, the smell of fresh paper and glue, and all of those shining people. At the register, one of the other children stood with a stack of clothes, seeming bored, elegant, casually stunning, and cold. His mother was next to him, chatting with another mother with rich black hair, and his father typed away on his cell phone. Jack couldn't help but imagine the sort of life they must have—galas and fundraisers and meals out, clothing and jewelry and shoes without holes.

He held a blue jacket under his chin, trying to imagine the next four years, what he would look like. Who he might be. His fingers delighted in the soft material, but—

"For fuck's sake, Jack. We can't—go look at the used pile." His mother's face was pinched and still somehow disinterested. She had tucked herself in a corner, maybe in an attempt to go unnoticed, but she stood out here just as much as he did. She didn't fit.

He'd learned not to blush, not to show shame. He turned away from the mirror and dug through the pile of used uniforms.

The blond boy at the counter slanted his eyes over, looked at Jack from his scuffed sneakers to his frayed collar, and Jack could feel his eyes like glaciers on his neck. The boy smirked. "This school's really been lowering its standards, Mother."

His mother turned from her conversation, glanced at Jack and his mom, and pursed her lips. Half an unkind smile, and then her tanned skin smoothed out into a blank haughtiness. "Be nice, Theo." She turned back toward the other parents, unbothered. Dismissing Jack—and maybe her own son—as if he were of no consequence.

A sigh from the boy, unnoticed. "If I must."

Everything that Jack had ever hated about himself was visible on the other boy's face. An unpleasant face, a jeering face. That child had seen right through him, right down to the root, and he had found him wanting.

And that boy—Theo—was everything that Jack yearned to be. His skin was pale, clear, white enough to show the blue tracery of his veins, and his hair was perfectly coiffed, and he wore a five-thousand-dollar watch, and he could afford to be cruel. Could afford to go to Gwynns without a scholarship, without working himself down to the nub, competing and scrapping and begging, Please, see me.

Jack gathered up two jackets, two pairs of trousers, three shirts, one tie. His mother dug in her handbag and looked at him as if he were a terrible burden. This was a big day, an important day—he didn't want to admit his mother's resentments. He could look at that later; his mother's attitude wouldn't go away.

Jack got in line, keeping a significant distance between himself and that boy, Theo, who was tall and lithe and perfect, who smelled like vanilla and gin, who was sparkling. Who belonged here, effortlessly.

No one could ever miss Theo Beaumont.

Jack hated him at once.

"For fuck's sake, Will."

Jack, if pressed, would admit with a sheepish grin and a tilt of his head that Gwilim Linwood Alistair—Will, now, since all of his kids were determined to have normal names, despite his best efforts—was his favorite child. He was quiet, a dreamer, with all of his father's sarcasm but none of his insecurity, and Jack maybe felt a bit bad about the name, but it was too late now.

He looked exactly like his dad. But he was better.

Though, admittedly, just as absentminded. Christ.

Johnny, of course, had set herself up in her room with little fanfare and a careless hug for each of her parents—a very clear "go away" signal—and was already prepared for her junior year. She'd been through the routine before. And she was never quite as—distractible as Will.

Jack looked at Will's Gwynns Academy blazer, forgotten in the back of the car. Meg, as pretty as ever but twice as worn out, strapped Amy into her seat belt, and gave Jack a *that's your kid, you idiot* stare.

He sighed. "I'll run it in, all right? Maybe check in with Charlie, catch a cab home."

"Mm."

He handed over the keys and leaned down to press a kiss to his wife's freckled cheek, and then they had that moment which many soon-to-be divorced people must have—oh, shit.

Not his wife. Not anymore.

Jack turned away, walked out of the parking lot and back to the mica-flecked granite of the school gates, school uniform in hand, and he tried not to think about what was coming next. The signing of the papers. Finding a new place to live. Splitting up the hours, the days—Will and Johnny at school, for now, but where would Amy live, and would he get to see her enough, and would they all hate him, maybe, for tearing down a marriage which must have looked, from the outside, unbreakable?

They'd settled Will into his dorm room, posters on the walls, bookshelves jammed with science fiction paperbacks and thick textbooks and all that literature they were paying a ridiculous amount for teachers to shove into his head. Jack jogged back through campus, passing the old Japanese maple he'd climbed and hid in for so many hours as a teenager, and the running stream he'd fallen into while skipping study hall, and the lacrosse field where he'd shed so much blood. Parents and their children were still milling about, and despite the long years between his youth and adulthood, Jack was full of excitement and dread and that old longing, a kid at the candy store, a child without a home. He barely looked around him, eager to get into the dorms and out without being noticed, and he ran right into the back of another parent.

Juniper. Sandalwood. Vanilla.

Fine, combed wool. Ice-blond hair.

Oh, shit.

He was going to throttle Will.

Theo Beaumont turned, elegant, still. He was wearing a perfectly tailored suit, tie loosened around his neck and top button undone, a gold watch, shined shoes. Jack suddenly felt underdressed and unfashionable, just as he had twenty years ago.

He'd spotted him in the distance—of course he had—while getting Will into his dorm, though he'd tried not to think about it; he had a son, too, in Will's year, with the same chilly looks but a big toothy grin. They'd been filling out forms at the reception desk, designer luggage handed over to be carried up by school staff, and Jack had turned away, face hot. He didn't want—he had really tried not to look—he forced himself not to even though, God, he needed—

Now Jack couldn't look away. Theo's hair was long again, no longer asymmetrical and uneven, and his skin was still flawless, enriched by the few fine lines showing the decades between that summer after their senior year and today. His eyes held a hint of warmth—maybe he'd been softened by fatherhood, by marriage—but they were gray and frosted as he regarded Jack. Despite the subtle differences, he looked— it was still him, unequivocally. Still Theo—still so beautiful.

Nothing had changed.

Jack hadn't talked to Theo in nineteen years.

And everything had changed since then.

"Gardner."

"Um, hi. Sorry, I—" Jack felt like he'd been hit with a blast of ice. He was frozen to his spot, here on the red brick lane, in the shade of pear blossom trees, the thick wet scent of Baltimore in September.

He looked so much the same. He even smelled the same.

Jack was, very quickly, losing the plot.

Theo rolled his eyes. "Is there a reason you're holding a Gwynns jacket?"

Jack looked down at his hand, eyes catching on gold stitching. Looked over at the dormitory building. Looked at Theo. He opened his mouth, but nothing came out.

"Oh, for God's sake." Theo rolled his eyes again, somehow more dramatic, and waved a hand. "Just go in, would you?"

"I—"

"The dorms are quite nice, now." His casual tone was forced in a way that only Jack would be able to notice.

"Yeah, I—"

"I think they have your picture up there, somewhere. Sure to be a thrill."

Still kind of a bastard, it seemed. Jack grimaced, embarrassed. "I wish they hadn't done that."

Theo scoffed. He was unbelievably good at scoffing. "You're the only person I know who could be ashamed of such a... significant donation."

"Yeah, well..." He trailed off, uncertain. He really was

uncomfortable with people—people thinking about—"I hate that they—"

"I remember." Theo looked him over, eyes just as sharp and critical as ever, and then his face softened, just a little. "Always so ashamed to be noticed."

Jack's face colored. He glanced away, staring at the brick pathway.

"It's been a long time." Theo's voice was hollow but gentle.

"Yeah." Jack rubbed the back of his neck, tried to smile. "We're old men now."

"Not that old." A lifted eyebrow.

"God." Jack felt the burden of too many years, so many joys and too many stupid decisions. "I feel old."

They both paused, silent. Jack felt the distance between them as if it were a physical thing, a solid thing, and he wanted to reach out, smell that place where Theo's shoulder met his neck—and he remembered those few months, the stone wall next to the River Lee, Cork at sunrise, cigarettes laced with hash, and the most beautiful and fucked-up time in his entire life.

And he thought about his three children, whom he loved more than anything. Meg, the girl who'd cared for him, and their family, and their failed marriage. And the rumor he'd heard, back in January, about Theo's divorce.

The moment he realized he couldn't lie anymore.

"Yes, well…" Theo breathed out, shaky, and ran a hand through his still-perfect hair. "Right, so this has been… awful, yeah. Absolutely terrible." A shrug. "Good luck with the jacket, Gardner."

"Theo, I—"

But he was already walking away.

Jack had watched him go so many times.

Above him, hopping from branch to branch in the pear

blossom tree, a blue jay yelled out its sharp call, and a damp breeze ruffled its feathers, and Jack remembered the apartment above, filled with exotic birds, and the skipping of old records, and the way the air felt at two o'clock in the morning when they'd had too much to drink and the rain came down, mizzling, and lamplight refracted in the spider silk strands of Theo's hair.

Something twisted inside him and he made a sound like spitting up concrete.

He gripped the jacket, too tight, in his left hand.

Don't miss All the Way Happy *by Kit Coltrane,*
available wherever Carina Adores books are sold.
www.CarinaPress.com